THE JUDGMENT

THE JUDGMENT

From the author of the Sarah Weston Chronicles

D.J. NIKO

MEDALLION

Medallion Press, Inc.
Printed in USA

DEDICATION

For my daughter, Anastasia,
and for all daughters brave enough to make a stand for
God and country

Published 2016 by Medallion Press, Inc.,
4222 Meridian Pkwy, Suite 110, Aurora, IL 60504

The MEDALLION PRESS LOGO
is a registered trademark of Medallion Press, Inc.

Names, characters, places, and incidents are the products of the author's imagination or are used fictionally. Any resemblance to actual events, locales, or persons, living or dead, is entirely coincidental.

Cataloging-in-Publication Data is on file with the Library of Congress

Typeset in Adobe Garamond Pro
Printed in the United States of America
ISBN # 978-1-94254-622-1

10 9 8 7 6 5 4 3 2 1
First Edition

"The wisest of women builds her house,
but folly with her own hands tears it down."

Proverbs 14:1

CHAPTER ONE

The saffron light that signaled the decline of day grew leaden while a cloud of dust, parched as the ground from whence it came, gathered on the western horizon. The plains stretching like earthen waves beneath the tell were consumed, little by little, by the haze rolling across the Way of the Sea. The faint sound of horses' hooves, thousands of them, was a slow torment, the harbinger of an inescapable fate. In the distance, a flash of gold flickered as the waning sun cast its rays upon bronze chariots: the lightning before the thunder.

It was Adar, the twenty-ninth day. In better years, this would be the season of promise, when buds sprang from the rock and newborn lambs struggled to find their legs, a time of deliverance from the melancholy storms that battered the land all winter. The valley to the east was only beginning to wear its coat of green, and the sea had given up its anger. But the naissance was as short-lived as the fragile spring flower. Life, new and old, would soon buckle under the iron grip of the advancing army.

There was no surprise as she regarded the onslaught. She knew they would come. Destruction followed moral decline as surely as vultures descended on decaying flesh. Even as the daughter of a king, she was powerless to stop it. Her will, however fierce, was a grain of sand in the face of divine wrath.

She lowered her head and gazed absently at the ashlar stones beneath her feet. So perfectly hewn they were. Her father had insisted on such precision. He built his fortress as he did his kingdom, and his kingdom as his character: formidable, abiding, immovable. She ran her sandal-bound foot across a hairline crack. Faults like this, left untended, could tear a stone asunder. That was how walls crumbled, making way for enemies to enter unchecked.

She looked up with a sigh and reminded herself who she was: Basemath, beloved daughter of King Solomon by the wife he adored like no other, the wife who loved him mightily and tainted him and ultimately destroyed him. For all his flaws, he was the most powerful king in history, the one in whom the Lord placed his trust, the one who made the world bow to Israel. To be the progeny of such a man, to honor his memory and keep his spirit alive, was a responsibility she did not take lightly.

"Mother?"

Basemath faced her twelve-year-old daughter, a honey-skinned, wild-eyed beauty with silken black hair cascading to her waist. The girl wore a simple gray cotton tunic hardly befitting her royal status. It was as if she, too, could sense that ruin drew nigh. She dressed like the commoners, for she would soon have to stand among them and fight on a battleground where there were no titles or privileges or stores of gold.

"I have searched the whole of the palace for you. The men have gathered in the courtyard and are saddling their horses. There is confusion among the people." She looked past her mother's shoulder and out the narrow window. "What is out there?"

Basemath drew a sharp breath. There was no reason to hide the truth from her. The way of the women of Judah was to be brutally honest, no matter what it cost. "What we feared has come to pass, Ana. The Egyptian enemy is upon us." She nodded toward the window. "They will be here by dusk. We must be ready."

"Is it why we fled Shechem to come here?"

"Megiddo is our fortress, girl. It will protect us. My father built it as he did his palace in Jerusalem. It is nigh on impenetrable." She believed it, and it gave her comfort. "Now make haste. We must guide the others. Have the women and children assemble in the courtyard."

Ana did not hesitate. She spun on her heel and started down the spiral stairway of the tower, her black locks billowing behind her like the mane of a trotting thoroughbred.

Basemath lingered a moment longer. She reached inside her white linen gown and pulled out the golden chain that hung on her bosom. She let the object dangling from it rest on her hand and felt the weight of it. The ring, forged of iron and crowned with a disc on which were embedded four gems, was a thing of substance, a physical manifestation of supreme power.

It was her most cherished possession, given to her by her father only days before he died. Solomon could have bequeathed it to his son and heir, the reigning King Rehoboam, but he chose against it.

"This must go to one who is pure of heart and spirit," the aging, emaciated king had said as he'd tucked his bony fingers into her palm, releasing the mystical symbol of his sovereignty. "You, and you alone, are worthy of it, my daughter. All others have failed in the eyes of the Lord."

When she protested, telling him the ring ought to accompany him to the world to come, he offered a pale smile. "There is much I cannot tell you. You must trust your old father. Take this ring and keep it close to your heart. Let it remind you the blood of the house of David runs through your veins. Kneel to no one, even when the winds change."

Basemath gazed out the window at the approaching column of men, their war cries suspended in the *ruach qadim*. Solomon's words seemed prophetic now, some five years after his death. He had known this day would come. In many ways, she had too.

She clutched the ring and made a silent promise to her father: *They will not win.*

She kissed it as if it were still around his finger and tucked it back inside her gown. She tightened the pins on the white gauze veil that covered the back of her head and draped down her back over a long sweep of chestnut waves. She placed a hand across her abdomen to calm the gnawing sensation. The serenity that was unequivocally hers during thirty-eight years of life was fading like the splendor of youth erased by age.

"God be with us," she whispered, and made her way to the courtyard.

On the ground level of the palace, a chaotic scene unfolded. Beyond the double arches that formed the wide terrace, in happier times a place of genteel repose, the men gathered to be fitted with armor. Army officers stood on stone altars and shouted: "Fight for the kingdom! Fight for your right to be on these lands! Fight in the name of the Lord!"

Basemath's husband, Ahimaaz, was one of the military leaders. He was on horseback, instructing his garrison of soldiers who were readying to ride out of the palace gates. In times of peace, Ahimaaz was governor of Naphtali by appointment of King Solomon; in wartime, he was a captain. She had not seen him step into that role before that day, and she felt a pang of anguish at the newness of it. She willed it away, for it was a futile sentiment. This was no time to fear the unknown but rather to charge it head-on.

Basemath had faith in her husband, for he had a holy man's heart and a warrior's instinct. In his youth Ahimaaz had been a priest, trained in the ways of the Lord by his father, the high priest of Solomon's kingdom. Yet he also knew how to wield a sword, and he had been called upon to quash a rebellion against his king. Solomon rewarded Ahimaaz's victory with an important governorship and the most precious prize of all—the hand of his first daughter.

She caught Ahimaaz's eye and held up a hand. He returned the gesture, and the two stood for a long moment facing each other, silently contemplating their fate. What awaited them wasn't good, and they both knew it. The man who hunted them, Pharaoh Shoshenq I, was a formidable foe. He took what he wanted, without warning, without mercy; this he had proven over and over during his reign.

Word of his campaign in Kush had reached Jerusalem years before. His men had ambushed the border towns in the middle of the night, burning villages and butchering people as they advanced toward Napata, in the name of controlling the gold trade that flourished there and expanding the boundaries of Upper Egypt to the fourth cataract of the River Nile.

Perhaps the Kushite invasion was training for Shoshenq's conquest of the lands on which he had ultimately set his sights: Israel and Judah. While King Solomon was alive, the Libyan-born pharaoh of Egypt didn't dare attempt to breach the impenetrable fortress of Jerusalem. But during the king's final years, it had become clear the state was hemorrhaging, politically as well as spiritually. Egypt had smelled the blood and circled round, waiting for the opportunity to strike.

Some weeks ago, the messengers spoke of Shoshenq's Egyptian army riding north along the Way, destroying everything and everyone standing between them and victory. Word came of threescore thousand men and five thousand chariots, some heading north along the sea route, others turning east toward the holy city. Canaan had been taken, the messengers said. Scores of cities had fallen. Houses had been torched, their inhabitants skewered. Blood had stained the rocky soil in the south. There was no way to know the death toll, but the mere imagining of it made Basemath shiver with dread.

Ahimaaz lowered his helmet over his shoulder-length, silver-threaded ebony hair and shouted to his men, igniting the spark of the offensive. Armed with their spears and their courage, the horsemen followed their captain out of the palace gates and spilled down the tell and onto the valley.

Basemath said a silent prayer for their safety. Ahimaaz led not a conventional army but rather a resistance movement. Men rode from all parts of Israel and Judah, organizing in the crags of Gilboa, southeast of Megiddo. The Gilboa wilderness was hostile to the Egyptians and therefore ideal for the resistance fighters, who knew the caprices of the mountains. Their mission was to weaken the enemy by gathering intelligence and mounting flash strikes while the Egyptians' guard was down. In the face of Shoshenq's mammoth army, it was the best, and perhaps the only, hope they had.

Basemath turned toward the terrace and scanned the faces of the women and children who had assembled, waiting for direction. The little ones blubbered, their plump tawny fingers clinging to the skirts of their mothers. Babies screamed inconsolably, prompting their mothers to insert their breasts into their mouths, offering whatever comfort they could. Even the women, usually stoic in the face of danger, were restless with fear. One young maiden had to be propped up by her kin, who took turns stroking her hair and her tear-soaked cheeks. Another kneeled by one of the columns and retched, expelling the demons that tormented her.

She turned her gaze to the old widow Hannah. Her face, though etched with the rivulets of age and trials, was as soft and peaceful as a virgin's beneath the shadow of her charcoal-gray head veil. As the others buzzed around her like bees in a honeycomb, Hannah stood still as a column, her gaze turned downward and her palms open to the heavens. Her lips moved ever so slightly as she offered up a prayer.

Basemath could not hear the old woman's entreaty, but she felt the loveliness of it. She was certain Hannah's was a call for divine union, a birdsong offered without expectation or conscious effort. She envied her peace.

Basemath searched the crowd for her daughter. Ana was instructing a group of girls her age on the art of wielding the *khopesh*, the Canaanite sickle-sword. She stood behind one, guiding her hand with her own, showing her how to parry. It was a maneuver her father had taught her, at her own insistence, when she was eleven. It was her rite, Ana had said, for becoming a woman.

Now almost thirteen, Basemath's only daughter was mature beyond her years, a reflection of her royal heritage and the line of leaders to which she was born. She watched Ana demonstrate a sickle-sword sequence to her young friends. She commanded the blade as if it were an extension of her arm, dodging a pretend enemy. She spun on her heel and swung round to strike, her uncovered hair whipping like long ribbons of black silk.

One day, Basemath thought, *she will marry a king.* It was more a premonition than a passing fancy, and it fueled her will to fight. She owed a future to her daughter, to all daughters.

"Hear me, sisters." She waited for the buzz among them to die down before continuing. "The Egyptian enemy is at the gates of Megiddo. Our men are doing all they can to hold back the army. The mightiest weapon we can wield now is our faith. Be strong in the eyes of the Lord. Pray for our soldiers. Pray for Israel."

"I want to fight, Mother," Ana said. "I want to show those men what the women of our country are made of."

"There will be time for that, girl. Now it is our duty to protect our children and ourselves so we may perpetuate life. We must retreat to the tunnel."

Ana's eyes widened. "But, Mother, that's cowardly . . ."

Basemath held up a hand. "Be silent and obey. Can you not smell the smoke of their torches? Can you not hear their savage cries? The Egyptians are ruthless. They mean to crush us. Our best defense is within the bowels of the fortress. Let us save ourselves lest they smite our breed."

The girl lowered her head and spoke not another word.

Basemath continued in a louder voice. "The enemy knows nothing of the tunnel of Megiddo. King Solomon built it to protect our water supply in times of war. It is secret to all but the royal family and the highest-ranking governors." She paused and held the gazes of several women to emphasize her point. "We will be safe there."

The women were afraid. She could see it in their pinched foreheads, in their clenched jaws, in the shadows behind their eyes. It was her duty to protect them, not only from the enemy but from themselves. Their faith was a fragile thing, cracking in the face of adversity. Only Hannah and a few of the elders held strong, for they had seen times like these and survived them.

She turned to Ana. "Lead the womenfolk to the tunnel. Do it now."

The girl did it without protest. For all her willfulness, she knew when not to challenge her parents. It was an unspoken dance among the three of them: each knew when to support the other. It was why there was harmony in their house.

The ground shook. Basemath snapped her head toward the ramparts and saw the massive boulder flung off a catapult break Megiddo's defenses. The screams of the men stabbed her gut. Her ebony eyes misted. It would be only moments before the Egyptians were through the gates.

She turned toward the bewildered women and children. "Make haste. There is little time."

She took up the rear of the column, ensuring no one was left behind, and spurred them on to the east side of the palace, stopping at a grassy patch by the vegetable gardens. The four-cubit-square stone covering the chamber entrance was so perfectly camouflaged by the vegetation that no one would know it was there.

Basemath kneeled down and felt for the handle in the brush. Her hand ran across the iron bar gritty with oxidation. It measured about two palms in width, big enough to be grasped by two male hands but small enough to be disguised in the thicket.

She felt a momentary pang of doubt. It took four men to move that stone, and that with some effort. How would a group of women accomplish such a task?

The ground quaked once more. Though she could not see the west side of the fortress, she could hear the wretched cries of men plunging to their death. She looked to the sky. *Give me the strength.*

She turned to the women and picked five of the youngest and most able. "Ana, Leah, Nava, Shifra, Sarai. Untie your waist sashes."

Each removed the strips of cloth binding her own gown and handed them to Basemath, who plaited them with nimble fingers. She tugged on either end of the makeshift rope and was satisfied with the weight. She threaded it through the handle and turned back to the women. "Now we pull."

The five rushed to her side and followed her hand gestures directing them to each side of the rope. They dug their feet into the ground and held tight.

"Heave!"

They pulled with all their might, but the stone barely budged.

Basemath's biceps burned and the tendons of her neck strained. She called again: "Heave!"

Without waiting for her command, some of the elders, though feeble, stepped out of the crowd to offer their assistance. Some twenty women pulled on the fabric rope's two ends, their heels scuffing the earth. Their grunts were drowned by the thumps of a heavy weapon battering the wooden planks of the palace gate.

At last, the stone gave way, popping open like a lid.

"The Lord be praised." Basemath wiped the perspiration from her forehead and gestured to the women to enter the shaft.

They scurried down the rough-hewn stone steps helter-skelter, each of them aware time had run out. In a matter of moments, the fortress of Megiddo would be overrun. When the last of them had gone inside, Basemath followed. She plucked a torch hanging from an iron brace on the wall and lit it by striking a piece of flint against the stone. She handed the torch to a pair of waiting hands and pulled the handle on the inside of the stone. It swung down with the help of gravity, shutting out the light of day.

Basemath collapsed onto the first step and caught her breath. Thoughts galloped through her mind like stallions: visions of Megiddo under attack, its walls crumbling beneath the fist of the heathen king.

Solomon's fortified chariot city was built high on the

tell to protect the Israelites in times of conflict. It was to be a gathering point for people from as far as the western harbor and the northern capital, Shechem. Within its sturdy stone walls and in the chambers of the magnificent *bit-hilani* palaces, the Israelites would hunker down as their cities and villages burned. But Solomon's vision quickly unraveled, for even Megiddo was not strong enough to hold back the onslaught of the insatiable colonists from the western banks of the Yam Suph.

Basemath was convinced the women and children were safe in the tunnel . . . but what of their men, including her own beloved Ahimaaz? With a shudder she expelled any dark notions of bloodshed and loss. The Egyptians were brutal, but her own countrymen were cunning and clever. They would not easily concede the lands they'd fought so hard to make their own, the lands the Lord himself bestowed upon their ancestors. She sighed deeply and told herself, *There is hope yet.*

She descended the twoscore steps in the dark. The cold, rough-cut stone felt like petrified sand against her hands. The slow drip of distant water filled her ears, and she thought of her father. It must have been divine guidance that gave him the foresight to engineer a network so complex that it could provide water to thousands of people. A vertical shaft reached deep into the earth and was connected to a spring outside the city walls by the very tunnel in which she stood, allowing Megiddo inhabitants access to water even in times of siege.

Solomon began the project toward the end of his life

and never saw it finished. He had left specific instructions to his son Rehoboam on how to complete it, but the great king's heir had proven himself unworthy of the task, and of so many others. Though Basemath loved her half-brother, she could see he was weak, indecisive, and unable to lead the people in the way their father had. Under his reign, the united monarchy of Israel and Judah that had been established three kings ago and reached its zenith during Solomon's time was now crumbling like limestone in an earthquake.

But perhaps Rehoboam wasn't all to blame. The collapse had begun in her father's lifetime. Though Solomon's forty-year reign was one of peace, he sat on a cauldron that was brewing unbeknownst to him. Anger seethed among the taxed masses like a toxic cocktail. Fattened by prosperity, they had grown accustomed to plenty and did not wish to be parted with their gold and comfort so that the state's power and influence could reach beyond Jerusalem. Solomon's vision to build chariot cities in the north, such as Megiddo, and to fortify the holy city against the intruders he knew would one day come was met with resistance. Without any regard for the future of their children, or for the divine wisdom that guided King Solomon since the crown was passed to him from his father, David, they sought to protect their own treasuries. The prevailing ideal had shifted from serving God and working toward Israel's greater good to cultivating self-interest. It was, she thought, an abomination.

At the base of the stairway, the women huddled

beneath the meager light of a single torch, shivering in the damp cold of the subterranean passage. They stared at Basemath with wide eyes, like frightened rabbits, as the ground above them quaked with the footfall of countless soldiers.

She stood on the last step, her shadow a black giant dancing on the limestone wall. "Women of Israel, the time has come for courage. We are the Lord's chosen people. As long as we have faith, we will be protected." She stepped down and stood among them. "Now we pray."

She dropped to her knees and waited for the others to follow. She lowered her head. "Almighty ruler of the heavens, Lord of our forefathers, who has bestowed your commandments upon us, hear the entreaty of your humble servants. Bless, O Lord, the house of the righteous and let it prevail over wickedness and violence. Let wisdom and understanding reign among your people. Let their hearts know peace in the face of injustice, and let them accept your will and judgment without protest. To the slain, give everlasting life. To the living, grant the prudence to walk on the narrow path of virtue and faithfulness. May your word be nourishment in the time of hunger, your way a beacon in darkness. Amen."

Silence fell upon the chamber for many moments. The energy of the group was sedate—not a deliberate calm that came with strength of heart but rather a numbness, a forlorn resignation to whatever would be.

A boy with a round face and golden curls tumbling into his eyes separated himself from the bosom of his mother and spoke. "Who are the men who have come here? What do they want with us?"

Basemath gave him a tight-lipped smile. "I will tell you a story, Elo'ah."

The boy put his thumb in his mouth and leaned back into his mother. His big, eager eyes told her to continue.

She spoke softly. "Many years ago, in the time of our ancestors, there was a terrible drought in Canaan and the people were dying of hunger. The old patriarch Israel, who was the son of Isaac and the grandson of Abraham, led his house to more fertile lands that were rich in grain and water. With his sons and their families, who numbered threescore and ten, he traveled south in a journey that took many moons and claimed the lives of their newborn lambs. At last they came to the Yam Suph, and they rejoiced. They crossed over to the west, to a kingdom called Egypt, and there they found pastures and water for their livestock, and they tended the land with care, taking only enough to survive.

"For seventeen years, Israel and his clan prospered and multiplied. They had the favor of the pharaoh and lived in harmony with the Egyptians. But Israel, who was quite old, died, and his son Joseph took him back to Canaan to be buried with his forefathers. Israel's house mourned for him together with the Egyptians, who were like their kin. Israel's clan continued to live in Egypt and now numbered many thousands.

"When the pharaoh died, a new king came to power who did not know Israel or his son Joseph or any of his offspring. He regarded the sons of Israel as foreigners in

Egyptian lands and loathed their multitudes and their vigor. Afraid they might rise up and fight Egypt, the new pharaoh subjected them to bondage. The Israelites, who were always a free and proud people, now slaved under the burden of a foreign king. They were made to build cities and carry heavy loads and do the work of oxen, all for a crust of bread.

"But Israel's people were mighty and clever, and they continued to multiply in the face of hardship. And the more they did so, the more the pharaoh hated them, until one day he commanded their sons be cast into the Nile lest they spread the seed of Israel."

She paused and smiled at the young boy, who was clutching his mother's gown to his lips.

"But hatred and oppression never last, Elo'ah. Even if many years pass, the righteous always win. By the grace of Yahweh, Israel's tribe was delivered from the yoke of Egypt and led by a man named Moses back to Canaan land, where they lived and prospered as free men once again. The pharaoh never forgave them for reclaiming their freedom, and that hatred was passed down through the generations, and the people of Egypt and Israel who once were brothers became lifelong enemies."

She shifted her gaze to the group and raised her voice a notch. "Just as Israel's tribes prevailed then, their descendants will do so again. Even if the blood on the ground rises to the horses' bridles and the sea is littered with corpses, the sons of Israel will stand on the mountains of their forefathers and claim victory over their enemies.

They may have terrible armies and bronze chariots and catapults that hurl great stones, but we have something they do not: the favor of the Lord, our God. Do not abandon your faith, even in such trying times, and you shall live to see the glory of Israel restored."

In the silent space, Basemath could hear the rise and fall of her people's breath. The fire of kinship warmed her. One of the elders sitting at the rear of the circle began a familiar song. Her clear words, tragic utterances of suffering delivered with the cadence of a war march, echoed in the stone womb and amplified as the other women joined in, one by one. Soon every mouth sang in unison, each note honeyed with hope and deliverance.

Basemath thought she heard something and withdrew from the impromptu chorus. Without alarming the others, she listened.

A shuffling sound came from the staircase.

She felt the icy grip of dread on her veins as the sound crept closer. The women continued singing, oblivious to the fact that someone had breached the chamber. Her heart thrashing like a caged wild animal, she turned her gaze to the dark staircase.

A man emerged from the shadow, then another. And another, each wearing against his bare chest the golden breastplate of the Egyptian warrior. She gasped. The singing stopped, and all heads turned toward the commotion.

Basemath slowly rose and regarded them with head held high. Ana ran to her side.

The men stood at attention in two rows, their spears

dug into the earth by their sides. Their leader made his way down the stairs and stood in front of his soldiers. Against his hips he wore a swath of white cotton gathered at the groin and covered by a golden shield that hung between his legs. A thick plate of bronze extended from his throat across his shoulders and to the base of his sternum. A bronze helmet in the shape of a wig crowned by a serpent protected his head. His wrists were bound by gold cuffs. He trained his kohl-ringed eyes on Basemath, then turned to Ana with a greedy glare.

"Leave us be," Basemath said, shielding her daughter's body with her own. "We are only women . . . children. We are no threat to your people."

He tossed his head back and laughed in short, baleful bursts. He spoke in a language she understood: the language of her mother. "Your fate is not yours to defend. You are the property of the pharaoh now." He turned to his men. "Seize them."

The men pointed their spears toward the bewildered Israelites. Children clung to their mothers, their hysterical cries filling every dark corner of the chamber.

Four soldiers went to work binding their prisoners with jute. The women sobbed softly as the men tied the rope around their waists and bound their wrists to their backs, passing the length to bind the next woman until they were all connected in a chain, immobilized by their shackles.

One of the men was charged with penning the children in one area. Some went quietly, others not so. Eliezer, son of Sarai, kicked one of the soldiers in the shin, then slipped out of the man's grip like a live fish as he clawed toward him. The boy, who had just entered his tenth year, was a maddening foe for the Egyptian, cleverly eluding his advances and taunting him.

"Eliezer, go quietly, my son," his mother called.

The boy did not listen, this time slipping under the soldier's legs and bolting toward the stairs. Two others grabbed him and threw him to the ground with no regard for his tender age. As he lay on his back, Eliezer drove his foot between the nearest soldier's legs, sending him to the ground with a howl.

Another Egyptian lifted his spear. "This boy is filled with the evil spirit. He must die." He thrust his spear into Eliezer's throat, bearing down with all his might as the boy gasped and spat blood.

Basemath fell to her knees and clutched her mouth with both hands. She shook as she witnessed the beastly crime against her people. Taking prisoners was a reality of war; taking a life, and that of a child, was unforgivable. Young Eliezer's blood seeped into the limestone as he flailed in a desperate attempt to cling to life. Three women held back his wailing mother from rushing to his side.

As the boy's movements grew weak and his body pale, the Egyptian yanked the spear out of his throat with a movement so coarse it almost split Eliezer's neck in two. "Challenge us and you shall suffer the same fate."

Bitterness rose to Basemath's mouth. What had been quiet resignation to the Israelites' fate turned to hot rage. She stood and spoke to him in his own language. "Coward.

Is this your notion of conquest and victory in the name of your king? Killing children and torturing women?"

He snarled and pointed his bloody spear at her. Saliva dribbled from the corner of his downturned mouth.

The leader stepped between them. "Lower your spear. She must be taken alive." He called over his shoulder to another of his men, "Bind her." Then he turned to Ana and let his gaze travel down her body. "This one is coming with me."

Basemath's eyes widened. "No . . . you cannot. My daughter belongs with me."

He ignored her plea and took Ana by the elbow.

The girl gritted her teeth as she struggled against his grip. She turned to her mother with the look of a frightened gazelle.

A rush of blood seared Basemath's face. She lunged at the Egyptian like a rabid cat, digging her nails into the flesh of his forearm. "Let her go!"

He flung his arm, breaking her grip and tossing her onto the ground. Her strength was no match for his, but that did not stop her. She scrambled to her feet and clutched Ana's other elbow with her fiercest grip. "You cannot take my daughter." She said it over and over, growing more hysterical with each utterance.

She tugged against the Egyptian's grip even as Ana's face twisted with pain. Basemath's arms shook from the effort. She could feel her grasp slipping.

Other soldiers came to the leader's aid, but he waved them away. With a swift movement he ripped the girl out of her mother's arms. A sinister laugh left his throat and echoed against the stone of the subterranean chamber. He grabbed Ana by the hair and led her up the staircase.

Basemath howled as she watched her only child disappear into the dark catacombs. She felt a pair of hands wrap jute around her waist. She did not fight. She dropped her head to the ground and wept, her body quaking as her wrists succumbed to the enemy's bindings.

CHAPTER TWO

Night came swiftly to the valley of Jezreel. Basemath sat on a worn carpet on the ground of her prison-tent, knees gathered to her chest. Even in spring, the night's breath was frigid as it blew across the open valley. A chill traveled down her spine, as much a response to the cold as to the fate that awaited her.

Though it would have offered her comfort, she refused the blanket that had been placed in the tent for her use. She recognized the coarse weave of the wool, striped in faded blue and violet and fringed on the ends, as the work of her people. She wondered which house Shoshenq's men had pillaged and from whose bed they had plucked it. She imagined the inhabitants, ordinary folk judging by the quality of their textiles, being driven from their house, if they survived at all, scattering from their towns like ants, frightened and stripped of everything. She viewed the stolen blanket as a symbol of their suffering and left it be, for accepting it would feel like a betrayal.

She was grateful for this: her bindings had been cut. She pushed the long trumpet sleeve of her gown back and regarded the bloodied skin of her wrists, scraped raw by the jute. It stung no more than the humiliation of being taken prisoner.

The tent of her captivity was barely big enough for four people to stand upright, shoulder to shoulder. It was made of woven goat hair strips that had been stitched together to make a broad cloth and secured to the ground with wooden pegs. A branch of olive wood held up the ceiling. A meager flame burning in a clay saucer lamp flickered against the tent walls, casting long shadows in the semidark.

Basemath heard a man clear his throat outside her tent and realized she was being guarded. Her face tightened. This was a foil to her plan to exit the tent in the thick of night and search for her daughter. Even if it cost her life, she was determined to save Ana's. The thought of her precious child in that heathen's hands ignited a fury she did not recognize in herself. Anger and violence were not her way. But if it came to that, she would disembowel the Egyptian before seeing him strip the girl of her purity.

She inhaled deeply to let the rage simmer down. She needed her wits about her. She stood and walked to the flap covering the tent door. She peered through a slit and gazed at the sky. The full moon hung low above the horizon; she was facing east. She parted the fabric ever so slightly, hoping her movements would go undetected.

It was a fool's hope. The guard noticed right away

and pointed his spear at her, barking something in a dialect she did not recognize. He was a tall man of great girth, whose eyes shone with a murderous glint.

She did not retreat. "My thirst is great. I want a cup of water."

He jabbed the air with his spear, urging her back inside.

She stood her ground, staring into his eyes, two obsidian marbles that seemed devoid of intelligence. "Bring me water."

The tip of his spear touched her ribs. He spat out more words. When again she did not move, he twisted the spear.

She heard the linen of her gown rip and felt a sting. She glanced down and saw blood seeping slowly from the flesh wound. "You are godless," she hissed in Hebrew.

"He is merely carrying out orders." A male voice came from the shadows.

Basemath was surprised to hear Hebrew spoken in the enemy camp. She watched the guard's reaction to the invisible intruder. He didn't flinch.

"Who are you?" she asked, uneasy. "Show your face."

He stepped into view. In the blackness of night, she could make out the lines of his *halug*, the long tunic that identified him as an Israelite. The decorations on the garment—a metal belt cinching the waist and embroidered trim along the sleeves, hem, and neckline—betrayed his status. She could barely see his face.

"Hello, Princess." He edged forward. "It has been long years since we last met."

Basemath froze when she realized who stood before her. There had been rumblings about the traitor's return to Israel after he had been driven out of the country for masterminding a rebellion against her father. She attempted to speak, but the words were trapped in the cage of shock.

"Aren't you going to greet your future king?"

"Do not assume a fate that is not yours, Jeroboam. It is blasphemy."

"You and I both know it is a matter of time before I will reign over the tribes of Israel."

"The people of Israel are loyal to the house of David. They will never allow—"

"They already have. There is nothing you, or any of Solomon's spawn, can do to stop it. The people of the northern tribes have separated themselves from the united kingdom. I am to lead them, as the prophecy foretold."

Bile rose to Basemath's throat, and she fought the urge to vomit. No longer able to look at him, she retreated into the tent.

Jeroboam followed her. "You will hear what I have to say. Face me."

Basemath turned her head slowly. He had not changed in the years since she'd last seen him. His dark, angry eyes were set deep beneath substantial eyebrows, and a short black beard covered his jaw and throat. His skin was the color of fired clay, with creases marking his hollow cheeks. His shoulder-length hair, an unruly mass of ebony waves, was bound by a tight turban in hues of indigo and myrtle.

Her mind flashed back to the day she'd met him. She was Ana's age when Jeroboam, some ten years her senior, was chosen by King Solomon to preside over the forced laborers in Jerusalem. Her father had singled him out from among thousands for his industry and honor and trusted him with his most important building projects. Jeroboam was to oversee the *burnden* for the building of the Millo, which encircled and fortified the king's city, and of the royal palace for her mother outside the holy compound.

Basemath had met him at the Passover feast. He sat at the long table with the king, partaking little of the food and wine, rarely loosing his lips. When welcoming his court, Solomon called upon his most beloved servants to recognize them before all who had gathered. It was the first time the young Jeroboam had been bestowed this favor, and it instantly changed his posture. He stood among the king's other lieutenants, head held high and chest inflated like a rooster's, pride visibly seeping into his soul.

It was a story as old as time: once they had tasted power, men were easily corrupted.

The wound on her side stung anew. "You will be judged for this act of betrayal, Jeroboam."

A burst of laughter laced with irony left his throat. "By whom? Your brother, the impotent king? I went to Rehoboam's coronation to bargain on behalf of the people. He was so arrogant that our pleas to ease the burden of your father's taxation evaporated like raindrops on hot stone. He insisted on raising taxes rather than reducing them. It was clear he has no idea what the people want, and for that the people are abandoning him. Surely you are aware the leaders of the ten tribes of Israel walked out of the coronation, humiliating Rehoboam on the day of his ascent to power." His face twisted into a look of disgust. "It was no more than he deserved."

She was all too aware of the incident and of the schism that followed it. Rehoboam had spent five years trying to alternately subdue the separatist tribes and make peace with them. It was no secret he was losing the battle, nor was it surprising that Jeroboam had arisen as the leader of the disgruntled north, for it was he who had given voice to the people and fanned the flames of revolt against the house of David.

"Why do you tell me this? Do you expect my sympathy? You shall not have it. The disrespect you have shown my father, and now my brother, is shameful."

"Shameful is your kins' disregard for the people. The unfairness with which they have treated us, all so they can line their coffers with gold." He held up a clenched fist. "I am loyal to these people . . . and I shall see them vindicated."

"Dare you use the word *loyal*, you who attempted to overthrow your king, the very man who trusted you and gave you everything?" A knot rose to her throat, strangling her words. She still winced at the recollection of Jeroboam's attempt to take the government into his own hands during Solomon's reign.

It was the most despicable of acts. Solomon had placed Jeroboam in charge of the levy from the house of Joseph, the most influential of the tribes. Jeroboam, an Ephraimite and thus a member of the tribe, was charismatic and had the respect of his people, so he was in the perfect position to exercise influence over them. Solomon had made him his personal representative to this all-important part of his constituency, entrusting him with imposing the will of the crown, even if it was unpopular.

But the king's plan backfired. Instead of remaining faithful to the reigning house of David, Jeroboam took up the cause of the house of Joseph and bargained on the people's behalf. Solomon viewed this as a betrayal and removed his once-favored officer from his post. Shortly after his dismissal, Jeroboam, who had retreated to his hometown of Zeredah, gathered three hundred horses and a rebel army to him and plotted a revolt against Jerusalem.

His paltry attempt to dethrone the mighty King Solomon was crushed by a unit of mercenaries led by her own Ahimaaz, but it sent a message: the kingdom was no longer secure or unchallenged. The bliss that ushered in Solomon's rule had soured. After his act of treason, Jeroboam was forced into exile, but with or without him, anti-Solomonic sentiment simmered.

"Tell me this, Jeroboam," she continued. "Where did you flee when my father drove you out of Israel?" She suspected she knew the answer but wanted to hear it from him.

A smile crept upon his pursed lips. "By sending me away, Solomon merely galvanized God's plan. He forced me into Egypt, surely thinking the enemy would feast upon my flesh and crush my bones. But it was not so. The pharaoh Shoshenq embraced me like a brother and took me into his court. He offered me protection and a royal bride—Ano, the sister of his own wife. And he helped me come back to claim my destiny.

"You see, Princess, it was prophesied long ago that I would rise as king of Israel. The prophet Ahijah the Shilonite came to me in secret one day and tore his mantle into twelve pieces. He gave me the ten and said, 'Behold the Lord's will. He has chosen you to lead the ten tribes of Israel, leaving only the tribes of Judah and Benjamin under the rule of the house of his servant David. The united kingdom will be no more.'" He banged on his chest with a closed fist. "I am only claiming what is rightfully mine."

News of the prophecy took her by surprise. So it had been done. The Lord had stripped the house of David of its glory, banishing the old decree that David's seed would rule forever. Divine anger could no longer be appeased, for the sins that ignited it were too great. It was too late for the house of David, too late for Israel. The darkness was upon them, and Jeroboam shepherded it in with his flock of Egyptians. She was grateful her father did not see it in his lifetime.

Basemath scanned Jeroboam's eyes for any trace of holiness that might cause the Lord to appoint him ruler of a new, divided kingdom. She saw nothing but death in his shallow gaze. Ambition and vanity he had plenty of, but righteousness he did not. Beneath the valiant front, fear stirred in his soul, and she predicted it would be his downfall.

She breathed in the cool night air perfumed with hawthorn embers from a distant campfire. "If what you say is true, what will become of King Rehoboam?"

"He will continue to reign as king of Judah. The two tribes of the south will be his to rule." He sneered. "They're nothing but chieftains and herders anyway. They are of no consequence to me."

"And Jerusalem?"

"Pharaoh Shoshenq's armies are marching toward Jerusalem this night. The pharaoh himself is leading the charge. He will sack the city and reclaim his property."

"His property? There is nothing in Jerusalem that belongs to him."

Jeroboam laughed. "There is so much you don't know, Princess. But do not be troubled by things you have no power to change. All will be revealed in due time. And then . . ." His gaze traveled down her body, then back up to her eyes. "You can decide what you wish to do with the truth."

How she despised him. The mere words *the truth* were blasphemy when uttered by his lips. She had no use for his enigmatic statements, his supercilious proclamations that he, a mere commoner and the son of a harlot, was privy to a secret.

He continued. "The glory of Jerusalem will be no more. Stripped of its dignity, Solomon's holy city will be as it once was, a small stronghold in the rocky backcountry.

Shechem will be the new seat of power. It is what the people want."

"You are mistaken. The people will never stop journeying to the temple of the Lord. It is where Yahweh dwells and where his tablets of law are kept. The faith that draws the Hebrews to Jerusalem is far more potent than anything you or your pharaoh can muster."

"You are the one who is mistaken. There will be no more need for the people to make the pilgrimage to Jerusalem. I will build temples in the great northern holy cities, Bethel and Dan, and the people will flock there to worship the Lord."

Her eyes widened. "The Levites will never stand for this . . ."

"Then they shall be banished from my kingdom."

"You cannot banish the priests. It is against the word of God."

"Need I remind you, Princess, God has chosen me? Anyone who stands in my path will be struck down."

"It is sacrilege—"

"Silence!"

Shaking her head, she took a step back. "This is madness. You are traveling down the path of destruction and taking an entire nation with you." She pointed to the tent flap. "Leave my tent at once."

He spoke through clenched teeth. "You can no longer order me. In a matter of days I will be crowned king. You will owe me your allegiance."

"Until such a day, you will bow to the house of David."

"You have one night to decide your own fate. You can be exiled to Egypt to serve the pharaoh, or you can be executed in your homeland. I will expect your decision by first light." He smirked, then turned to leave the tent. "If you don't choose," he said over his shoulder, "the choice will be made for you."

Basemath was thankful to be alone again. With an exhale she lowered her head into her palms. Jeroboam's presence had rattled her more than she wanted to admit. She searched for the peaceful place inside her heart, but it eluded her. So many thoughts circled her mind, refusing to alight. Facing east, she kneeled down on the old carpet and folded her upper body forward. With the crown of her head touching the carpet, she inhaled the scent entwined in the fibers: a combination of dry earth, wood-fire smoke, and livestock.

It was the smell of her land—the territory promised by the Lord to the children of Israel, which they had reached after forty years of wandering plagued by trials and hardship. They had watered the earth with their blood, calcified the soil with the bones of their dead. However many struggles they faced, it was worth it to inhale the scent of their inherited land—the sweet perfume of deliverance and freedom.

The twelve tribes of Israel had earned their place there, yet they never had assured it. Their right had been challenged throughout their history, the gift of their God scorned by the heathen nations encircling their own. The campaign of Shoshenq was just another manifestation of the tribulations the Hebrews had faced since their seed was planted on the earth.

But to be betrayed by one of their own was unforgivable. Basemath shuddered at the thought of a high-ranking Israelite ensconced with the pharaoh, drinking his wine and tasting the flesh of his women. Surely Jeroboam had sold the Egyptians state secrets—how else could they have known about the water tunnel?—in exchange for their military support. He needed Shoshenq and his ten thousand warriors to charge into the fortified cities of Jerusalem and Megiddo and to strike terror into the hearts of the people—*his* people, whom he preferred to frighten into submission than inspire to greatness.

Regardless of how he posed, Jeroboam was not a man of God; of that she was certain. He was cunning and clever and golden of tongue, but divinely guided he was not. Why the Lord would choose him to lead the ten tribes of Israel was a mystery she did not comprehend, but neither did she question it. She had learned long ago the will of the Almighty would be done, and no human could cry injustice.

She sat with her head to the earth for a long time, offering her body and spirit but praying for nothing. With eyes closed, she let thoughts enter and leave unchecked, hoping for a vision of the future. Her mind drifted as if in slumber, yet she was awake. In that coveted realm of awareness without conscious thought, she saw the face of Ana, unblemished and beaming. She stood on a pile of rocks in a hostile wilderness, beneath a shaft of light.

Though everything around her was still, her white flax *halug* and her unbound raven locks billowed in a rogue breeze. The light caught her eyes, making them shine with the intensity of polished agate.

Basemath thought she heard the girl say, *I have come to help you. Do not be afraid, my love, my love.*

She opened her eyes with a start. A profound chill settled upon her bones, making her shiver.

She felt a hand on her shoulder and froze.

She was not alone.

CHAPTER THREE

"Do not be afraid."

Basemath knew that voice. She sighed and sat up to face her husband. Ahimaaz's skin was blackened with dirt and soot, his graying beard unruly. His blue *halug* had been ripped at the shoulder, and the fabric hung over the bronze armor that covered his torso.

Ahimaaz took off his red woolen mantle and placed it over her shoulders.

She took his hands in hers. "You are safe. Praise the Lord."

He blew out the oil lamp, plunging the tent into darkness. "There isn't much time," he whispered. "We must leave under cover of night. The moon shines full. It will light our path."

"I will not go without our daughter. She is in one of the tents. I do not know which."

"Verily, I know."

She could not see his face but heard the confidence in his voice. "How . . . ? How is it you know?"

"When we got word the tunnel had been breached, three of the men and I followed the Egyptians to this camp. We hid in the copse beyond the vale and watched. It is how I knew you were here. Ana is across camp, in an officer's tent."

"Then you must know Jeroboam is here."

"Yes."

"He claims he will be crowned king, ruling over the ten tribes of the north."

"It is true. God save us." He paused. "Has he made mention of Jerusalem?"

"The pharaoh's army marches to Jerusalem this very night. Jeroboam said Shoshenq wishes to reclaim his property. Know you what that means?"

Ahimaaz was silent for a long moment. "I do not."

After thirteen years of marriage, Basemath knew when her husband hid something from her. Though she could not examine his gaze for sincerity, she knew that tone: a bit hesitant, weak. "I must know the truth, Ahimaaz."

He exhaled. She felt the warm puff of air on her cheeks and smelled his slightly sour breath.

"I will tell you what I know. There are murmurs of the pharaoh wanting to take your mother back to Tanis. Back to her home."

Basemath sat up straighter. "My mother may be Egyptian, but she's nobody's property."

"She was a pharaoh's daughter before marrying your father. Now that Solomon is dead, her kin may want her to live out the rest of her days in her homeland. They have a custom of burying royalty in family tombs, just as we do."

Jeroboam's words rang in her ears. *There is so much you don't know, Princess.* She was certain Ahimaaz's theory, though sound, was incomplete. But she had no answers.

"Someone must warn my mother . . . and the king." She grasped his shoulders. "You must ride to Jerusalem, my husband."

"I fear it is too late. If Shoshenq's troops are on the move, we will not catch up to them in time. Jerusalem must make her own fate. My first responsibility is to my family . . . to you and Ana. We must escape this camp alive so we can fight the Egyptian enemy. That is our priority now."

"How can you say that?" Though she whispered the words, her tone was resolute. "Our first and only responsibility is to the Lord our God. If we don't endeavor to save Jerusalem, everything my grandfather fought for and all my father built in the name of the Lord will fall to ruin—and with it, a nation's faith. I would sooner die than see that come to pass."

"The road to Jerusalem is long and treacherous. Even if we do make it out of this camp alive, I fear for your safety during the journey. The enemy lurks at every bend. We may be called upon to fight. It is no place for women and girls."

She squeezed his shoulders. "Listen to me, Ahimaaz. There is no time to mount a rescue scheme. You must ride to Jerusalem alone. It is our only hope."

"I cannot leave you . . . leave my child."

"Our plight is much bigger than we are. Everything we believe, everything our people have fought to build since the time of our forefathers, is at peril. My father built Jerusalem and the Lord's magnificent temple by divine grace. The holy city and the temple therein symbolize God's favor upon the Hebrews. We must never forsake this. We must not yield Jerusalem or allow the heathens to defile the temple . . . even if it means spilling our blood upon the earth."

His calloused hand touched her face. "My wise and courageous wife. Even if I perish in battle, I die a happy man, for I have known the grace of Basemath."

She leaned forward and rested her forehead on his. She remained in that position for a long while, listening to the sound of his breath. She was keenly aware this might be their last encounter.

She sat back. "I ask one last thing of you."

"Anything."

"Leave your *khopesh* with me."

She heard the sickle-sword scrape against his woven metal waist sash. He placed the small *khopesh* on the ground next to her knees.

She squeezed his hands. "Now go."

Without another word, Ahimaaz lifted a tent peg and slipped out the unguarded back.

Basemath raised a hand to her mouth. She felt a vague stabbing sensation in her chest. For all her valor and conviction, she was still a wife, a mother, a woman. She did not want to make the choices she did, but circumstances did not permit an alternative. She was sickened at the thought of Ahimaaz potentially riding to his death, of Ana alone in an Egyptian officer's tent, of herself choosing between captivity and execution.

She picked up the *khopesh*. In spite of its size, it was a heavy instrument, one that could exact damage. She ran a finger across its cutting edge and smarted at the sting as her skin was sliced open. She sucked the wound, tasting the metallic tang of her own blood.

Fatigue weighed down her eyelids. She pushed up her gown and tucked the *khopesh* into the folds of her loincloth. She let herself collapse onto the carpet and drew her knees and elbows close to her body. Curled up like an unborn babe, she thought of her mother.

Nicaule Tashere was born to the Pharaoh Psusennes II by one of his consorts and given to Solomon in marriage to ensure healthy relations between the two nations. Indeed, while Nicaule lived in Jerusalem, Egypt did not raise a hand toward Israel. While Psusennes was living, there was trade between the two nations and mutual aid in the form of labor. Upon his passing, Shoshenq, his successor, had different urges and political aspirations. While Psusennes was content with the Egyptian boundaries, Shoshenq, the progeny of tribal warriors, aimed to push them—at whatever cost.

But what did he want with Nicaule? Was it merely his way of gathering all Egyptian royalty back to Tanis? Was it a promise to the dying pharaoh, a pledge to the man who had trained him to be his successor? Surely Shoshenq did not want Nicaule for himself; she was well past the prime of her seductive powers.

Had her mother been younger, Basemath would have allowed for that possibility. In her youth, Nicaule was unlike anyone in the whole of Israel, her exquisite presence a combination of her loveliness, her Egyptian heritage, and her indomitable spirit. When she attended feasts alongside her husband, people diverted their eyes, such was her beauty. It was said she could hypnotize men.

She certainly had that effect on Solomon. She was one of his many wives, but by far his favorite. Basemath had witnessed the power she had over him. After Solomon announced their eldest daughter was to marry, Nicaule had stormed out in anger. She had retreated to her own palace and would not reemerge, ignoring Solomon's pleas.

Basemath watched from the shadows on the night Solomon came to Nicaule's door, begging her to let him in. His wife appeared in the doorway wearing a transparent gown. She stood behind a web of scarlet that kept the door from opening all the way. She told him, "Enter my chamber without breaking the scarlet thread. It is how a husband begs forgiveness of his wife in my homeland."

Solomon looked bewildered.

"On your knees," she'd said, pointing to the stone floor.

Basemath was certain he would not do it, for he was the anointed king of Israel. Surely his pride would not allow such an act. But he desired his wife so much that he crouched like an animal on all fours and crawled into her chamber.

Basemath grimaced at the recollection of the detestable demand and the clear message it had sent: Solomon's spirit had weakened to the point of becoming slave to a woman, of beseeching corporal pleasure. Nicaule had manipulated him without regard for his soul, and he had given her permission to do it.

There was much in her mother she did not want to forgive, but her own covenant with the Lord did not permit dishonoring a parent, no matter how questionable the actions. Whatever her mother stood for, she accepted it. But her own allegiance always and unconditionally belonged to her father.

It was difficult for her to watch his decline. It had come little by little, but Basemath could see the signs even if he could not. The incident with the scarlet thread was only one case in which he should have reviled the perpetrator and walked away, keeping his spirit intact. Rather, he gave in to the rapture of the flesh.

It wasn't the only time that had happened. In his quest to maintain peaceful relations with surrounding nations, he had taken a number of foreign wives and had loved each of them with gusto. He let his wife Naamah the Ammonite worship her god, Molek, on a hill outside of Jerusalem's walled compound. When the act was condemned by the kingdom's holy men, Solomon explained Naamah was the mother of his heir, Rehoboam, and thus entitled to worship as she wished. He insisted his permissiveness did not corrupt his own soul, even as the priests warned him of being guilty by association.

But Solomon believed he was above all that. Basemath would never forget the day she overheard a confrontation between her father and his high priest, Zadok. The holy man had related to the king a vision he'd had the previous night.

"I have seen enemies at the gates of Jerusalem, my lord. There was a young man who chipped away the stone of the terraces using a stone hammer and a peg from the old tabernacle. His face was covered so I could not see. But he wore the garments of your people. I fear someone from within your ranks is conspiring against you."

Solomon scoffed. "It is nonsense. My men are loyal to me. I have given them all they could want . . . fair pay, status, honor. To some I have even given my daughters as brides. Why would any one of them forsake me?"

Zadok issued a harsh rebuke. "Perhaps you trust too much. Perhaps you have grown too complacent and do not see what is crumbling around you."

"Dare you speak this way to the king who was placed upon the throne of Israel by God himself? The favor of the Almighty is with me always. It was the Lord's promise to my father." He raised his voice. "If anyone opposes me, let him come. I will crush him with the staff of divine power and watch him beg for mercy. No one challenges the rule of King Solomon."

Basemath reeled at the veracity of Zadok's dream. Soon after, Jeroboam had emerged as the king's adversary.

Though he was indeed knocked down, he rose again, waving the peg and hammer of God. Had Solomon not been so haughty as to believe himself invincible, perhaps the outcome would have been different.

Or perhaps not.

She sighed and closed her eyes. She wanted so badly to be overcome by sleep. She wanted to not feel, if even for one moment, to be released from the shackles of her memory. She let the tears flow onto the fibers of the old carpet as the words of Jeroboam's ultimatum melted into her mind.

You can be exiled to Egypt to serve the pharaoh, or you can be executed in your homeland.

When she opened her eyes again, she felt rested and lucid, though she was certain she hadn't slept. She sat up and peered through the slit on the tent flap. The sky was the color of tekhelet, streaked with great plumes of violet and crimson that reached to the heavens like a prayer. A sliver of gold appeared between the crests of the mountains to the east, heralding the new day.

The moment of her judgment was upon her.

CHAPTER FOUR

Zadok, the son of Ahitub, stood upon Mount Moriah, gazing at the city sprawled beneath his feet. He contemplated the foundation of the royal palace, a year in the making by twoscore stonemasons, the finest in Israel and Tyre. There was much work yet to be done, but its scale and substance already were to be feared.

A bit farther down lay the citadel, the fort of protection that stood between the city's treasures and the flat-roofed, square stone structures where the people dwelled. At the foot of the city walls flowed the life-giving Gihon Spring, which fed the arid desert and supported the inhabitants of the holiest place in all of Israel.

It was a splendid sight, this Jerusalem his king was building. Never in the history of the Hebrews had there been a city of such magnitude, a city dedicated to Yahweh. Jerusalem was more than a fortress and the seat of power; it also was the site the Lord chose for the building of his house, a monumental task appointed to only the most worthy. Though it would take several years and an enormous amount of resources, the king was undaunted and launched into construction with fervor.

This pleased Zadok, the high priest of the united kingdom of Israel and Judah under King Solomon and, prior to that, the trusted priest of King David. As a descendant of Eleazar, who was the third son of Aaron, Zadok traced his patrilineage to the brother of Moses and the nation's first high priest. His line had been established by God himself since the exodus into the promised land, and he had given himself completely to his appointed duty, which was to him more than a birthright: it was a privilege.

Zadok felt a firm hand on his shoulder and turned his head. King Solomon stood to his left, his gaze fixed upon the city. He wore a white flaxen gown with long sleeves and a generously draped fringed skirt tied at the waist with a leather girdle. Over it a red woolen mantle was secured at the shoulder with a gold pin bearing the likeness of a lion's head. His shoulder-length curls, gleaming beneath the midday sun like oiled onyx, were crowned by a pointed skullcap woven of yellow silk.

He rubbed the short black beard that grew across his square jaw and encircled his fleshy lips. "Magnificent, isn't it?" He turned to Zadok and regarded him with smiling eyes. "I wish my father had lived to see it."

"He would have been a proud father. His son is doing exactly as commanded of him."

Solomon looked over his shoulder to the construction

taking place on the highest point of Mount Moriah. "So many years have passed since the Lord appeared to King David on this very mountain and said to him, 'Build me a house.' It pleases me to fulfill my father's debt and bring honor to his name."

Zadok delighted in the king's humble nature. Though Solomon was only twenty-three years of age and had scarcely completed his fifth year on the throne, he was not hotheaded or vainglorious, as were so many of his peers. He possessed a modesty that could stem only from authentic self-assurance. The youngest son of King David, born to his wife Bathsheba, was blessed with a regal quality, an aura of a kind. Even before he was a monarch, people were drawn to him and transfixed by his presence. It was as if he was destined for the role he had stepped into: leading God's chosen people into a new era of greatness and prosperity.

Zadok looked toward the construction site. "Everything is progressing well, then?"

"Come. Walk with me."

The two ascended a series of rough-hewn stone steps placed along the hillside temporarily so the workers could transport with ease the multitude of building materials for the temple of the Lord. Upon completion of this most holy of structures, proper steps would be installed so every Israelite, even the eldest and most infirm, could comfortably make the journey to the Lord's house.

Zadok used his staff to steady himself. He was in his fifty-eighth year, and his physical ability had begun to deteriorate. Silver streaks had colored his waist-length black hair, which he pinned beneath a blue turban, and his gray beard hung to his chest. He ate little, for he considered gluttony a sin, and it was evident in his emaciated form. Despite his advancing age, he had the energy of a man much younger. He was determined to see the temple of Solomon completed and to venerate the Lord in its hallowed chambers. Long had he and his forebears prayed for that moment.

On the highest peak of Mount Moriah, hundreds of men labored. The leaders barked urgent commands as sweating laborers grunted under the burden of the ashlars they hauled with pulleys. The stones had been cut and dressed by the finest stonemasons at the limestone quarry beneath the mount so that no hammer or chisel or other iron instrument would be used in the vicinity of the holy house. The outer walls had been erected to a height of thirty cubits, towering toward the heavens. Around the main structure, a series of chambers and a porch leading up to the entrance began to take shape.

Zadok lowered his head before the edifice in construction and offered a silent prayer.

"Come, old friend," said Solomon. "Let us walk in the footsteps of our fathers."

The king and the priest walked toward the entrance and stood in front of the porch. The king said, "All those who come to the Lord's temple will walk through this doorway. Here will stand two columns made of bronze, with molten bronze chapiters carved with lily work and pomegranates. I have found the most skilled bronze worker in all the land, a man from Naphtali who hails from a long line of sculptors. He is already at work on the columns and the brazen sea." He turned away from the doorway and pointed to the empty space. "The sea will stand here. Ten were the commandments laid forth by the Lord, so ten will be the cubits measured from one brim to the other. It will rest on the backs of twelve oxen, each representing a tribe of Israel, which will be arranged in a circle and face the sky. And it will be filled with living water flowing from the spring."

"A magnificent way to take *mikveh*," said Zadok. The ritual bath, intended to purify the priests before they entered the temple, was paramount to the Hebrews' faith. Though Zadok's own sensibility was far simpler, he marveled at the young king's ingenuity in venerating their God in the most exalted way imaginable.

Solomon turned again and walked toward the edifice, standing in the open doorway. He gestured toward the west side of the temple. "Behold the place that will be the oracle of the house. It will be constructed in perfect symmetry, twenty cubits on each side, and will rise ten cubits above the floor. Its floor and ceiling and every wall will be covered in gold, and beneath the gold will be planks of cedar pledged by Hiram, the king of Tyre, who was a friend to my father.

"And when it is finished, the ark holding the Lord's covenant with our people will be taken up from the old tabernacle and brought hither, as will all the treasures amassed by my father." He looked to Zadok. "You will carry the ark to this temple, Zadok, old friend, and you will preside over the oracle for all your days. This is your charge and your destiny."

The priest bowed before the king. "My lord, I vow to protect the holy of holies and the tablets of law within it, as my fathers have done before me."

"This would please my father. You have been a loyal servant to him and to me."

Zadok had adored King David. Since David's early days in Hebron, where he was anointed king of Judah, Zadok had been faithful to him as a high-ranking priest, second only to Abiathar of the house of Eli. While Abiathar betrayed David in his old age, supporting the treacherous Prince Adonijah for accession to the throne, Zadok remained steadfast, backing Prince Solomon, who was God's chosen.

On his deathbed, David at last had understood the difference between the two priests: one was acting from self-interest, the other from divine direction. He relieved Abiathar of his duties, naming Zadok to the post of high priest. He had served in that capacity since, his authority reinforced by Solomon, who was ever grateful to Zadok for helping him rise to the throne of Israel.

From the day Solomon was anointed king at Gihon by Zadok's own hand, he set about fulfilling the vision of his father and realizing all David could not, or was forbidden to. Solomon's first charge was to crush his father's old enemies and those who had brought shame to his house: Joab, the captain of the army, who had shed innocent blood in the time of peace, and Shimei of the house of Saul, who had cursed David but later begged his forgiveness.

Ordering the deaths of these men was Solomon's initiation into manhood. Zadok had stood by the eighteen-year-old king through these executions and watched him transform from a fawn with shaking legs to a strong buck.

It had taken all his strength to call for the death of his own brother.

On the day Solomon had been made king, one of the guards came to Zadok in a panic, saying, "Adonijah has gone into the tabernacle. He hides behind the altar in fear for his life. He believes the king will have him slain."

Zadok nodded his thanks to the guard. "I will speak to the king."

The priest made haste for the throne room, where Solomon sat in solitude, his thin limbs draped awkwardly over David's ruling chair, as if trying to own it. Zadok bowed before him. "My lord, I bring tidings of your brother."

Solomon sat up. "Say what you will."

"Adonijah, son of Haggith, has taken hold of the horns on the altar and waits for your pardon, my lord. What do you command?"

The king looked off into the distance as he weighed his decision. "He has sinned against my father."

"He has, my lord."

"The throne may have been rightfully his, but he proclaimed himself king without asking for my father's blessing. That is a disgrace."

"It is, my lord."

Solomon rested his chin on his fist. "He knows of his trespasses and has run to the altar. So he admits his guilt." He fell silent for several breaths. "What would my father do, Zadok?"

"I advise you to search your own heart and let the decision be yours. You are king now. Being king means having to make difficult choices."

"Very well." The newly anointed monarch thought for a while before speaking. "My decision is to let him live. If he proves himself a good man, he shall always have my protection. But if he strays, he shall die. Give him these instructions, and tell him he is free to go to his house."

That was Zadok's first glimpse into Solomon's heart. Though the hair on his face was still soft, he had the wisdom to grant a second chance and give a man the opportunity to show his character. Once in a while, wicked men would have a change of heart and follow the righteous path, but more often they would craft their own demise. Zadok was certain Adonijah would interpret Solomon's decree as weakness and dig for himself a deep grave.

And so it happened.

At the end of fall that year, after David had breathed his last, Bathsheba requested audience with her son. Zadok brought her into the throne room and waited in the shadows as she put forth her request.

Solomon rose from the throne and stepped down to meet his mother. He took her hands and bowed. "My dear mother, what brings you to the room of judgment?"

"My lord, King Solomon, I have something to ask of you."

The king guided her toward a chair to the right of his throne. They both sat facing each other. "Tell me, Mother. What is it you ask?"

"I ask not for myself. I come as a messenger for your brother Adonijah. He sends me here this day."

His face hardened. "Adonijah, who is not even your son. Why has he come to you?"

Bathsheba lowered her eyes. "He believes you will not deny me."

"I have never denied you; it is true. But each request must be judged by its merit. I do not promise I will grant this thing, but ask it anyway."

"Adonijah wants to take a wife. He asks to be given Abishag the Shunammite."

Solomon took hold of the throne's armrests and slowly sat back. His face was expressionless, but his eyes burned with insult. "Does he, indeed? Does he truly think he deserves the virgin who ministered to my father as he lay dying, all while Adonijah"—he spat out the name—"made merry with the men of the court, exalting his own name? What he asks is an affront to my father, to me, and to my kingdom." He stood. "I never should have let him live."

"My lord . . . what do I say to him?"

"Tell him nothing. I must deliberate on this. I will give you my answer by sundown." He offered a hand to help her rise from the chair. "Good day, Mother."

Bathsheba's golden bracelets chimed as she hurried out of the room. Solomon wrapped his mantle around his shoulders and walked out behind her.

On the hour before sundown, Zadok received word that the king wanted to meet him at Gibeon. The priest made his way to the mountain posthaste. There he found Solomon sitting beneath an olive tree, his arms wrapped around his knees and his gaze fixed upon the city. He did not turn around as Zadok approached him from the back.

"I have spoken to the Lord," Solomon said.

Zadok lowered himself with some effort and sat next to the king. He offered no words.

Solomon spoke in a soft, even voice. "As I sat here weighing my decision, sleep came over my eyes and I leaned into this old tree trunk. In my dreams I saw a brilliant light and heard a thundering voice say, 'What is it you wish for, Solomon?' I looked away for fear of being blinded. I didn't know what to say. And the voice continued: 'Your father, David, was my loyal servant. This I do for his sake. Now ask what you will, and I shall grant it.'

"I realized then the voice was the Lord's and fell to the ground, lying prostrate before him. And I said, 'O Lord, beloved God of Israel, I am but a child. How can I judge your people, whom you have chosen, when I know so little about the ways of the world? If I ask anything, O Lord, it is an understanding heart to know the difference between good and bad, so I can lead your nation with fairness and compassion but also with a firm hand toward those who trespass against you.'

"And the Lord said, 'Do you not ask for honor and abundance and long life?' And I replied, 'What good are those things if a heart is empty of truth?' Then the light diminished and in its place came a terrible darkness, and I thought I had displeased the Lord." He turned to Zadok.

"Do not fear the darkness, Solomon," the priest said. "The divine takes many forms. Spirit can exist in absolute beauty as easily as it can in bleakness. There is a duality to all things."

The young king nodded. "This I know now, for the Lord said, 'You shall have what you ask and more also. Behold, I grant you wisdom the likes of which has never dwelled in the heart of a mortal. And though you have not asked it, you shall have boundless riches, victory over your enemies, and peace in your kingdom for all your days. You shall stand apart from all who came before you and all who will follow you.'"

"This fate has been written," said Zadok. "The Lord has chosen you. Do you remember what your father said to you before he died?"

A stiff breeze swept across the mountaintop, tousling Solomon's raven curls. He wrapped his mantle more snugly about him. "He said, 'My son, I go the way of all the earth. The time has come for you to be strong and to lead our people. First and foremost, keep the ways of the Lord as it is written in the law of Moses. If you shall keep the Lord's commandments and fear his judgments, you will be shielded from enemies and our nation Israel will prosper. Behold the Lord's promise to me: 'If your children and their children walk along the righteous path and stand before me pure of heart and mind, your kingdom will be established forever.' This is your legacy, Solomon. Do not forsake it."

Zadok had stood beside King David as he spoke to his son for the last time. He was pleased Solomon had taken heed of the words, for he would have to bear their weight for his lifetime. "The Lord gives generously to those he favors. But such favor does not come without conventions. You must put Yahweh first, before your own earthly desires. Hear the advice of this old man: do not stray, or all will be taken from you."

Solomon gazed at the far horizon and sat in silence. His face was radiant, yet a vague sadness dwelled behind his eyes.

Zadok knew what he was thinking. "What of Adonijah, my lord? Have you considered his fate?"

"I have," he said softly. "By wanting to wed Abishag, who was chosen from young women in all the land for the sacred duty of caring for the king of Israel, my brother is sending a clear message. Though he knows she must remain pure for carrying out with honor the grave task appointed her, he asks to defile her virginity. That is a sin before the Lord and a challenge to my sovereignty. This I cannot allow. I have sent word to Benaiah, the captain of the host, that Adonijah must die this day."

There was no uncertainty in Solomon's voice. Zadok admired his resolve. It could not have been easy to order the death of a man who shared his own blood. "Your brother had the opportunity to live. In spite of his trespasses, you gave him his freedom; all he needed do was follow the path of virtue."

"Adonijah chose his own destiny." Solomon sprang to his feet and offered a hand to the old man. "Come, Zadok. Let us not delay the inevitable."

As the sun painted the clouded sky above Jerusalem in shades of copper and pearl, Solomon and Zadok came down from the high place. By the time they returned to the city, day had departed—and with it a youth's naïveté.

From that moment, Solomon never looked back but plunged into his appointed task. Now, five years on, they stood before the stone shell that would become the temple of the Lord and the fulfillment of a promise.

"My lord."

Solomon turned around.

With head bowed and hand over his heart, the superintendent of the temple construction project stood a few steps behind the king.

"What is it, Itai?"

"My lord, a young man seeks to see you. He has traveled on foot from the hill country of Ephraim to ask for work."

"You need not bring such matters to me, Itai. It is up to you to evaluate and hire the workers." Solomon started to leave.

"My lord, he insists. He says his father was in service to your father."

The king looked annoyed. "Many men dedicated their lives to King David. That does not put me in their debt."

"He brings you this." Itai held out a hand. In it was a triangle of faded indigo wool with frayed edges.

Solomon frowned as he regarded the piece of cloth. He took it from Itai's hand and rolled the wool between his fingers. "Bring him to me."

The prefect bowed and hurried away.

Solomon studied the wool by turning it and holding it up to the light.

Itai returned with a man who looked to be about Solomon's age. He wore the knee-length tunic of a simple man and a turban of blue and white braided tightly around his head. The hard angles of his face were exaggerated: his nose was straight and sharp as the chisel of the stonemasons; his brow jutted forward; his cheeks were hollow beneath protruding bones. He was of thin build but didn't appear weak. Zadok attributed it less to his constitution than to the raptorlike look in his eye.

"This is he, my lord," Itai said. "He calls himself Jeroboam, son of Nebat the Ephraimite."

Jeroboam kneeled before the king and bent forward so that his forehead scraped the dusty ground.

"Rise, Jeroboam." Solomon's voice boomed across the mount.

He did as commanded and stood tall with his eyes fixed upon the king.

Solomon held up the fabric. "What is the meaning of this?"

"My lord the king, it is a piece of the cloak of King Saul, who hunted your father. It was cut by David's sword in the cave at Ein Gedi."

"How have you come to have it?"

"My father was with David in the cave. He was one of the men who followed him during the days of his rebellion and wished to see him anointed king. In Ein Gedi, your father's enemy was delivered into his hands, but he chose not to kill him. Instead, he cut a corner of Saul's mantle with a sword that could have just as easily been used to claim a life.

"Even Saul, who was consumed with hatred, realized how admirable David's actions were. There could have been a bloody battle in Ein Gedi that day, but because of this"—he pointed to the fabric—"King Saul retreated, sealing David's fate.

"Your father discarded the piece of the cloak, but my father saw something in it and picked it up. He kept it for long years as a reminder of what a man's moral character should be." Jeroboam placed a hand upon his heart. "Now it belongs with you."

A slight smile crept upon Solomon's lips. Without moving his gaze from the bold stranger, he handed the cloth to Zadok. "What is it you want, Jeroboam of Ephraim?"

"Work, my lord. I am able of body and strong of mind. Before he died, a year ago, my father instructed me to walk from Zeredah to Jerusalem"—he gestured toward the temple construction—"to help build the Lord's house. I need not be paid. The honor would be enough reward."

"It is a long journey from Zeredah," Solomon said. "And it would be a long journey back."

"I would be prepared to undertake it should you send me away. But I beg you not to."

The king turned to his superintendent. "Itai. Do you need stone haulers?"

"I do, my lord."

"Show Jeroboam what to do."

Jeroboam again lowered himself on bent knee and bowed his head. "Thank you, my lord. I will not fail you."

"It is not easy work. You will labor hard." He swung one end of his mantle over his shoulder. "It is how a man proves himself." He walked away.

Zadok followed, barely able to keep up with the young king's spry gait. He contemplated Solomon's sense of fairness, his tendency to give trust and generosity up front and let people either earn it or chip away at it. Those who proved themselves worthy prospered; there was no tolerance for the rest. That pliability born of benevolence, combined with unwavering strength when the situation called for it, had won him the favor of everyone from kings to paupers.

Solomon spoke over his shoulder. "We must make haste, Zadok. Tonight we feast in honor of Hiram of Tyre. His caravan will arrive at any moment."

"Yes, my lord." Zadok's voice was labored.

The king stopped and waited for the old man to catch up. It was almost as if he had forgotten his priest's age.

Zadok stopped before him, leaning onto his walking stick with both hands.

Solomon put a hand on his shoulder. "I want you and Benaiah to sit on my right tonight. And make sure my mother and Nathan the prophet are honored guests."

The priest nodded.

"Hiram has been a good friend to Israel—first to my father and now to me. This evening's feast is most important. We must take our alliance with Tyre to the next level." He narrowed his eyes and looked toward the city. "Jerusalem will be the greatest city in the East. It will be exalted by the faithful and feared by its enemies. It is the Lord's plan; I am merely executing it." He turned back to Zadok. "Many negotiations will take place tonight. I will need your experience and wisdom, Zadok, old friend. I want you to speak in my ear."

"I always have and always will, my lord." It warmed him to utter those words. He was unconditionally devoted to his king.

Solomon squeezed Zadok's shoulder with a firm hand and said no more. He turned and walked toward the palace.

Zadok straightened his back and braced himself for the long journey down. He mulled the king's words: *We must take our alliance with Tyre to the next level.* Foreign lands and their monarchs were central to Solomon's rule and instrumental in the expansion of his kingdom. Zadok felt a vague needling sensation in the pit of his stomach. The law of Yahweh warned against aligning with non-Hebrews, for they could turn the hearts of Israel's children toward strange gods.

Solomon was walking a fine line.

CHAPTER FIVE

The banquet room was set with a cedar-plank table that stretched from one end of the hall to the other. On each place setting sat a glazed pottery bowl stamped with the winged lion insignia that had become the king's mark. Clay cups were placed next to the bowls, ready to receive wine. In the middle of the table were vessels filled with fruit and footed dishes piled high with plump dates.

Around the table were long benches and at least a score chairs, each seat occupied by a member of Solomon's court: captains and officers of the army, mighty men bred for war, governors, judges, brothers and kin, decorated servants, prophets. The king and his honored guest had not yet arrived.

Chatter, like the drone of bees, filled every corner of the room. Zadok took his place at the middle of the table, next to the high-back, carved-wood seat reserved for Solomon. He nodded to Benaiah, the stout army captain whose presence was so calm and quiet it was hard to imagine the lethal nature of his sword.

No sooner had Zadok lowered himself onto his chair than a footman stood by the doorway, sounding an elongated brass trumpet. Following five short bursts and one long one, everyone stood. The room was as still and quiet as a tomb.

"Their Highnesses King Solomon of Israel and King Hiram of Tyre," the footman announced.

Solomon walked in first. He was dressed in a long gown the color of the Mediterranean in summertime, cinched at the waist with a belt woven of metal and leather. A violet mantle with fringed ivory lining was draped luxuriously across his body and secured at one shoulder with a round buckle encrusted with jewels. The twelve points of his golden crown radiated from his head like the rays of the sun.

In unison, the banquet guests placed their right hands upon their hearts and bowed to their king.

Solomon turned toward the doorway and held out a hand in welcome to his guest. Hiram entered the room, and the two kings bowed to each other. Hiram's dress was exotic, flamboyant even, surely influenced by the extensive trade his country had undertaken with Egypt and the lands to the east. He wore a brocade gown of Tyrian purple silk with golden embroidery at the hem, neckline, and trumpet sleeves. His bejeweled gold headdress extended his head by a span, making up for his lack of height. He was resplendent in his finery, though he had aged since Zadok last saw him, during the reign of David: now his full black beard looked as if it had been dusted with flour.

The two men walked past Solomon's genuflecting subjects to their place at the table. Solomon sat to Zadok's left and bade everyone be seated. Servants came in through the back door with platters of charred meat and bladders full of wine.

After the wine had been poured, Solomon raised his cup. "Tonight we feast in honor of Hiram, esteemed king of Tyre. Eat and drink to your hearts' content, friends. The Lord be praised for our plenitude."

He took a loud gulp and turned to Hiram. "How was your journey, old friend?"

"Alas, it gets longer as the years pass." He laughed jovially. "But it was worth undertaking to witness what the son of the great David has achieved with his kingdom. Construction of the temple seems to be coming along magnificently. This surely would have pleased your father."

"We are proud of our progress," Solomon said. "Thanks in no small measure to you and your generosity. The cedar logs you have sent by sea are the finest my eyes have seen."

"I have asked the best craftsmen in all of Lebanon to hew the timber. This I pledged to your father near the end of his life. He came to me and said, 'Hiram, I endeavor to collect the finest and most precious materials so my son and successor can build a house for the God of Israel. My son is but a babe; what does he know about such things? I want you to send me your best cedar and fir and algum that I may provide for Solomon. In exchange I shall give you all the food you desire for your house and for your servants' houses.'"

Solomon reached for a date and bit into it. "I have ordered my men to load your camels with wheat, oil, and honey. When you desire more, send word to me and I shall provide it."

"Your kindness overwhelms me."

"Speak nothing of it."

Hiram gnawed on a lamb rib until all that was left was bone. When he finished, he dipped his fingers in a clay bowl filled with rosewater. "Tell me, Solomon. What more can I do for you?"

Solomon sat back and glanced furtively at Zadok.

The priest nodded slightly, indicating the fruit was ripe for picking.

"There is something," the young king said.

Hiram leaned forward. "Name it."

"Gold." He paused. "I require a thousand talents of gold of supreme quality for overlaying the cedars that will cover the holy of holies from the floor to the roof, and for carving the cherubim that will guard the ark of the covenant, and for the chain that will be set in front of the altar. Whatever the sacrifice to glorify the Lord's house in the highest, I will make it."

"You ask a great deal. Tyre—nay, all of Lebanon—does not have that kind of gold."

"I speak not of your own supply, only of your ability to procure it. You have a fleet of ships . . . and your men know the sea in a way my men do not. I can send a hundred servants to sail together with your seamen to the source of the finest gold: Ophir."

"Ophir is very far away, my lord Solomon. The journey there and back again will take three years at the least. And the waters are very treacherous."

Solomon put a hand on his ally's shoulder. "If we do not venture, we will not gain. There are enough riches there for both our kingdoms. I say we should claim them."

Hiram pursed his lips and fell silent.

Zadok leaned into his king's ear and whispered. "Offer him cities in Galilee."

Solomon drew a sharp breath. Zadok continued. "Twenty of them."

The king turned to the priest in surprise. Zadok affirmed his position with a nod, hoping Solomon would see his logic: the mountainous terrain of Galilee, though beautiful and fertile, would be foreign to a seafaring people. Hiram would be impressed enough by the magnitude of the gift to accept it in exchange for services. Later, when he would find himself unable to take advantage of it, Solomon would offer to help develop it—for a price.

Solomon turned nearly in slow motion to his guest. "Of course, I do not expect a favor. I mean to pay. You have been a good friend, my lord Hiram. I wish to reward you with land in my own country. If you honor me by accepting it, I shall deed you twenty cities in the land of Galilee, in the mountains of Naphtali, very near your kingdom."

Hiram sat up. "It is a generous offer you make, my lord."

"Then say you will take it."

The Tyrian king took a long sip of wine and firmly set the empty cup on the table. "Yes. I will accept your gift. My navy shall set sail for Ophir in a fortnight. Ready your men."

"You shall have a hundred of my best."

The two kings placed their hands on each other's shoulders and touched foreheads.

When Hiram pulled away, a look of concern crossed his face.

"What is it, brother?" Solomon asked.

He held up his cup and a servant rushed to him with the bladder of wine. "There is also the matter of Egypt. The Egyptians have long dominated the trade with Ophir. As you know, they have a voracious appetite for gold. It will be difficult to negotiate for so great a quantity as you require. The pharaoh does not like to share his resources."

"Leave the pharaoh to me. Continue with your preparations, and I will ensure we are well received at Ophir." Solomon signaled to one of his footmen. "Music!"

Two young men, one holding a lyre and the other a harp, entered the banquet hall and sat on low stools in direct view of Solomon and his honored guest. The harp player plucked the strings, releasing a sweet, angelic sound. Zadok closed his eyes and listened to the melodic prayer offered to the heavens, every note resonating within his core. He sent up thoughts of gratitude for the triumphant negotiations that would ultimately bring more wealth to Israel and glory to Yahweh. There was every indication that God's promise to his people would be fulfilled by the son of David. Tears formed behind his eyelids as he was filled with profound joy and thankfulness that he had lived to see the dawn of the greatest epoch in the Hebrews' history.

The lyrist joined in with a somber cadence, which dissolved into a rapid strum that was downright playful. The mood in the room was instantly buoyed. Zadok looked toward his left. The young king was transfixed, as he often was when music played. It was a gift from his father, this love of melody. "When I play the lyre, I am closest to God," King David had always said. David had mastered the instrument, and in his hands it became a tool for calling the divine and subduing the wicked.

When the first psalm ended, Solomon acknowledged Zadok's gaze. "We must bring the lyrist with us."

The priest inferred the answer but asked anyway. "Where to, my lord?"

"Tomorrow we ride for Zoan and the palace of Psusennes II. We shall take gifts of gold, silver, wine, olive oil, and golden honey to the pharaoh."

"My lord, it is my duty to caution you. Relations between Israel and Egypt have been strained . . ."

Solomon raised a hand. "It is time for change. What we need now are allies, not foes. Egypt is weak. Its leader lacks vision. Trade has all but ceased, and the state's wealth has dried up. Pharaoh cannot even build a water network for his people." He leaned forward and spoke softly. "He is spending all the state's money on gold for funereal masks to glorify himself and his kin, to the detriment of infrastructure. In exchange for some of that gold, there is much we can offer Egypt."

Zadok hesitated. Solomon's political agenda had never reached this far afield, and he wondered if his decision was a sound one. The Egyptians, in his estimation, could not be trusted. They swayed like reeds in the wind. And their attitude toward the people of Israel, though unspoken, was not a favorable one: since the days of the exodus, when the Hebrews escaped bondage in search of their promised land, the Egyptians considered them an inferior breed. But other than his own instinct, Zadok did not have a good argument for quelling the king's plan.

The musicians launched into a merry tune that seemed to speak of optimism and dreams fulfilled.

As if reading his priest's thoughts, Solomon said, "Trust me, Zadok. This journey will change everything."

CHAPTER SIX

The king's caravan arrived in Zoan—or Tanis, as the traders knew it—on the third day of the last month of the great flood. The sand mounds on the outskirts of the city opened like red maws and gave way to a fertile valley in the desert's belly. The arid land suddenly was thick with palms and orchards fed by the high waters of the Nile, which splayed into a delta on its way to the sea.

Zadok sat up on his camel and glanced at Solomon, a slim figure cloaked in white from head to foot. His youthful vigor showed in his riding posture, which had not wilted despite the distance traveled by the royal caravan of two hundred camels and donkeys and nearly as many men. As was the custom for kings, Solomon could have spent the twelve-day journey inside a fringed silk carriage on the backs of the beasts of burden. He chose to ride like a common man. The stretch between Canaan and Egypt was full of raiders and thieves, he'd said, so it was prudent to keep status hidden.

Even the gifts intended for Pharaoh Psusennes II were humbly packaged. Wrapped in black sackcloth woven of goat's hair, the kind used to store grain or house desert dwellers, were treasures worthy of a king: forty talents of the finest imported silver and gold, earthen pots full of thick thyme honey from the Levant, olive oil and jars of cured black olives from the groves outside Jerusalem, and enough wine to warm the royal household through the season of the emergence.

As they entered the city through a tunnel of palms, Zadok halted his camel and took a moment in stillness to observe the unfolding panorama of the capital of Lower Egypt, wrestled from the sodden banks of the Nile by the pharaohs of the twenty-first dynasty. Zoan was a sprawling oasis, its tree boughs bent with clusters of fruit—dates, sycamore figs, pomegranates. The scent of wet earth was everywhere, a sweet fragrance that called to mind fecundity and renewal.

Swallows circled above, their forked tails slicing the cool wind blowing in from Mediterranea, the sea beyond the river valley. A pair of hoopoes, their crowns of golden feathers splayed open, flitted among the fig trees, inserting their long beaks into the hollows of the trunks to coax out the tastiest beetles. The musical *hoo-hoo-hoo* of their song hung in the air like a welcome.

Though winter was not yet upon the land, the sky was low and thick with pewter clouds. The chill of autumn's breath went through Zadok's old bones, making him shiver. He pulled a woolen blanket from his saddlebag and tossed it across his lap.

Solomon caught up to him. "This is it, old friend. The land from which our people escaped slavery so long ago." He pointed to the river in the distance. "The Nile Delta. It is where the children of Israel were subjugated in the most deplorable manner, hoisting silt from the river to make mud bricks for the Egyptians' houses." His jaw tightened. "Every injustice has its day of reckoning."

Zadok knew he was referring to the ten plagues that swept over Zoan, a series of warnings from the Lord to the reigning pharaoh. It wasn't until the tenth plague struck and all Egyptian firstborns died that the pharaoh was brought to his knees and finally released the Hebrews from their servitude. It was from this very city they escaped and made their way back to Canaan, their patriarchal home. Zadok imagined the throngs passing through the same avenue of date palms, heads bent and backs whipped raw, and was struck by the irony of a royal Israelite caravan entering the city for the first time since the exodus.

The king prodded his camel with a braided goat-hair crop, and the priest followed. As they made their way toward the riverbanks, a great temple structure came into view. A high wall of dressed stones encircled the compound so that only the tops of the pylons were visible from ground level. Zadok imagined the builders' intention was to keep the temple and the worship therein cloaked in mystery.

Breaks in the wall, which was as thick as six camels

standing side by side, offered some glimpses inside. One opening revealed a processional way into the temple, lined by two rows of obelisks and statues glorifying past kings. At the end of the way was the temple forecourt, delineated by four high columns with capitals carved in the likeness of palm fronds and a score of lower ones, fluted all around and capped with delicate engravings depicting papyrus brooms.

It was impossible to see inside the temple—that surely was by design—but beyond its closed facade there must have been a courtyard, for a colossal statue towered behind it. Ramesses II, the one the Egyptians called "the great ancestor" and the one reviled by the Israelites for his brutal campaigns into the Levant, kept silent watch over the temple and the whole of Zoan, his stone effigy a reminder of the nation's long since expired glory days.

When it reached the banks of the Nile, the caravan stopped beneath a canopy of sycamores. Across the river was the royal palace, built upon a manmade mountain of stone. The pylons of the pharaonic dwelling rose some fifty cubits above the river's swollen levels, and their flag-poles reached even higher as banners whipped the air between heaven and earth.

The riders already had been given their orders: the royal entourage would camp riverside within view of the palace. Only the king and his top officers would be collected by Psusennes' personal barge and taken across the river, where they would stay in quarters reserved for state visits.

The pharaoh's men were waiting for their passengers by the riverbanks. They had been alerted weeks ago of the royal arrival, when Solomon had sent word to his counterpart requesting audience for trade talks.

"Egypt will welcome the king of Israel with trumpets and pipes," Psusennes wrote back in a message.

Zadok was suspicious of the pharaoh's enthusiasm and doubtful that centuries of animosity could be so easily forgotten. He kept his reservations to himself so as to not dampen Solomon's spirit on the eve of crucial negotiations.

The Egyptians had lined up in two rows flanking an aisle lined with brilliantly colored carpets. They wore white cotton, knee-length kilts with vertical knife pleats, and belts of woven wool. Their chests were bare and smooth, the color of cured mud. The only ornament on their bodies was a pair of brass armbands wrapped around the tops of their biceps. Their eyes were ringed in kohl and exaggerated; yet their gazes were vacant, almost idiotic.

They stood at attention and waved green papyrus brooms as Solomon and his men descended the riverbanks and proceeded to the barge, an impressive vessel carved of ebony and decorated with gold. Twelve oars, also of ebony, protruded from each side, and a rectangular sail hung from a mast claimed from the trunk of a date palm. Three young women dressed in white serenaded the passengers with lutes, harps, and song as fragile as a meadowlark's as they came onboard.

As the inundation came to an end, the Nile was at its fullest. The water, which took on the hue of a dove's wing under the moody sky, had risen above the midway point of the Nilometer, a stepped structure abutting the stone mound on which the palace was built. It would be a good year for the Egyptians, who counted on the annual coming of the floods for irrigation of their crops.

If nothing else, the pharaoh would be in good spirits, Zadok thought. He sat back on a gilded chair and listened to the maidens' high-pitched lilt, which competed for his attention with the cadenced whoosh of the oars as they sliced the river. Tranquil as the surroundings were, he could not find peace. He vowed to not let his guard down despite the warm welcome.

The boat came to rest on the shore of the promontory that housed the palace and its auxiliary structures. To underscore the godlike aura of the pharaoh, no other dwelling stood nearby. The royal compound was shielded from the common existence by a thicket of palms that formed an amphitheater around the finger of land dedicated to the regal court.

Solomon and his entourage ascended the steps leading to the entrance courtyard. The low, mud-brick walls of the T-shaped forecourt facing the Nile were freshly coated in brilliant white that dazzled the eyes even on a misty autumn day. In the midst of the court was a series of rectangular lotus ponds lined by rows of date palms, straight as poles and perfectly maintained. On the fringes were the walking gardens, encircled by clumps of salt cedars whose leaves had yellowed in response to the cold, and shaded by mighty sycamores and willows. In the center were planted all manner of flowers that were foreign to Zadok's eyes. A gentle breeze coming in from the river carried the scent of sweet anise from the herb beds around the footpaths. The bucolic scene was as close to Eden as anything Zadok had witnessed in the lower heavens, but he knew with all conviction that within it lay a toxic temptation he could not yet name.

The hour advanced, and a melancholy dusk fell upon Zoan. The clouds had parted now, revealing a lilac sky and a sliver of a moon afloat in the void. The moisture was so thick that breathing was like inhaling a fine mist.

Zadok steadied himself upon his staff and waited on the edge of the open terrace set upon the high point of the palace mound. Soon the banquet room would be filled with important Egyptians coming to pay tribute to his master. Solomon had gone alone to meet Psusennes prior to the festivities. It was an unofficial meeting, and no business was to be discussed. As was royal protocol, the two would arrive together at the gathering, a move symbolic of their pending alliance.

He felt a presence behind him and turned around with some effort. Benaiah, the army captain, stood there like a statue, rigid and expressionless. Though he came alive on the battlefield, Benaiah was awkward in social situations. He was there as a bodyguard to the king because duty called for it, but it was obvious he'd rather be in the trenches, belching and guffawing with his mighty men.

"What news, Benaiah?" Zadok asked.

"I met the pharaoh's commander in chief; they call him Shoshenq." The captain rubbed his short black beard and squinted toward the Nile.

His words are as few as his sword cuts are many, Zadok thought. He tried to encourage him. "This Shoshenq . . . is he worthy of his post?"

Benaiah laid a hand upon his waist sash, onto which was tied a small but lethal knife. "He has a taste for blood. And a certain disdain for the Hebrews."

"He is a Libyan, is he not?"

He nodded. "Son of the chief of the Ma, the tent dwellers and warriors of the desert lands. Also the nephew of Osorkon the Elder, who reigned in Egypt before Psusennes and his predecessor."

"Royal descent. But a foreigner nonetheless."

"He looks and thinks like an Egyptian. And wants to fight like one, though he does not have many opportunities under Psusennes. He has made no secret of his desire to push east into Canaan and the Transjordan, but the pharaoh is more interested in pleasures of the flesh than in conquests." Benaiah's rotund brown face hardened. "In my mind, Shoshenq is a threat."

"So long as the pharaoh lives, I think not," Zadok said. "Psusennes is too lazy and content to wage a campaign."

"But he is also in want of tribute. If he cannot get enough in his own country . . ."

Zadok laid a hand on the captain's shoulder. "This is why we are here, Benaiah. To avert any plans of invasion by forging an alliance. If Psusennes can get what he wants by peaceful means, there will be no need for bloodshed."

The trumpet of the pharaoh sounded. It was time to go inside. Zadok cast a glance toward the banquet room, which was filling with Egyptians dressed to celebrate, and turned back to Benaiah. "I know a captain must always be on his guard. But we are here to bring about peace. Let us not forget."

The two made their way to the great hall and stood among the masses that had gathered to celebrate the royal visit. There must have been six-score pairs of kohl-ringed eyes in the room, all turned toward the massive gilt wood doors that would be the gateway for the procession. The guests were dressed in impeccable white linen and wore black wigs cut in styles so similar it was difficult to distinguish one from the other. Some of the women braided their wigs and crowned them with enameled headdresses and perfume cones that released a pleasant myrrh scent, masking the odor of perspiration. Jewelry was dazzling. There were enough gold and precious gems to decorate a temple, yet these people wore them for their own aggrandizement. Zadok, who stood out in his draped gray gown and blue mantle like a beggar in a crowd of noblemen, cringed at the display of excess.

The heavy doors, carved with Egyptian deities and symbols, creaked open and a pair of trumpeters marched into the room as their horns delivered short, fanciful bursts. Behind them were pipers chiming in with shrill but happy notes and percussionists tapping frame drums. A servant girl with breasts exposed walked backward, lining the king's path with lotus blossoms.

The pharaoh, seated on a gilded chair with purple cushions, entered on the backs of eight male servants with bare chests and shaven heads. The members of the crowd, standing on either side of the pharaoh's passage, bowed simultaneously.

He was a sight to behold. His hairless torso gleamed in the torchlight, for it was rubbed with perfumed oils that released the scent of bitter almond as he passed. His breastplate was shaped like outstretched eagle's wings and inlaid with stones as big as fists and carved in the shape of scarabs. He held a flail in one arm and a crook in another: the symbols of his kingship. A tall, tapered headdress rendered in silver and bronze bore a coiled serpent with lapis lazuli eyes to match his own, which were gray with flecks of deep blue.

Solomon entered behind him. Though he did not display wealth and power in the Egyptian fashion, the king of Israel was resplendent in his youth, something Psusennes, though new to the throne, no longer had. Solomon scanned the room and caught Zadok's gaze for a long moment. The priest bowed deeply to his king.

Behind the regal men came the women of the court: Psusennes' mother, Neskhonsu of Thebes, followed by the Great Royal Wife and her two daughters. When the royals had been delivered to a platform meant to separate them from their subjects, the others scattered onto seats placed around the room. The servants entered the room carrying big trays of fruit on their shoulders, which they placed on low tables next to each seat, and clay jars full of beer.

Zadok partook meagerly of what was offered. The guests around him were talking in a low murmur and holding up their glasses for the servants to refill. The young women who sat together fed morsels to each other with their henna-dyed fingertips and giggled, their eyes darting around the room. Everything smelled of myrrh and musk.

He felt uncomfortable, not only because the Egyptian culture was so unfamiliar but also because he was so detached from Solomon. Since the beginning of the king's reign, Zadok had been by his side, advising him and nurturing his spirit. Seeing Solomon separate from his people, with the greedy Egyptian pharaoh whispering in his ear, made him recoil.

After a period that seemed eternal, Zadok could no longer sit in the stuffy room and pretend to be merry. He clutched his chest and gasped for a fresh breath, but only the scent of stewed mutton and charred waterfowl filled his nostrils. He rose and made his way to the terrace as quickly as he could.

The Nile was as black as spilled ink, and its waters rose and fell gently, like a sigh. Zadok looked to the sky and saw a myriad stars, none of which he recognized. Somewhere up there, he thought, was the bright star that always hung above Jerusalem like a promise, lighting the path of the Hebrews even in the darkest nights.

"Zadok." Solomon's deep voice was a comforting sound. "Are you well?"

The priest turned around. "My lord, you should not be here. You mustn't leave the pharaoh's side. It's protocol."

"I sought permission from our host to check on you. When you stood to leave, you looked pale and ill."

"Do not worry about me, my lord. I only needed air."

"Very well, then." Solomon paused and looked out to the river. "I know this place is strange to you. It is to me as well. But we must bear it for a few more days until we make a pact. If all goes according to my plan, it will be a worthwhile sacrifice."

"Yes, my lord." Zadok's voice sounded more tentative than he intended.

The king smiled. His countenance was so serene as to seem angelic. Zadok was struck as never before by his beauty. The sculpted bones of his face were defined by the wan torchlight and his honey-colored skin glowed like polished amber. His glossy black curls spilled haphazardly around his face, framing eyes the color of new chestnuts. The golden, twelve-pointed crown that encircled his head seemed like a natural extension of him, as if he'd been born with it.

"Come, Zadok," Solomon said. "It is impolite to keep Pharaoh waiting."

Zadok followed the king inside, remaining ten paces behind as protocol commanded. Solomon's scarlet mantle billowed behind him as he walked with that regal gait of his. With every stride, the ample woolen fabric swelled like a flag in the breeze, and he seemed to float above the ashlar floor.

A few steps before the entrance to the banquet hall, the mantle deflated as Solomon stopped abruptly. Zadok approached to see what the matter was and saw a young woman standing opposite the king.

She seemed as surprised as he did by the chance encounter. Her eyes, the color of the Nile at midnight and outlined in a smear of black kohl that extended to her temples, betrayed her bewilderment. She was an exquisite creature, obviously a member of the upper class. Lustrous raven hair, held in place by a silver band with inlaid colored glass, hung to her shoulder blades. Her brown skin, unblemished and taut, shimmered beneath diaphanous white linen draped artfully around a white modesty sheath. Around her neck hung a golden collar with spokes that recalled the sun's rays, and on her feet were sandals of leather decorated with feathers.

She did not wear the perfume cone, yet she was redolent of roses and myrrh with a vague hint of cinnamon. Solomon stared at her, clearly taken by her beauty.

Like a frightened cat, she diverted her eyes and dashed away, disappearing inside the arcade of stone pillars.

The king's gaze followed her until she was completely out of view.

"My lord," Zadok said.

For a long moment there was silence. He repeated: "My lord?"

"A lily among thorns." Solomon inhaled the air still perfumed by her presence. "I must know who she is."

CHAPTER SEVEN

Three days passed before Psusennes was ready to grant audience. There was much to tend to, he'd said, as the inundation began to retreat and a new season of harvest was upon the people of Egypt.

Solomon and his men were well cared for in the interim. Every two hours, servants came to the guest quarters bearing jugs of pomegranate wine and great platters of food: goat seasoned with cumin, fish from the Nile, pigeons roasted in earthen ovens, bread loaves with coriander seeds, figs, dates, plums, and melons. Music was a staple as harpists were stationed on the courtyard and ordered to play day until night.

On the morning of the meeting with the pharaoh, Zadok went outside to greet the dawn. The humid air lubricated his aging bones and put a measure of swiftness in his step, so he went for a long walk in the gardens.

The song of the hoopoe kept him company as he navigated the moist red earth paths meandering through the plum orchards. The mud soaked the bottom of his tunic and felt cold against his bare feet. He often walked shoeless; it brought him closer to the ground and put him in a meditative disposition.

As the first light broke through the gray clouds, he thought of Solomon. Since the night of the banquet, the king had been pensive. When Zadok questioned him, he said he was gathering his wits for the day of negotiation. But a priest always knew what was in a man's heart.

He hoped the obsession with the foreign girl was a passing fancy. Zadok entertained a vague worry but did not let it settle. He wanted to believe Solomon's trained mind had told him she was an exotic stranger and nothing more.

There he was. Beneath a plum tree, the king kneeled toward the rising sun and prayed. Zadok walked in a wide arc so as not to disturb his peace and stood behind him.

Solomon extended a hand. "Come, Zadok."

The priest sat next to him. He gazed toward the clouded horizon and the fingers of light piercing through it. "Every time I think I have strayed too far from home," Zadok said, "I look at the dawn and am reminded of the Lord's ubiquitous presence."

"If only we realized we all live beneath the same sky, warmed by the same sun, there would not be so much conflict," Solomon said.

"Not every man is as wise as you, my lord."

Solomon squinted toward the light. "I have been thinking, Zadok. It is time for me to take a wife."

"It is, my lord. When we return, the men will find

Israel's most beautiful and gentle-hearted maidens that you may choose your heart's desire."

"The girl from the banquet . . . did you find out who she was, as I asked you?"

Zadok felt a needling in his gut. "She is Pharaoh's daughter by one of his minor wives. Her name is Nicaule Tashere."

"A princess."

"Far removed. She has no rights to the throne."

"Does she have her father's favor?"

"I do not know this." He cast a hard look at Solomon. "The rumor is Shoshenq, the commander of the army, has his eye on her."

The corner of Solomon's mouth curled into a smile. "Does he, indeed?"

"My lord, what thoughts go through your mind? Surely you don't intend—"

Solomon put a hand up. "Leave me be, Zadok. I am seeking the Lord's counsel. That is all I will say." He got to his feet. "I will go now and prepare. We meet with Psusennes after the morning meal."

Zadok bit his lip. "Yes, my lord."

He watched the king walk away and sighed. He had learned that if Solomon made up his mind about something, swaying him from it would be like stopping the headwaters of the Nile.

The pharaoh's throne sat at the end of a long, narrow corridor lined on either side with thick papyrus columns painted in brilliant shades of crimson and indigo and decorated with gold leaf. The walls were painted with scenes from palace life: the pharaoh being crowned by the sun god Ra, royal subjects sitting beneath trees of plenty, slaves tilling the ripe soil on the banks of the Nile.

Solomon and his entourage entered the throne room in a formal procession. First came four men bearing gifts on a platform they carried upon their shoulders. They stopped in front of the pharaoh and presented the bounty of foodstuffs and wine from the Levant and silver and gold from Solomon's private cache. The Egyptian ruler nodded in approval and sent the men away. Then he gestured to Solomon to sit in the chair next to his.

Psusennes was dressed in full court regalia. His head was covered with an indigo-striped cloth held in place at the forehead by a golden band. A black false beard, woven like a tight braid, protruded from his chin. Around his neck he wore a necklace depicting a winged scarab holding a sun disc of polished amber. Two gold cuffs with inlaid lapis bound his wrists.

He was accompanied by a female leopard with fierce green eyes and a killer's gaze. As he sat, the paunch of plenty hung over his waist, which was cinched by a band of lion's hide culminating in a set of claws. The cat curled itself around his feet.

"Solomon, esteemed king of Israel." His voice was surprisingly high-pitched. "What brings you here this day?"

"Psusennes, lord and overseer of the vast Egyptian empire, I come in peace. Our nations can benefit greatly from one another."

The pharaoh fingered the tip of his false beard. "And what is it you propose?"

"I have observed the building of your water network connecting the river with the sea—an ambitious undertaking considering the capricious behavior of the Nile."

"Our progress is slow. We must work only when the river is at its lowest point, for the water is a hindrance."

"If you had twice the labor force, it would go more quickly. It appears you need more men. Trained men."

"We have every able-bodied man in Lower Egypt working on the project."

Solomon sat back on his chair and tapped his fingers together. "We have constructed an elaborate water system in Jerusalem, and my men know the challenges of such a venture. I can offer you my best engineers as well as thirty-score laborers to work alongside your men. You need not pay them, for they will be in Israel's employ; you simply will provide them with shelter and food." He paused and scanned Psusennes' eyes. "But be mindful these are guests in your kingdom, not slaves. They must be treated well. We must not repeat the mistakes of our forefathers."

The pharaoh raised an eyebrow painted with black kohl. "Your generosity overwhelms me. Very well. You have my word your men will be treated fairly and honorably." He leaned forward. "Tell me, Solomon. What is it you require in return?"

Solomon smiled. "Word may have traveled that a great temple is rising on the highest place in Jerusalem. This is the house I promised my father I would build to glorify our God, and I mean to keep my promise. So help me, it will be the finest structure in all of Israel and the Near East. I hope you will honor me and come to see it when it is finished."

"Of course. But what does this have to do with Egypt?"

"In order to finish the temple, there is something I need that you, my lord Psusennes, can help me acquire."

"Say it."

"The most sanctified part of this house will be covered from the floor to the roof in pure gold—so much of it, we must look beyond our boundaries to find it. I have trained my eyes on Ophir, for I need a thousand talents to finish the work."

The pharaoh's slate eyes widened. "A thousand talents! That is more than all the gold in all the tombs of Egypt's great kings." He looked Solomon up and down. "The king of Israel has a taste for splendor."

Zadok read the insult in Psusennes' words. The Egyptians had long thought the Israelites inferior. Despite the amicable climate of their meeting and the mutual appetite for cooperation, that ingrained prejudice seeped out like milk from an old, threadbare bladder. He watched Solomon's reaction. The king blinked slowly but did not change his expression. Zadok knew he was wise enough to let it go and refocus on the task at hand.

"My men sail to Ophir with the Tyrians," Solomon said. "Their mission is to come back with a ship full of gold. But, alas, the lion's portion of that gold is spoken for by Egypt."

"And you wish for me to relinquish my hold on that supply. The hold it took me and my forefathers long years to establish." He laughed.

"I could pay the Ophirians double and test their loyalty. But it is not my way to employ such underhanded means. I like to conduct my business man to man." He leaned forward and extended an open palm. "So I will pay that money to you. I want you to sell me part of your supply at a profit."

Psusennes swallowed hard. He was rendered mute by the offer.

"Moreover, I am prepared to forgo levies on trade between our two nations, so long as there is peace. Israel will not charge Egypt tariffs on livestock, foodstuffs, pottery, or spices—and, of course, we would expect the same courtesy."

The pharaoh folded his arms across his chest. The gold of his wrist cuff gleamed as a ray of light entered through a window shaft. "You are a smart man, Solomon. There has not been a leader like you in Canaan land. A new day dawns for Israel."

"A new day dawns for peace between old enemies. Do you accept my offer?"

Psusennes smiled sideways. "I accept. I will order my scribes to record a treaty, and it will stand testament for all to see."

Zadok exhaled. It was done. It was a costly alliance, but the end would justify the means. In a climate of peace and open trade, Israel could also count on Egypt's support on the military front should it be attacked by neighboring nations. In the ever-warring territories of the Near East, this was a prospect as good as all the gold in Ophir. Zadok caught Solomon's eye for a moment and nodded his approval.

"To mark the treaty," the pharaoh continued, "I offer you gifts of precious gems and gold to take back to your kingdom. And twoscore of my best horses besides."

"You are most gracious, my lord," Solomon said. "But the only way to seal our alliance is through marriage."

Zadok started. This was not part of the plan.

The pharaoh shook his head. "Egyptian royal daughters are not given to foreigners. Not even to kings."

"Your daughters by your queen are to wed Egyptian royalty; I know this. I ask for one who does not aspire to the throne. A daughter by a minor wife."

Psusennes looked at the bold king in silence.

Solomon continued. "The beauty of Nicaule Tashere is like none other. I wish to make her my queen. She will want for nothing. And you, my lord Psusennes, will be assured of a supreme ally in the Near East to the end of your days. Israel and Egypt will be bound not only by a pact but also by blood."

Zadok closed his eyes and lowered his head. Solomon had gone too far. Surely he knew the Lord opposed such a union. *Do not marry foreign women*, Yahweh had warned his people Israel, *for they will turn your heart to other gods.* Zadok viewed Nicaule as particularly dangerous in that regard. Solomon may have claimed he was merely trying to cement a political alliance, but the bare truth was he desired her in a way that robbed him of sleep at night. How far would he go to please such a woman?

"If I were to grant your request," Psusennes said, "I would have conditions. First, my daughter must never be required to venerate your god. She must be free to practice her customs and worship in her own way. Second, she must have her own palace with every comfort and be tended to by her own staff of Egyptians who will accompany her from the motherland. Third, any children she bears must learn the Egyptian tongue and be schooled in the heritage of their mother as well as their father. None of these are optional."

Solomon did not hesitate. "I accept your conditions. Every one."

"Then it shall be done. She will be ready to depart with your caravan tomorrow morning. We will celebrate the union this eve." He stood and bowed, and Solomon mirrored his movements. "Go in peace, Hebrew brother."

Zadok followed his king out of the room and into the courtyard. He squinted as the daylight assaulted his eyes.

Solomon spoke over his shoulder. "I know you don't approve of what I've done, but time will prove my actions prudent."

Zadok did not hold back. "You have disregarded the Lord's covenant. He will not be pleased."

The king halted and swung round. "Blasphemy! Do you think I did not seek the Lord's counsel? Do you believe I would do this if the Lord our God did not sanction it? You must remember this, Zadok: I am Yahweh's chosen. I communicate with him on a deeper level than you can imagine."

Zadok stood his ground. "You are navigating dark waters, my lord."

"There will be no more said of this." He drew a deep breath and spoke calmly. "I do not wish to quarrel with you, Zadok. Go now and ready yourself, for tonight we celebrate my marriage."

The priest looked away as his king turned and walked across the courtyard. In his mind's eye flashed an image of fire . . . villages burning, women and children running scared, black smoke rising like an infernal beast. It was Yahweh's wrath, and it was coming.

CHAPTER EIGHT

Nicaule languished in the bath despite the lateness of the hour. The banquet feast would begin at any moment, but she was in no hurry to get there.

She ran a hand slowly across the warm water, watching the ripples it created. She closed her eyes and inhaled the scent of myrrh and frankincense released by the gentle agitation. It was the perfume of her identity, the fragrance she had come to associate with blithe days at the palace and sultry nights at the banks of the Nile.

So it had come: the day of her betrothal. It wasn't how she imagined it as a girl or how she plotted it as a woman. Her own designs, secure in her mind until that day, were crumbling like mud bricks in the *khamsin*.

The wife of a king. She repeated the phrase in her mind, hoping it would take on weight. Though it was what she'd always wanted and worked fiercely to earn despite her marginal rank in the royal lineage, she was nauseated at the thought of marrying a king of slave stock. It was utter irony. All those years of making herself desirable to the man she was certain would succeed her father were now for naught. The prospect of being crowned an Egyptian queen had been yanked from her.

"My lady." The soft voice of her bath attendant was a bell in the tortured silence. "It is time."

Nicaule closed her eyes and sighed. *It is time.* She stood and watched the water stream down her dark body. She let the attendant wrap her in a shroud of linen and lead her to the marble slab for the perfume ritual.

The girl removed the linen from Nicaule's shoulders and draped it on the marble. Still damp from the bath, Nicaule lay upon it, offering the attendant her naked backside. She felt the girl's velvet hands upon her back, rubbing into her skin with long, rhythmic strokes a potion of crushed rose petals, cinnamon, and myrrh blended with rare balanos oil. The spiced floral fragrance, made to her specifications by the court perfumer, had become her signature: exquisite with an ever-so-subtle bite.

When the ritual was complete, Nicaule slipped into a fresh linen wrap and walked into an adjacent dressing room, where her lady-in-waiting, Irisi, had readied the evening's attire: a floor-length, fitted coral linen sheath embroidered with a honeycomb pattern, a sheer, pleated cape dyed the same color, and a long blue sash to tie around her slim waist.

Irisi bowed. "My lady."

Nicaule placed a gentle hand under Irisi's chin and lifted her head. When their gazes met, Nicaule smiled.

Though bowing was a court formality, it was not necessary between friends. Nicaule stood in a well-lit spot between two oil lamps and let her wrap fall to the floor. She drew a deep breath as her lady-in-waiting fastened a loincloth between her legs.

"Did you deliver what I asked?" Her voice betrayed her anxiety.

Irisi looked up with sparkling brown eyes. Though she was ten years Nicaule's senior, she had a youthful gaze and the spirit of a swallow, with a diminutive stature to match. "It has been done, my lady. Written on a square of papyrus as you commanded and delivered unto his hand."

She exhaled. "How good that my lady-in-waiting is also the finest scribe in Lower Egypt."

Irisi helped Nicaule step into her sheath and adjusted the seams to follow the curves of her body. The linen felt snug against her, like a second skin. She lifted her arms and let Irisi wrap the blue horsehair sash twice around her waist and knot it so the loose ends draped to her ankles.

"His reply came but a moment ago," Irisi said.

"So quickly?"

"A man in love does not waste time."

She sat in a chair next to the cosmetics box. Her heart raced. "Do not torture me with this anticipation. I must know what he said."

Irisi smiled sideways as she opened the cosmetics box and placed some galena and malachite powder onto her palette. She reached into her bosom and pulled out a roll of papyrus. "Read for yourself."

Nicaule snatched the paper from her hands and unfurled it. She read aloud. "'My beloved, my heart cries at the thought of your absence. Life without you will be like a rose without perfume. I must see you one last time before you go. Look for my signal.'" She clutched the note to her chest and sighed. "Oh, Irisi. How can my father be so cruel?"

Irisi applied galena around Nicaule's eyes using an ivory stick. "Men have their own plans, my lady. What is love when empires are at stake? What meaning has a woman's passion when there are roads to be built and rivers to be harnessed?" She smirked. "We are bargaining chips to help them win their game."

Nicaule closed her eyes so Irisi could apply the crushed malachite paste onto her eyelids. "How is it you are so wise?"

"I have lived longer than you. I have seen firsthand the betrayal of men. They can't be loyal to each other, let alone their women."

Nicaule understood the reference. Ten years ago, on the eve of Irisi's nineteenth year, Irisi had witnessed the slaughter of her husband, the royal scribe Ptah. She had told the story with such vivid detail that Nicaule felt as if she, too, had been there as Pharaoh Siamun's mercenary drove a knife into Ptah's throat for falsifying a document detailing the pharaoh's conquests. As Irisi told it, Ptah had done so at Siamun's behest and was eliminated lest anyone discover the truth.

She opened her eyes and parted her lips for the

application of red ochre paste.

Irisi daubed the paste lightly and took a step back. "My lady, you look like a dream. I hope this king knows what treasure he has been granted."

"He's a savage. He knows nothing." She tossed back the glossy black ribbons of her wig. "I suppose we ought to get this charade done. My jewelry."

Irisi slipped a gold cuff around each of Nicaule's wrists and fastened a delicate necklace of colored glass around her neck. As a final touch, she tied a ribbon into her hair, securing it at the crown with a lapis scarab pin.

"Finished," she said.

Nicaule slipped the cape over her shoulders. She squeezed her friend's hands and gave her a look of solidarity. "Do not wait for me tonight."

All the faces, even the most familiar ones, looked strange to Nicaule. It was as if she had drunk too much wine and seen them through the distorted filter of inebriation. They had gathered to wish her well, to celebrate the new union. Yet she could feel their eyes throwing darts of pity in her direction even as their lips wished her good fortune. Hypocrites, every one.

She glanced at her father, seated to her right, from the corner of her eye. He had stuffed himself with food and drink and looked rather content upon his bejeweled eagle throne. Why wouldn't he? He had all he wished for: a strong ally in the Near East, an unobstructed road to Mesopotamia, silver and gold to line his coffers, and disposable foreign men to build his city.

No matter that he had bargained her happiness.

The pharaoh stood and raised his hands, and the crowd fell silent. "Today we celebrate the betrothal of two young people and the union of two nations. Egypt and Israel will soon be bound by royal blood." He turned to Nicaule and offered her his left hand. "My beautiful daughter Nicaule Tashere has been chosen by Solomon, King of Israel, to be his queen." He offered Solomon his right hand. "May Amun-Ra bestow his favor on this union." As the crowd cheered, he brought the two palms together.

Nicaule's knees felt shaky as she touched Solomon for the first time and looked in his eyes. His hand was soft and supple, as if he had never known conflict or held a weapon. There was not a shade of doubt in the almond-shaped eyes that held her gaze with an unexpected intensity. This was a man who knew what he wanted—and was accustomed to obtaining it. But not everything could be bargained for like a mound of spices.

She broke away from his stare, shifting her gaze downward. To him, it might have looked demure. To her, it was an act of defiance.

"Let there be music," Psusennes bellowed.

The musicians plucked at their stringed instruments, filling the room with the ethereal notes of harps and citharas as everyone reclaimed their seats.

The pharaoh leaned down and spoke to Nicaule, his voice just above a whisper. "You will soon be a queen, my daughter. Do not take your role lightly, for much rides upon it. A prosperous and peaceful alliance between two nations depends on you being a good and dutiful wife . . . and mother."

She exhaled a trembling breath. The thought of having a child with him . . .

"You must not let Egypt down," he continued. "Do you understand?"

She felt the color drain from her face. "Yes, Father."

He gave her a superficial smile and sat back on his chair.

Nicaule cast a few furtive glances around the room, hoping to capture the eye of her beloved. She knew he was there, among the crowd; being absent from a celebration such as this would be an egregious breach of protocol. Yet she had not seen him since the festivities had begun. She imagined how he must have felt seeing her with the man she was to marry. His warrior nature bristled over far lesser offenses. Faced with the inevitability of this marriage, which was beyond the control of either of them, he would've been boiling with rage.

In her peripheral vision she saw someone standing between the arches at the edge of the room. She turned her head slowly and was rewarded by the sight of him. He stood in the shadows of the stone arcade, a hand over the mace tied to his waist. His gaze met hers for a moment, and arousal flooded her body like a rushing river. Her heart beat so loudly she was certain her father could hear it. She turned away and consciously assumed a look of nonchalance, an exercise of discipline she had gotten quite good at. By the time she glanced back at the arched passageway a few seconds later, he was gone.

Look for my signal.

She felt her cheeks flush. Thoughts of him embracing her were wild stallions that could not be tamed. She signaled to one of the attendants to fan her with a palm frond. The air calmed her and set her mind to plotting her exit.

The pharaoh was engrossed in a conversation with Solomon, his tongue loosened by the free-flowing wine. The Israelite monarch listened more than talked, probably unable to wedge a word into Psusennes' bombastic monologue. She was certain her father was oblivious to her agitation. About Solomon she could not be sure. The young king's eyes were never fixed upon one object or subject for too long. He observed everything in a quiet manner that made her uncomfortable. She preferred it when men of power ignored women and left them to tend their webs.

She absently regarded the crowd. How empty their gazes! The depth of their engagement centered on gossip and consumption. She pitied them not being in love. Her own cause was far loftier and thus justified her absence, she told herself.

Nicaule placed a hand on her stomach and doubled over in her chair. A murmur fell over the crowd as two ladies-in-waiting rushed to her side.

"She is stricken with nerves," she heard her father say. "Such is the constitution of women."

She sat up slowly. "Father, I am unwell. Will you

grant me permission to retire?"

Psusennes nodded and waved her off. She bowed to him and her future husband, avoiding his gaze, and let the servants lead her out of the room.

Irisi was in Nicaule's bedchamber, laying out the clothes and personal items for the next day's journey. The bed was decorated with a woven linen and silk shawl, created by Nicaule's mother and female kin for the wedding day. The room was crowded with white roses and lotus flowers, papyrus brooms, and cornflower. The latter, an import from the Near East, symbolized the union between the two cultures.

"My lady," Irisi said in surprise. "But it is so early."

Nicaule ran to her. The two women grasped each other's elbows and touched foreheads. "He waits for me, Irisi. I must go to him."

"It is risky . . ."

"You must help me." She took off her wig and offered Irisi her back, speaking over her shoulder. "Remove my clothes and jewelry, and change it with yours. Then paint my face like yours and give me your wig."

"My lady . . ."

"Make haste. His voice in my ear is a sweet torment. I am sick with love."

She could feel Irisi's trembling hands as she unfastened the necklace and peeled off her clothes one by one. Her heart hammered against her ribs like a caged animal struggling to escape. Her plan was fraught with hazard, but it was her last chance—and nothing could keep her from taking it.

Grateful for the indigo night that kept her hidden, Nicaule skulked down the steps of the palace mound and plunged into the shadows of the city that lay beyond the thicket of palms. Breathless, she looked over her shoulder periodically to make sure she wasn't followed.

His house was the one closest to the palace, indicating his status as protector of the pharaoh and his great city. She pushed the door slightly open and slipped in.

He started when he saw her. She was pleased her disguise was so effective that even he didn't recognize her.

"Shoshenq," she whispered. "It is I."

He picked up an oil lamp and walked slowly to her. He held its light next to her face and looked into her eyes. A golden halo surrounded him, illuminating his smoothly shaven head and the well-defined muscles of his bare chest and arms. He placed the lamp on a shelf and stroked her cheek with the back of his fingers. A faint whimper escaped from her lips.

"I should not be here," she said. "If they find us, you will be banished from the kingdom and all your dreams will crumble to dust."

"My dream stands before me." His voice was hard but lustrous, like a rare pearl. He dropped to one knee and took her hands in his. "I would sacrifice a thousand chances at the throne to have this night." He gently pulled her hands down.

Nicaule kneeled in front of Shoshenq, their faces a palm's width apart. Emotion strangled her throat. She could only stare at the cinnamon-colored face that was so perfectly proportioned it seemed hewn by a mason and the kohl-smudged ebony eyes, slanted like a cat's and burning with the ferocity of a jungle beast, hinting at a violent nature that both terrified and excited her.

"Such a beautiful, rare flower." He inhaled deeply. "Your perfume would draw a thousand bees, yet you belong to me."

She guided his right hand to her bosom. "My heart beats for you only. Know this, even when we are apart."

His gaze hardened, and he spoke behind clenched teeth. "I curse this king who takes you from me."

She touched his cheek lightly and let the tips of her fingers move across his bottom lip and down his neck. She watched the mighty commander of the army, the man who had crushed his enemies with his hands and who had led thousands of warriors to battle, surrender to her touch. The power she held over him surged through her body.

"The king of Israel will never know my heart. He cannot take what I do not give him. Your soul and mine are forever tied, now unto the afterlife."

He moved closer, his breath warm and sweet. "If it takes all my years and all my strength, one day I will come for you. This I promise."

She knew he meant it. Shoshenq was a simple man whose words were few but potent as an iron spear. It was the way of his ancestors, the great chiefs of the Ma, who wandered the desert from Libya to Egypt. The blood of nomad warriors coursed through his veins, making him impervious to hardship and rabid to make those who challenged his honor kneel before him.

"Come for me a king," she said. "This is the path that has been laid before you. Do not be swayed from it." She leaned into his ear and whispered, "I will wait for you even unto my old age."

His strong hand embraced her waist and traveled up her spine to her bare shoulder blades. His touch made her tremble. She kissed the side of his neck and his ear. When a soft moan left his throat, she grazed his skin with her teeth.

He turned his face to meet hers, and their lips touched. Nicaule crumbled in his arms, giving him the signal that she was his, body and soul. Her pulse pounded violently in her temples and ears, robbing her of all rational thought. Even if she had to pay for this moment with her life, she was prepared to do it.

She parted her lips and let him taste her tongue. His breath rose and fell like waves in a raging sea. She whispered into his mouth, "Plant your seed in me."

He stood and lifted her up, sweeping her with one swift motion into his arms. He snuffed the lamplight with his fingers and carried her into the darkness.

CHAPTER NINE

The stones of Nicaule's betrothal house closed in around her, suffocating her with the stench of wet earth and animal manure. It was the house of Solomon's mother, Bathsheba, vacant since her death the year prior and now appointed to the woman who would soon be the king's wife.

Nicaule had been there almost four weeks, waiting in isolation as Solomon readied the wedding canopy at his father's house. Though they were betrothed, they had not seen or spoken to each other since the king's retinue, with his prize in tow, returned to Israel. It suited her just fine. She did not care to parade herself around Jerusalem, the detestable city of Judahite kings, nor to have the Hebrews gawk at her and whisper over each other's shoulders, "There walks the foreigner King Solomon bought."

She looked down upon her bare arm and stroked it with her fingertips. Her skin was soft as a dove's feathers, dark as the red clay of her beloved Nile. She was so different from these people, who gulped wine and tore their meat like animals. Coarse swine. Living among them for the rest of her days felt like a punishment, even if they would call her queen.

Any time now he would come for her. Word had arrived the night before through Solomon's emissary, Azariah, a son of Zadok the priest, that the king was ready for the marriage ceremony. She was to bathe and perfume herself, dress in her finest white clothing, veil her head, and wait. She would know of his imminent approach when the horn sounded.

She drew a deep breath. How would she lie with this man for seven days knowing her beloved longed for her on the other side of the Sea of Reeds? The distance between her and Shoshenq seemed impossible to bridge. She had departed Egypt only weeks ago, but already her former life seemed like faded letters on a forgotten papyrus.

Would he remember his promise?

"My lady Nicaule." Irisi came into the bedchamber with a tray of jewels.

Nicaule offered a weak smile. Irisi's face was a boon in this godforsaken place.

Irisi approached and sat next to her on the bed. "Azariah says the king will come for you at sundown. The time nears." She gently cradled Nicaule's hands and glanced at her from head to foot. "You are like the sacred blue lotus from the pools of Nun, so sweet-smelling and lovely."

Nicaule sighed. "I go with heavy heart."

"You must be strong, my lady. This is your destiny. The gods have willed it, and you cannot but accept it."

Nicaule squeezed her hands. "You are wise, my dearest and most loyal friend. Your mere presence gives me solace."

The deep, solemn wail of the shofar sounded in the distance, alerting the entire city of the ceremony under way. A violent knock came from the other side of the door, then the voice of Azariah. "The bridegroom comes. Be ready."

Nicaule sprang from the bed and wrapped her arms around her chest. A wave of nausea overcame her. She jerked her head to and fro, looking for an escape, though she knew there was none.

Irisi rose. "Calm your nerves, my lady. You are about to be crowned queen. You will have the life so many women dream of." She chose from the tray of jewelry two gold cuffs with moonstone scarabs.

Nicaule held her arms out as Irisi fastened the cuffs. "I cannot do it, Irisi. I cannot lie with him."

Irisi looked deep into her eyes. "You must. It is your duty to Egypt. The way you conduct yourself will either magnify the glory of your fathers or diminish it."

A bitter smile crossed her lips. Irisi was right.

The rapid cadence of a hundred drums, accompanied by a carefree flute song, sounded as the wedding party approached Bathsheba's house. She imagined the man whose face she had gazed upon but twice, who spoke a different language and believed in a foreign god, who looked and smelled unlike her people, leading her by the hand to the royal marriage chamber. Anxiety stirred her belly with the fury of a maelstrom, and she bent over a pot, heaving.

The music grew closer. The singing voices of the attendants were now within earshot. She raised her hands to her ears to escape the vulgar sound. She wanted to cry, but no tears came.

Irisi's gentle hands lifted her to her feet, then wiped her mouth and forehead with linen gauze. Irisi said nothing—not a word of judgment or of encouragement—as she reapplied ochre paste to Nicaule's lips.

Another hard knock.

Irisi held up the veil, a diaphanous silk cloth embroidered with tiny flowers in red and white thread and edged in delicate golden fringe. She slipped it over Nicaule's head and let it hang to the floor.

Covered completely by the fine silken shroud, Nicaule felt safe. It was a curtain separating her from the activities unfolding around her, a barrier between her and him, a symbol of her detachment. In her country, only the dead would be swathed in such a manner.

The door creaked open, and Irisi stepped back into the shadows of the room. Nicaule stood alone, clenching her fists to control her trembling limbs.

Azariah stepped into the doorway. "Behold, the bridegroom has arrived. Go out and meet him."

Nicaule drew a long breath, her last as a single woman. With head high, she did as told.

As she stepped out into the autumn night, a cool breeze kissed her cheeks and delivered the scent of molten beeswax. The whole of Jerusalem had come out to witness the occasion, cramming the path between Bathsheba's house and King David's palace and spilling down the hillside. They held candle lanterns, their flickering lights like a thousand stars fallen from the sky, and chanted a happy tune whose words Nicaule could not comprehend. They craned their necks to get a glimpse at the object of Solomon's affection.

At the top of a narrow passageway through the swarm of gawking Israelites stood the bridegroom and two white horses with garlands of white lilies hanging around their necks. He stepped onto the stoop of his mother's house and gazed at his bride. He was dressed in a long white tunic over which was wrapped a white linen coat with wide sleeves, cinched at the waist with a belt of silver. A crown with twelve golden fingers reaching toward the heavens encircled the soft black curls that tumbled to his shoulders.

He signaled to one of his attendants, who promptly delivered the bride's gift on a cedar tray inlaid with mother-of-pearl. Solomon took up the golden crown, a smaller and more delicate version of his own, and placed it on her veiled head. He said something in Hebrew that she loosely understood to mean *Welcome to my house*.

Emboldened by her gossamer shield, she met his gaze. Orbs the color of post-flood Nile silt regarded her with the voracity of a raptor. The intensity of his gaze held her captive, and she forced herself to look away lest she be mesmerized. She shuddered.

He walked down the steps, and she followed him. He stopped in front of the horses and stroked the neck of one. He turned to his bride and lifted her from the waist, as effortlessly as if she were a feather, onto the horse's bare back. He mounted the other horse and led the way through the crowd of witnesses.

Nicaule's eyes darted from face to face. Glowing like molten copper in the lantern light, they seemed like wraiths from the underworld haunting her steps, mocking her. Their gazes were like whips, their toothless smiles like spurs, goading her to the embrace of their king so she could become one of them, insipid and vulgar and stinking of too much wine.

The palace of King David stood at the end of the ascending path, its two wings like open arms. Torches surrounded a tented canopy at the entrance, sealing her fate by fire. The rhythmic clop of the horses' hooves on the cobbled stones, the sound of her fleeting freedom, grew slower until it stopped altogether. She issued a trembling sigh only she could hear.

Solomon dismounted and walked to Nicaule, offering his hand. Together they walked to the wedding canopy and stood before the cheering crowd. Trumpets sounded, then drums and flutes. She felt like an impostor, posing as the happy bride when in reality there was nothing about that moment she wanted to own. She wanted to flee into the cold arms of the night, to be swallowed by its dark womb.

He turned to her. She thought he said, "My rose, come into my father's house." She said nothing as he lifted her into his arms and led her into the chamber he had prepared for her. With one voice, his people sang them into matrimony. The door closed behind them. They were alone, save for one groomsman on the other side of the door, who would wait for the fateful knock signifying the union had been consummated.

Even to her cynical eyes, the room was lovely. It was filled with lilies, whiter than alabaster and so profuse they recalled a valley in springtime. Their sweet perfume filled the air so that no breath could escape it. Perched on the carpets lining the floor from wall to wall, candle lanterns cast their halcyon light onto the ashlars, magnifying the texture of the stone. In the center of the room was a mattress covered in violet silk and draped with a swathe of white linen. Pillows of the same fabric, perhaps twoscore of them, enclosed the bed like a fortress. Silver-footed trays and red-slipped pottery bowls held grapes, figs, pomegranates, and apricots, a loaf of bread, and a honeycomb dripping with its golden gift. A skin of wine and two silver chalices sat on a low table nearby.

Solomon kneeled before Nicaule and took hold of the edge of her veil, rolling it upward as he stood. He lifted it away from her face and let it fall to the floor.

With nothing separating her from him, she could see the unadorned greed in his eyes as he drank her beauty. She instinctively took a step back.

"Do not be afraid," he said in her language, walking toward her.

It disoriented her to hear Egyptian come from that mouth. Shaking her head, she inched backward. The thought of him touching her revolted her. It was inevitable, but she wasn't going to surrender without a fight.

He followed. "Why do you run from me? I want only to love you."

"No. I am not ready."

"That is the first time I've heard you speak. Your voice is like honey dripping from the belly of a fig."

She walked backward until her shoulders scraped against a wall. She let out a soft gasp.

He caught up and placed a hand on her waist, holding her in place while he raised his other hand to her shoulder. He slipped his fingers under one of her dress straps and slid it down her arm, exposing a breast. He kissed her shoulder with fleshy, moist lips.

Images of Shoshenq flashed in her mind, and a knot rose to her throat. She pushed Solomon away and slipped out of his grasp, darting to the other side of the room.

He pursued her, removing his bridegroom's coat and throwing it onto the floor. He untied his tunic. His chest was barely dusted with black hair. "I will not hurt you, my dove. I feel only affection for you."

She wrapped her arms around her, covering her naked breast. "Stay away."

He stopped. "You are trembling. Why do you fear me so?"

She wanted to spew a litany of reasons but recalled the words of her father: *A prosperous and peaceful alliance between two nations depends on you being a good and dutiful wife.* Without thinking, she let a hand fall to her lower abdomen. "Please. I need more time."

Solomon's gaze traveled slowly down her body. The voracity in his eyes was replaced with scrutiny. "Very well. I will grant you time. I shall hasten my journey to the northern stronghold, Megiddo. I shall leave tomorrow."

She exhaled.

"I will be gone for a time, Wife." He paused, his gaze boring through her. "Nine months."

The blood drained from Nicaule's face. Her eyes grew wide as the realization settled upon her: he knew or at least suspected. She imagined the consequences if she was indeed with Shoshenq's child. All of Jerusalem would know the royal marriage was not consummated, for they waited for the telling knock that, should Solomon abandon the seduction and depart for Megiddo, would not come. If her belly were to swell with child in Solomon's absence, everyone would know of her perfidy. Banned from Jerusalem in shame, she would never be accepted back into her father's house. She was standing on the slender edge of a chasm with a steep drop on each side.

The oppressive perfume of the lilies choked her. They were everywhere she looked, swallowing her in their great white jaws.

He picked up his coat and belt and gave her a triumphant smile. "Until then, my dove." He turned and walked toward the door.

She clenched her teeth to suppress a cry of despair. She wasn't accustomed to being backed into corners. She called to him. "Wait."

He turned around slowly. His face was expressionless.

With trembling hands, she lowered her other dress strap. She stood bare-breasted before him for a moment before lowering her gown past her hips and letting it drop to the floor. She untied the kerchief wrapped around her hips and let it fall from her hand. She could see beneath his tunic how she had moved him.

"Come claim what you have bought," she said with no attempt to mask her rancor.

He approached, standing so close she could feel his breath on her cheeks. "I can see you are a lioness that must be tamed." He motioned toward the bed. "Lie down."

She did as he commanded, choking back tears.

Solomon stood over her and removed his tunic and loincloth. He didn't even afford her the decency of the dark. Without the light, she could pretend none of this was happening, that it was merely a passing dream. But no. He would force her to look upon his nakedness, to watch as he laid claim to her body, to witness the look of ecstasy as he satisfied himself.

He kneeled next to her. She could feel the heat radiating from his body.

He picked up a pomegranate from the silver tray and tore it in two. The blood of the fruit dripped down his forearms. "Your pleasure is my pleasure," he whispered.

He put one half down and tore into the other with his fingers, excavating a handful of the red seeds. He sprinkled them onto her body.

Each seed felt like a drop of cold rain as it landed,

first on the notch of her collarbone, then between her breasts, then on her abdomen and navel. The tiny hairs on her skin stood on end as she considered his intention.

He leaned over her. His hair brushed her neck as his lips explored her throat. His beard pricked her skin, and then his warm tongue tasted the seed in the hollow at the base of her neck.

Nicaule quivered. She hated him for this. It would have been far easier to accept her fate if he would have snuffed out the candles and done the deed quickly without subjecting her to the spice of his passion.

His lips traveled slowly down her sternum, sucking seeds along the way. He lingered on her breasts. *Curse him!* She wrapped her arms around him and dug her fingernails into the flesh between his shoulder blades, pushing hard until she felt his blood on her fingertips.

Solomon groaned but did not stop. He picked up every seed from her abdomen with assertive sweeps of his tongue. When he reached her navel, she quaked, resenting him for taking that reaction from her without her wanting to give it.

She could feel the mist of perspiration on his body as he draped himself over her, pushing upward with his forearms until their lips were a finger's width apart and his locks encircled her face like a raven prison. She expected his kiss, but he withheld it. Instead he whispered, "My wife, my queen."

He parted her legs and entered her.

She let out a gasp, louder than she'd intended.

Sickened at the notion of being one with him, she bore down with her nails, further tearing his flesh. She lifted her hands off his back and shuddered at how much of his blood she had drawn. Her palms were smeared with it.

She listened to his rapid, steady breath and felt warm beads of his perspiration drip onto her skin. She closed her eyes to escape her reality. She let herself drift into a daydream, imagining she was lying on the banks of the Nile beneath the new moon, dark water lapping her bare skin, and the man on top of her was a different husband.

CHAPTER TEN

A staccato sound echoed off the ceiling of the breezeway of King David's palace as Zadok's cane hit the pavement. Late summer's hot, dry breath had descended upon the landlocked capital, causing his step to be slower than usual. Yet summer, for all its lung-strangling heat, imbued him with the carefree spirit of a much younger man, the man he used to be before age and hardship deformed his limbs and robbed him of mobility.

He paused to catch his breath and heard the song of the cicadas. Their rhythmic trilling, like grain shaken inside a dried goatskin, was pervasive in summertime, signaling the last vestige of ataraxia before the changing of the seasons.

All was shifting, and not only because of the passage of time. Soon the king's first child would be born. If it were a boy, a healthy one, he could be heir to the kingdom. Zadok had hoped Solomon's firstborn would not be out of his Egyptian wife, but God's plan had it otherwise.

All that remained now was to hope the child would be a girl with no rights to the throne.

Zadok thought it important for Solomon—of all the kings—to continue the untainted bloodline of the Hebrews. Solomon was the chosen one, the one in whom Yahweh placed his most sacred duty and whom David, his father, trusted to perpetuate his kingdom, which was to rule over Jerusalem forever. Would there be an heir worthy of this?

Though he was a man of faith, Zadok could see the faintest glimmer of destiny written on the hewn stones. Since marrying Nicaule, Solomon had taken two other wives, a Moabite and an Ammonite. The latter was just beginning to show pregnant with child. The king had also identified the daughter of a Phoenician king as the next addition to his harem and was to draw the contract with her father on his next trip to Sidon.

Against his high priest's advice, Solomon insisted on marrying foreign wives for the security and prosperity of the kingdom. In some ways, it was wise. In others, it was an abomination. Zadok knew better than to challenge the king on this matter. It was an argument he could not win.

Zadok came to the quarters of the pharaoh's daughter, on the tip of the west wing, and knocked on the door. A nurse with kindly eyes opened it and bowed.

"Have you any news?" he asked.

"She still labors." The sound of a woman screaming came from inside the room. "I must go to her."

"I will wait here. Bring me word as soon as the child arrives."

The nurse nodded and closed the door.

There was a bench on the garden just beyond the breezeway, but Zadok was too restless to sit. Fueled by nerves, he paced the corridor. He heard the faint sound of Nicaule's howls through the thick slabs of stone. They came more rapidly now. It would be any moment.

Zadok knew Solomon was in the vineyard with one of his concubines, for it was a sin to touch his pregnant wives. He had not visited Nicaule in months but not only because she was swollen with child. When it was announced she was expecting, Solomon had confided in Zadok his apprehension. Though Solomon had been loathe to believe his dove had been delivered to him impure, there was evidence on their wedding night that he was not the first. Now he feared the child was not his own and retreated from his first wife as a result.

Zadok could tell how much it haunted him. He suspected that was partly the reason for his taking other wives so quickly: not only to spread his seed but also to find solace in another. Only that solace never came, for none had the power over Solomon that Nicaule Tashere did.

The door opened with a long creak, and the nurse emerged. She bowed once again.

"Speak, woman."

"It is a girl, *Kohain*."

Zadok closed his eyes and silently thanked the Lord. "Send word to the king. Do it quickly."

She bowed and took her leave.

Zadok walked to the office of the court scribe at the opposite end of the palace. Elihorcph, bent over an earthenware jug, looked up with a start when Zadok entered without knocking. He stood and approached the priest, taking his right hand in both of his own and touching his forehead to it.

"Rise, Elihoreph. We have much to do."

The young man with sunken cheeks and deep-set eyes met Zadok's gaze. "I await your command."

"We must send word to the pharaoh of Egypt. A child has been born to his daughter."

"A joyous occasion."

Zadok raised both eyebrows. "Indeed. Let us make haste now." It was important to waste no time in delivering the news to Solomon's father-in-law and greatest ally.

Elihoreph returned to his table and pulled a stretch of papyrus from a shelf. Though papyrus was not endemic to Israel, it was one of the privileges of the now-robust trade with Egypt. The scribe smoothed it with his hands, picked up a reed stylus, and waited.

Zadok dictated. "Esteemed Psusennes, great pharaoh of Lower Egypt, greetings come your way from the house of Solomon." He paused to let Elihoreph work. Writing was painstaking business, and it could take hours.

After a period that seemed interminable, the scribe looked up and signaled to Zadok to continue.

"Today the kingdom rejoices in the birth of the first royal child, the offspring of your daughter." He paused again, later adding, "A girl whose name shall be Basemath."

It was tradition for highborn children to be named by

the kingdom's high priest. Zadok had chosen the name for its meaning—sweet-smelling. It was a benign choice, devoid of symbolism or lofty references to faith and piety, since the mother was a nonbeliever. Besides, Solomon had made a covenant with Psusennes about the child's dual education, which included the religions of both her parents.

"See that this is delivered to the pharaoh right away," he told the scribe, who was still laboring over the letters. "The king's swiftest horses have been readied for this moment."

He turned to leave. As he walked, there was a bang at the wooden door. "Enter."

The door opened slowly, and a shaft of saffron light shone onto the floor. A messenger stood at the threshold. "The king requires your appearance at the birth chamber, *Kohain*. He asks that you not delay."

As Zadok exited the room, he felt the warm kiss of late afternoon on his face. He raised the hood of his garment to protect his head from the blazing sun and walked toward the west wing.

Solomon waited in the antechamber as the nurses prepared mother and baby for his visit. He smiled when he saw his priest. "Ah, Zadok. You have arrived in time. We will meet her together."

"May she have a long and blessed life, my lord." Zadok studied the king's face: his forehead was tight, betraying his worry. He decided to say nothing about it; there were others in the room.

A nurse stood at the doorway, bowing deeply before the king. "They are ready, my lord."

Two guards entered first. "All hail King Solomon," they announced in unison.

Solomon, dressed in a short garment the color of the sea with a red linen scarf draped across his body, walked into the room. Zadok followed.

Nicaule was sitting upright on the bed, her lap covered by a sheepskin. Her face was fully made up, and her straight black hair appeared neat and glossy. Her chin was high, her countenance devoid of emotion.

"Bring me the child," Solomon said.

A nurse reached into the cradle next to the mother's bed and lifted the crying infant. The tiny girl's face was bright red, a stark contrast to her white swaddling clothes. The nurse handed the baby to Solomon.

He held her in the crook of his left arm and gazed upon her face, which was twisted with displeasure. He held his right pinkie to the corner of her mouth, and she suckled it. She ceased to cry and looked at him with wide eyes. King and infant gazed at each other for a long moment. Then Solomon reached inside the baby's linen blanket and freed her right hand. He gently lifted her tiny, curled fingers and exposed her palm. He ran his thumb across a birthmark that looked like a brown stain inside the child's hand.

The hair on Zadok's arms stood on end.

Solomon and David both had the same mark on their right palms.

As Solomon regarded the newborn, the tension on his face vanished; in its place was a soft smile that spoke of a deep serenity. There was no question in Zadok's mind: Solomon saw himself in the baby girl's face.

The king turned to his priest. "Zadok. What name do you give this child?"

Zadok bowed slightly. "Basemath, my lord."

Solomon held the girl high and looked up at her. "Behold my firstborn: Princess Basemath. Blessed be she"—he glanced at Nicaule—"and her mother."

He handed the baby to the nurse, who delivered her to Nicaule. The new mother parted her gown to reveal a breast and let the baby feed.

Solomon kneeled next to her bed. She turned to him. There was a vacant look in her dark eyes, as if she were incapable of feeling. He took her free hand and touched his forehead to it but said nothing. He stood and left the room.

Zadok stayed a moment longer and intoned a prayer. When he looked up, he noticed Nicaule's eyes were misting. She turned away.

He let her be and retreated to the antechamber. He looked for Solomon, but he was long gone.

CHAPTER ELEVEN

In the thick of night, Nicaule rapped on the door of Irisi's chamber. It had been days since she could sleep. She wandered the halls of the west wing like the undead, bound to torment.

Her friend came to the door. Her eyes were heavy with sleep. "My lady?"

Nicaule spoke softly. "I have something important to ask of you."

Irisi held the door open, checking up and down the corridor for activity. When Nicaule was inside, she closed and boarded the door. "What keeps you awake at such an hour, my lady?"

"I have no rest. There is something I must do, and it haunts me."

Irisi lit a small clay oil lamp. Its meager flame cast a copper glow onto the shadows, making the peaks and valleys of her facial bones look like desert dunes in twilight. "What is it that cannot wait until morning?"

Nicaule grasped both of Irisi's arms. "I need your help. I must send a message to Shoshenq. I cannot risk doing it by day. It is far too . . . sensitive."

Irisi frowned. "I do not think this is a good idea."

"I care not what you think." Nicaule's voice was harsher than she intended. She sighed. "Just do as I ask."

The scribe walked to the back of the room, where she kept her papyri, inks, and writing implements. She laid everything onto a table next to the lamplight.

"Do I have your word that you will breathe nothing of this to anyone?"

"My lady, when have I disappointed you that you ask this?"

Nicaule smiled. "Not once."

"You seem distraught. What has you in such a state?"

"It is about the child." She felt emotion rise to her throat, and she swallowed hard to contain it. "I must inform him he is the father."

Irisi's eyes widened. "You mean—?"

She nodded. "Yes. On the eve of our departure from Egypt."

Irisi clutched her chest, twisting the linen of her nightgown. "Oh, my lady . . ." She lifted a hand to her mouth as if she were trying to hold back the stream of words.

"Do not judge me. Love rules over prudence."

"How can you be certain of this? He was not the only one, after all."

Nicaule looked away. "A woman knows."

"My lady, as your trusted friend, it is my duty to

speak my mind, is it not?"

"It is."

"Sending word to Shoshenq is a mistake. What if the missive falls into the wrong hands? That would be catastrophic to you—and to Egypt. Men have gone to war over less than this."

"I would rather die than keep this from him." She squeezed Irisi's hands. "He loves me. He will come for me—and our child."

Irisi shook her head. "You must not long for this, my lady. Think of what you're saying: you are putting your desire before the good of the state. You are a princess married to a foreign king. The marriage was an alliance between two countries, not a union between two people. For the sake of your ancestors, you must honor this. You must forget Shoshenq."

Nicaule jerked her hands away. Tears welled in her eyes. "I will not."

Irisi's expression grew somber. "Yesterday, word came from Tanis that Shoshenq has married another. A woman of his own race. She is already with child. I did not know how to tell you."

Nicaule went numb. She took a step backward. "Lies!"

"It is the truth. I swear it." Irisi opened an alabaster box and lifted out a scroll. "See for yourself."

Nicaule scanned the missive. It began with a message about her father. He had been ill, it said, and the doctors had not identified the cause. She read on, looking for the part that interested her. She read aloud. "Shoshenq, captain of the army, has wed a Meshwesh princess, Kara-mat. A child is expected in the season of the emergence."

She let the scroll drop from her hands. How could he? She had been gone for three seasons, and already her lover had moved on. While she despised her own husband and devised ways to escape the bondage to which he had subjected her, Shoshenq was willfully loving another. It maddened her to be so far removed, to be oblivious to the circumstances. Did his kin force him to marry one of his own kind? Was it some rite of passage particular to the Ma? Surely it was a forced marriage; it comforted her to think so.

The child complicated things. Her beloved was favored to succeed her father to the throne. If Shoshenq's legitimate firstborn was male, that child surely would be next in line to be king. Nicaule's love child, born of Shoshenq's seed, was a mere female and, as such, had no rights to the throne. If he had a son on the other side of the Sea of Reeds, Shoshenq would not hesitate to come claim him and raise him in the court. A daughter was another matter.

Once again, Nicaule's schemes had crumbled. If she could not be queen of Egypt, as was always her dream, she wanted her child to rule in the land of her ancestors. Even that seemed like an impossibility now. Nicaule felt condemned to look in on Egypt's royal court, the only world that mattered to her, from the periphery, never more than an outsider.

If only Basemath were male. If only . . .

Nicaule grabbed a sheet of papyrus from the table and held it up to the scribe's face. "Write the message." She raised her voice a notch. "Do it."

Irisi took the sheet and sat at the table.

"God of my river," Nicaule began. She used a term known only to him and her that no one might suspect the source or the recipient of the message. "A child has been born unto me who shares your eyes, your strength, your spirit. Come for me and claim your heir."

Irisi looked up, startled. "I cannot do what you ask. It is deceitful."

"Please, Irisi." She kneeled by her friend and grasped her forearm. "It is my only hope."

"You know as well as I do that Basemath could never be heir to anything. Your words will lead Shoshenq to believe his child is a male. Whip me, torture me, send me away if you must, but that is a lie I cannot enable."

Nicaule twisted her face in disgust. "Suddenly you are full of morals? Must I remind you of the death of your husband? That you spoke nothing of it, that you covered up justice, for no better reason than to preserve your own life? Do not lecture me about lies."

"What has possessed you that you spew such venom?"

She stood. "My patience wears thin, Irisi. Once more, I command you to write the missive."

Irisi hesitated, then picked up the writing instrument. Her hand shook as she set to work.

"Good." Nicaule exhaled. "We must be sure no one knows the source of the letter. Do not use your seal. And let no one see it. My personal guard will deliver it into Shoshenq's hand."

Irisi looked up, her gaze hard as iron. "You cannot escape your fate, my lady. Whatever it is, it will hunt you and draw level to you. It is the way of the gods; no man, or woman, can will it otherwise."

Nicaule smirked. She had tired of waiting for fate to smile at her. She would make her own destiny.

She left Irisi to her task and hurried out of the room. Her mind was a maelstrom fueled by sleeplessness and emotion, but she was clear on the next phase of her plan. She launched down the corridor, her mantle billowing around her. A part of her wanted to run until her legs buckled and her lungs were depleted of air, to release a primal scream that would echo all the way to her motherland. She resisted the urge, for there was work to be done.

At the end of the stone arcade was a terrace with steps leading to the garden. She stopped and caught her breath. In the distant horizon, a strip of light cracked open the darkness. She regarded the darkened treetops and the rows of vines cloaked in shadow.

He was somewhere down there. The king had a habit of rising early and taking a predawn walk to "bear witness to the awakening of a new day," as he liked to say. She smoothed her hair with her hands and started down the steps.

She came first to the orchard. She stopped beneath the dark canopy of an old fig tree and rested against its trunk. She unfastened her mantle and let it fall to the ground, leaving only a light cotton night tunic. A gentle breeze whispered through the leaves, carrying the scent of the ripe fruit. She inhaled the fragrant air as night gave way to day.

She continued through the beds of myrrh to the vine-yards. This time of year, the vines were heavy with grapes. The clusters looked like black pearls in the gathering dawn. They were like the grapes of Egypt, yet their wine tasted so different. She ran her fingers over the plump beads, plucking one and bringing it to her mouth. It erupted between her teeth, and she found its tangy sweet-ness strangely comforting.

"The vine flourishes with tender grapes."

At the sound of the voice, a sly smile crossed her lips. A hand rested on her bare arm, making her flesh come alive with tiny bumps. She turned to face her husband.

"But none is as tender as you." He stroked her arm with a downy touch.

In the fragile light, he was like a wraith. He wore none of his king's paraphernalia—only a short gown of gauzy cotton and no shoes. Without a crown to bind them, his mussed curls fell carelessly, softening the hard angles of his face. For the first time, she saw a man, not a monarch.

"How fair you are, my lonesome dove," he continued, speaking flawlessly in her mother tongue. "You are per-fection, the work of the most skilled artisan in all the land. Your eyes shimmer with the fire of a thousand jewels. Your neck"—he drew a long, slow breath as he stroked her throat with the tips of his fingers—"is graceful as a swan's."

"Your words are like the tender morn," she whispered, surprised at how easy it was to utter the words. "Like the wind rising up from the north and rippling the waters of Gihon."

He placed gentle hands on her waist and pulled her to him. Her heart told her to break free of his hold and flee to the safety of her chamber, where she could be alone with her sorrow and the memories that haunted her even as they grew distant. But her mind held back those girlish sentiments, clearing the way for the cunning woman to rise like a mandrake bursting forth from the rocky ground.

It was the moment of her transformation. She should have feared it, but instead she reveled in it.

One of his hands traveled slowly up her torso and stopped on her breast, rolling her nipple between his thumb and forefinger. Without willing it to, her mouth let a faint whimper escape. Her heart pounded violently.

Solomon drew closer. His breath was warm and redolent of figs. "The dawn comes with a terrible fury, yet it is my beloved who is the light breaking in the night sky. Your perfume is sweeter than all the myrrh in the garden, your hair as soft as the young goats of Gilead." He brushed her cheek with his lips. "I want to know what you taste of." He lightly kissed her face, his mouth moving closer to her own.

It was the first time he'd kissed her. His lips were soft and gentle, speaking more of love than of raw desire. Nicaule relaxed into his embrace in an act of submission she knew he'd appreciate. When she felt his arousal, she gave him a taste of her own passion. She suckled his upper lip, then thrust her tongue into his mouth and searched for a vulnerable spot.

The king moaned with pleasure, and she knew there was nothing he wouldn't do for her.

"Give me a son," she whispered.

Solomon did not bother to look for a spot on which they could lie. He placed his hands on her hips and lifted her, her cue to wrap her legs around his waist. In an instant he was one with her, thrusting and panting like an animal in heat.

Nicaule let her head fall back and gazed at the violet sky. The new day was perfectly clear and free of cloud. She felt powerful, unstoppable. Whatever the cost, she would finally claim her destiny.

CHAPTER TWELVE

It was Ethanim, the seventh day. The Hebrews had waited seven years for it, and at last it was upon them.

Zadok rose with the dawn and took himself to Mount Moriah for the ritual cleansing demanded by the Law on exalted days, of which this was foremost. He stood at the edge of the *mikveh* pool, fed by the living waters of Ein Eitam high above Jerusalem, and intoned a silent prayer, imploring the Lord to judge him worthy of the task appointed to him.

On that day, Zadok and the priests of the kingdom, together with the leaders of each of the twelve tribes, would take up the ark of the covenant from its place in the tabernacle and bring it to the house of the Lord, at long last complete. It was imperative he be pure of body, mind, and spirit to lead Israel's most blessed men on so grave a mission—the gravest, in fact, of their lifetimes.

He stepped into the frigid water. His flesh tingled as he lowered himself into the pool one palm's width at a time until the water came to his chest. He reveled for a moment in the chill of the autumn morning and the bracing freshness of the water. Then he immersed himself, holding his breath for as long as his lungs allowed. He floated in darkness, thinking of nothing.

His head pierced the water's surface, and he opened his eyes. He felt the kiss of a wind gust and looked through the quivering leaves of the olive trees at the early morning sky. Its roof was a perfect tekhelet, the color of the heavens. The hue grew progressively lighter as the fingers of the rising sun touched it. Without a cloud to impede the panorama, the horizon seemed infinite. He took it as a sign: Yahweh was pleased at the work of his children.

Shivering, Zadok stepped out of the water and dried himself. He dressed in the ceremonial garments of the high priest, reserved for the most important of occasions. First he slipped on a long white tunic made of spotless linen. Over that he wore a robe of the same blue as the sky, whose edges were trimmed in fabric pomegranates and tiny bells that would sound as he walked, calling the faithful to attention.

With reverence he picked up the ephod, the holy outer garment that could be worn by no one but the high priest. It was magnificent. Woven of fine linen in a pattern of blue, purple, and scarlet squares intersected by threads of gold and trimmed in golden fringe, it surpassed in beauty the clothing of any king.

The ephod was made of two pieces—to cover both the front and back of the body—joined by shoulder straps decorated with two onyx stones engraved with the names of the twelve sons of Israel, in order of their birth. The stones served as a memorial to their forefathers, whose struggles defined the Israelites' identity and granted them a permanent home away from the cruel hand of oppression.

His shaking fingers touched the breastplate of judgment. Attached to the onyx stones with two braided cords of pure gold and measuring a span on all four sides, it was woven of the same threads as the ephod and encrusted with precious stones, four on each of three rows. Each stone bore the name of a son of Israel so that the priest would keep the names close to his heart as he entered the holiest confines of the temple. His ancestors would guide him, it was said, in divining the judgment.

In a pocket sewn onto the back of the breastplate were the two seeing stones, Urim and Thummim. He removed them and placed them in his hand, running his fingers over the smooth, polished surface of the black Thummim, which symbolized darkness, then the white Urim, which stood for light: the duality of the human spirit. He held them with reverence close to his heart before securing them in their place.

He slipped the ephod over his head and felt the weight of it on his shoulders. It grew heavier as the years passed and the tribes grew more populous. Where there were more voices, there was a greater potential for discord. He feared that eventuality, though the winds blew favorably at that moment. Under Solomon's rule, Israel was indeed the land of milk and honey. The people wanted for nothing. Leaders of surrounding nations did not raise a hand against Solomon, nor he against them. The era he had ushered in was unprecedented.

But would it last?

Zadok tied the substantial sash—a fringed band of the same workmanship as the ephod—around his waist and drew a deep breath. He felt the cool soil beneath his bare feet and was reminded of his place on Earth. His flesh was a conduit for the word of Yahweh. Though he had a grave purpose, he had no sense of self. He was but a mediator between the Lord and his people Israel.

He picked up the final piece of his priestly ensemble. He coiled the white linen mitre around his head in the manner of a turban. With ribbons of blue lace he attached the golden plate engraved with the words *Holiness to the Lord*. It rested on his forehead like a crown, marking him as the bearer of the people's iniquities—the heaviest of burdens—and the instrument of their earthly judgment.

He stood tall. The sun gleamed on the eastern horizon like a promise. It was time.

Solomon was already at the tent of meeting when Zadok arrived. The king was splendidly arrayed in clothing fit for the occasion: a long white tunic with wide sleeves, over which lay a white silk robe embroidered with gold thread and cinched with a fringed sash of the same fabric, and a crimson mantle attached at the shoulders with ruby-encrusted bindings, which cascaded down his back and to the ground.

Solomon bowed deeply to Zadok, then regarded him

with sparkling eyes. "Seven years it has taken to fulfill my father's promise. Blessed be this day."

"So be it. A new day dawns for Israel. All the trials of our fathers, all the years of oppression and deliverance, they are rewarded today." Zadok brought a hand to his chest, touching the corner of the breastplate. "You, my lord, have led us here."

Solomon looked over Zadok's shoulder. "The Levites come. Soon we will sound the trumpet of glory."

Zadok turned. The elders of the tribe of Levi, the *kohanim* of the kingdom, had begun to gather before the tent of meeting. They were dressed in pure white tunics bound at the waist with red embroidered sashes. Their heads were wrapped with white turbans. Many held instruments, for part of their role as priests was to make the joyous music that could be heard in the high heavens.

When all the Levites, some fourscore of them, and the leaders of each tribe had arrived in the City of David, Solomon signaled to the shofar blower to announce the beginning of the ceremonies that would last seven days. The Levite raised the ram's horn to his lips and delivered a long blast that resonated throughout the city.

Within moments, the people exited their homes and took up their places along the path leading to Jerusalem so they, too, could accompany the Hebrews' most precious relic to its new home.

Zadok regarded the tabernacle King David had made in his youth, a copy of the original tabernacle of Moses, when he brought the ark of the Lord from Gibeon to his city. Zadok, then at the threshold of manhood, was one of the ark bearers for David, just as he would be for his son.

The tabernacle was a tent sanctuary much like the original that dated from the days of the Exodus, but far less tattered. It was covered with rams' skins that stretched from the roof of the structure to the ground on two sides. Curtains made of goat hair dyed in crimson, blue, and violet concealed and protected the inner sanctum, where the divine presence dwelled.

Within the sanctuary courtyard sat the laver for ablutions and the altar of burnt offering for ritual sacrifices. Solomon stood next to the altar, addressing the assembly. "Since the day our fathers escaped from Egypt, the tablets of the Law have dwelled inside a temple of cloth. It has been a symbol of the Hebrews' wanderings, our ancestors' quest for their promised land. Just as the ark will be committed to its eternal place today, so the children of Israel will dwell on this land forever."

The old song master Chenaniah, chief of the Levites since the days of David, sang a verse without accompaniment, then signaled to his fellow priests to start the music. The happy notes of psalteries and harps, trumpets and cymbals sounded across the city as Chenaniah sang the ancient tune said to have been written by Aaron, their forebear.

Zadok felt the clang of the cymbals in the pit of his stomach. Pride filled him to the tips of his fingers and the soles of his bare feet. He walked toward the tent's entrance, followed by the Levite elders to whom the task of carrying the ark had been appointed. He kneeled before the curtain with head scraping the ground, humbling himself before the creator, before entering the holy shrine.

They walked in single file past the tables of shewbread, the altars of incense, and the golden lamps until they came to the veil separating the holy of holies. He turned to the men and gestured to them to gather round him in a circle. He touched their turbaned heads, and they all bowed toward the center of the circle, whispering a prayer in unison.

Zadok parted the veil, a heavy wool curtain with stripes of crimson, violet, and blue, and entered the innermost sanctum. Though he had gone inside the holiest place scores of times, on this occasion he was overcome with emotion. Mostly he was elated that the ark would have a permanent home befitting its importance. Yet he could not deny a vague sadness. On this day, the tabernacle that had served as the holy sanctuary for hundreds of years would be no more. It would be folded and taken, along with the holy vessels, to the new temple, where the memory of what it stood for would slowly fade. The prosperity brought forth by Solomon was glorious, a blessing from the Lord, but a part of Zadok longed for the simplicity of their nation's humble beginnings and the modesty inherent in scarcity.

Perhaps he was too old a man to truly appreciate progress. Or maybe he feared the fine line between plenty and excess, for crossing it would surely corrupt men's hearts.

The four Levites took their places at each of the four handles of the stretcher beneath the acacia box that held the two stone tablets of testimony. These were the gravest of relics, inscribed by Yahweh himself as a covenant with his people Israel. Since the day Moses brought them down from Mount Sinai, the tablets had been a guiding force for the people. More than a prescription of conduct, it was a reminder that, for all their scheming, mortals were not in charge.

Chanting, the Levites picked up the sacred object and followed Zadok out of the sanctuary. When they reemerged in daylight, the priests' tune swelled into a sort of rapture. Zadok scanned the faces of the gathered and saw untarnished optimism in them as the old gave way to the new. As trumpets blew with a fevered pitch, the congregation sang a song of hope, eager to embrace Solomon's temple and the new Jerusalem it symbolized.

On the highest point of Mount Moriah, the temple stood thirty cubits high, as was mandated in the plans drawn up by King David, who had received instruction from the angels of heaven.

The ashlars had been hewn to perfection and fitted together in a manner so flawless it surpassed Zadok's estimation of human capabilities. It was as if the work had been done not by the hand of man but by the angels themselves. A gilt door carved with lilies and palm trees offered entrance into the sanctuary. Two monumental bronze columns with chapiters carved with pomegranates and lilies demarcated the vestibule leading to the entrance. Solomon called one pillar Boaz, the other Jachin, for each was a sentinel deserving of a name. Silently they guarded the treasures of the earthly kingdom of heaven.

In the courtyard stood the brazen sea that held two thousand baths for the priests' ablutions. Solomon had described it years ago: *It will rest on the backs of twelve oxen, each representing a tribe of Israel, which will be arranged in a circle and face the sky. And it will be filled with living water flowing from the spring.* Zadok could not visualize it then and thought it an exaggeration. Now, standing before the bronze sea that stood five cubits high, he marveled anew at the king's vision.

Sharing space with the sea in the courtyard was the altar of burnt offering, built of hewn stones with twelve steps leading up to the massive fire pit. The altar was made as Yahweh had commanded centuries ago, when the children of Israel came out of Egypt: a square frame of acacia wood overlaid with bronze, with horns on each corner and a grate of bronze. The fire's swirling copper flames reached through the network of the grate, ready to swallow the sacrificial animals that would die in the place of man.

Zadok inhaled the fragrant acacia wood smoke wafting toward the heavens as he watched Solomon ascend the steps to make the first, symbolic sacrifice. The priests assembled in a line from the washbasins to the altar, passing the skinned and washed animals from hand to hand. The priest standing closest to the altar handed Solomon the first of the animals, a sheep that had not yet reached its prime. The king held it up before the thousands of

Israelites that had gathered on Mount Moriah and threw it into the fire. The process continued until the sacrificial sheep numbered seven.

The air was filled with the pleasing scent of scorched meat. When the animals had been so consumed by the fire that the flesh separated from the bone, Solomon descended the altar and signaled to Zadok that it was time.

The trumpets and the goat skin drums sounded as the Levites picked up the ark and the holy vessels. Zadok led the procession, stepping gingerly as if to not disturb the sacred ground. His heart pounded as he stood between Boaz and Jachin. Though he had prepared for this moment and had come before the temple with pure heart, mind, and body, he did not deem himself fully worthy. He dropped to his knees and kissed the ground, not bothering to hold back the tears that flooded his eyes. With a soft sob, he stood and pushed open the heavy gilt doors.

It was the first time he'd seen the nave since its completion. He was in awe. The walls, soaring thirty cubits to the beamed ceiling, had been carved of cedar in patterns of open lilies, palm trees, and cherubim and covered with pure gold from Ophir. Not a single stone was seen inside the sanctuary, and no metal nails had been used, only pegs of gold. Softer and more pliable than stone, and finer besides, wood and gold symbolized the yielding of the soul before God, and nowhere had they been used more magnificently.

Solomon, like all men, was flawed, but in this he had come as close to perfection as a mortal could. That would be his legacy unto the ages of ages.

Zadok stopped before the altar of incense, on which sat a censer with live coals from the altar of burnt offering. On his right hand, Zadok held a pan of incense he himself had pounded the night prior. It was an amalgam of four ingredients—balsam gum, frankincense, galbanum resin, and the operculum of a Sea of Reeds mollusk—representing the four elements of the universe.

With the assistance of one of his priests, he spread the incense over the coals as an offering of atonement for the sins of the people. As wisps of aromatic smoke wafted skyward, he breathed in the quintessence of Israel. It was a most pleasing scent redolent of wood and spice with hints of sea air in summertime.

He walked to the rear of the nave and ascended the steps to the most holy place. He pushed open the folding doors. A gossamer linen veil dyed in the three holy shades—crimson for earth, tekhelet for the heavens, purple for the marriage of the two—offered a clouded glimpse of the innermost sanctum. The windowless room had been built as a perfect square, twenty cubits on each side, and decorated in the same manner as the sanctuary. In its midst stood two cherubim—human faces with the bodies of lions and outstretched wings touching the walls.

Zadok parted the veil and was dazzled as if he'd walked into a room full of treasure. Every surface from the fir floor to the ceiling to the cedar walls had been covered with gold that shone with an inextinguishable radiance.

He held back the veil, and the Levites entered the holy of holies, depositing the sacred tablets of the covenant within a golden box beneath the wings of the cherubim. And Zadok said, "Lord, our God, may your word rest here for all eternity, guiding your people Israel that their souls might not fall into darkness. May the wings of these cherubs serve as your throne and the ark box as your footstool as you judge this people. Come now and fill your house with your holy presence that it may be consecrated before all who have come to bear witness."

One by one, the priests backed away from the holy of holies and exited the sanctuary. As the last of them closed the doors behind him, there came a low rumble like distant thunder, and dark clouds gathered in the sky. A gust of wind swept across the mountaintop, and the cloud, like rolling gray smoke, hung above the temple. There was no rain, nor lightning; this storm was silent but sure, an omen and a promise.

Solomon lifted his arms to the sky. As the wind blew his kingly robes and raven curls, he shouted to the assembled masses. "The Lord said he would dwell in the thick darkness. Now, as surely as I have built this house for his glory, the divine presence has descended from heaven and walks among us. Fall, one and all, to your knees and bow your heads in reverence, for the Lord sees you and knows what is in your hearts."

With arms stretched toward heaven, Solomon kneeled before the congregation, which numbered in the tens of thousands. "O Lord, God of Israel, all-powerful and divine, bless your children who have come before you to dedicate this house in your name. It is but a humble gesture from your children, a manifestation of the covenant you made with your servant David, my father. You said, 'Build me a house, but do not let it be done by your bloodied hand. Let it be the duty and the legacy of your son, who comes forth from your loins.' Just as you deemed, O Lord, it has been done.

"And when your children come before you in the altar of your house with pure heart, judge them for their righteousness. But should they swear against you at this altar or harbor darkness in their hearts, condemn them for their wickedness. For this house is your throne room in the lower heavens, from whence divine judgment springs forth like the eternal waters of Gihon.

"When your people Israel sin against you, for none among us is without sin, when they are afflicted with ills, or taken up by the enemy and held captive in foreign lands, if the same people kneel before you and turn their eyes toward this holy city you have chosen and this house I have built in your name, hear their pleas, O Lord, and deliver them from their iniquities.

"When heaven is shut up and there is no rain, and the animals and people thirst and the trees wither, if your children walk upright before you with goodness in their hearts, and sacrifice in your name at this place, let there be water to feed the land which you have given them for an inheritance.

"For these are your people who you have brought

forth from the land of the Nile and delivered from oppression and injustice, the people to whom you spoke through Moses your servant and who are your inheritance upon this earth."

Solomon stood and addressed the crowd. "Our Lord has never faltered on his promise to us, his chosen people, nor has he forsaken us in our hour of need. Neither shall we falter on our promise to him but rather keep his commandments and laws, which he gave unto our fathers. Let everyone gathered here today, and all the people of Israel, know there is but one God. There is no other. Those who turn against him, or open the doors of their hearts to let false gods enter, shall be cast to the barren desert of the wicked, and those who glorify him shall dwell in a valley of fragrant lilies. Be, therefore, pure before this temple as on this day. Bring forth your livestock and let its blood soak the earth and its flesh feed the fire in the name of the most holy."

The crowd, a sea stretching from the courtyard of the temple down the mountainside and into the cobbled alleys of the city, cheered with one voice. Trumpets sounded, then drums and cymbals, overtaking the joyous cries of the people. Then they approached, one by one, delivering their young sheep and oxen to the priests, their tribute for the blessing of their souls.

Zadok watched as the priests slashed the living things' throats, delivering a quick death. The sheep were stripped of their skins and the oxen of their horns, then washed dutifully in the lavers and delivered up to the altar of fire. This went on until night fell, such was the number of sacrifices.

As smoke from the dancing pyre billowed upward, the storm cloud parted and revealed a ribbon of clear sky. Zadok recognized the omen. He thought of his father, and of his father's father, and every one of his ancestors since the day of Aaron, and he recalled the old stories. When the animals were sacrificed by the old tabernacle, it was said, fire came down from the sky and consumed the offering, and the people gasped at the spectacle and fell prostrate to the ground. The Lord revealed his power in such a manner—in the fire rushing forth from heaven, in the parting of the clouds—when he sensed harmony among the people and goodness in their hearts.

But when the opposite was true, the consequences were dire. Just as Aaron and his brother Moses were not permitted to enter the promised land after all the years of wandering in the desert, for a reason no better than taking with the hand of man what should have been granted by divine power, even the slightest missteps were punished. The Law was a knife-edge and keeping it a precarious balance. There was not a man in history who had maintained it without feeling the sharp sting of the blade of justice.

For now, at least, the Lord was pleased and had said so to Solomon the night before. Zadok recalled the private meeting with the king on the eve of the dedication.

"The Lord has spoken to me, Zadok," Solomon had said. "He came to me in a dream and said, 'I have hallowed this house, which you have built, and have placed my name upon it, and there I shall walk among you forever.'"

"He is pleased, then," Zadok replied. "My heart rejoices at this news."

"Yes." Solomon looked away. "But there was a warning. The Lord said, 'If you walk upright before me, as David your father did, your kingdom over Israel shall be established forever. Just as I promised your father, no man from your house shall fail you upon the throne of Israel. But should you or your children falter, should you break my commandments or serve other gods, I will strike down Israel and cast out of my sight the house which I have hallowed. This land I have given to these people will be barren and bleak and vulnerable to enemies. And this house in which I once dwelled will crumble to ruin and cause those who pass by it to shudder and hiss. And Israel, once great, will be a proverb and a byword among all people.'"

"It is a warning not to be taken lightly, my lord."

"Eleven years I have sat upon this throne, Zadok. Twice the Lord has come to me. I know the gravity of his warnings. I shall not falter."

"It is a lot to ask of one man: to walk upright that an entire nation will not suffer."

Solomon pressed his lips together. "Trust in your king."

Now, Zadok watched as David's favored son held court over tens of thousands. The ignorant youth the priest had anointed into kingship had grown into a man so strong, competent, and confident that the people of

Israel loved to linger in his shadow. His every word was water for the thirsty, his every deed a ray of light in the darkness.

Israel, it seemed, had finally been granted the leader who would guide it into the future it deserved.

CHAPTER THIRTEEN

For seven days and seven nights the Israelites came to the top of Mount Moriah, dragging their bleating animals to the courtyard of the temple, where they would meet the most honorable death. The smoke of the altar of sacrifice was profuse, and the entire city smelled of roasting animal flesh.

For those seven days, the people did not work. It was a time of rest and reflection, a time to honor their Lord Yahweh. Every day they offered prayers at the temple, and the priests delivered their blessings to the troubled, old, and infirm. Zadok marveled at the solemnity and sincerity of the worshippers. It seemed as if, by its very existence, the temple had stricken fear in their hearts. Now that there was a magnificent house to contain the divine presence, Yahweh seemed more real to the people, who believed he dwelled within the perfectly hewn ashlars and gold-covered walls. In all Zadok's years it had been the same: the people professed their faith, but secretly they needed proof—a sign from heaven—to truly believe.

By night, every citizen was invited to the courtyard of Solomon's palace, the chambers of which were, for years now, a work in progress. The people came and went, partaking of the plentiful food and drink and music.

On the seventh night, when the temple dedications subsided, Zadok and the Levites joined the celebrations. The courtyard, which measured forty cubits on one side and twenty on the other and housed a garden in miniature, was buzzing with murmurs and bursts of laughter that drowned the incessant song of the psalteries and harps. A fire in a stone pit at the center cast a glow like molten bronze on the happy faces.

As Zadok made his way to the far side of the courtyard, the crowd parted and the revelers bowed. Some rushed forth to kiss his hand. He waved a hand over their bent heads, conferring his favor upon them.

A raised platform within the pillared arcade at the edge of the courtyard was the domain of the king. Torches burned in a wide circle around the royal seat, creating a barrier of fire. Within the ring of flames, on the highest point of the platform, sat Solomon. To his left were his Egyptian wife, Nicaule, and their eldest daughter, Basemath, now four. The king's right was open for his advisors, who came and went during the course of the evening. At the moment, it was occupied by the captain of the host.

Zadok paused for a moment and watched from a distance. Despite the excitement of the festivities, Nicaule looked disengaged and perhaps a bit sad. It had been three years since her loss, but she was still mourning. Even her aloof Egyptian nature did not bolster her when she found out her son, born less than a year after Basemath, had been strangled by the umbilical cord inside her womb. The boy was a terrible shade of blue when he was delivered. All the doctors in the kingdom had tried to save him, but it was too late.

Nicaule had displayed more emotion on that day than Zadok had ever thought her capable of. Her howls had sounded across the City of David, desperate pleas to the gods who had sealed her fortune. Though Zadok had not trusted her in all the years he'd known her, it was hard not to sympathize with her anguish. For any parent it was difficult to lose a child, but losing a son was a grave blow—especially to the wife of a king.

On the night of feasting, Solomon seemed oblivious to her temperament as he was deep in conversation with Benaiah. When he noticed Zadok, he waved the high priest over.

Zadok approached, noting the king's pinched brow beneath his crown. In a day of celebration, he looked worried. Solomon and Benaiah bowed at him, and he returned the gesture.

"Benaiah has just informed me of old enemies stirring against us," Solomon said. "Hadad the Edomite lives."

Zadok tilted his head. Had he heard correctly? "That cannot be. His entire family was slaughtered years ago by order of your father."

"I was there," Benaiah said. "I saw the treacherous lot

of them fall to Joab's sword. We left them all lying in their blood. There was no escape from their wounds."

"And yet, by some miracle, Hadad survived." Solomon glanced over his shoulder at his wife and daughter. He lowered his voice. "He had been hiding in Egypt under protection of the pharaoh Siamun. He was but a child then. The pharaoh brought him up in the Egyptian way and made him a lieutenant in his army. He even gave him the queen's sister to wife. When Siamun died, he remained in the court of Psusennes, rising in the military ranks. All these years, this was unbeknownst to me."

"What became of him?" Zadok asked.

"He has resettled in Edom. It is said he is organizing his return to the throne." Benaiah placed a hand on the *khopesh* tied to his waist and turned to Solomon. "The army awaits your word, my lord. We will fall on him if that is what you command."

Solomon stroked his beard. "No. He is an ally of Egypt. We cannot risk angering the pharaoh." He shifted his gaze to his left, then back to his advisors. "I have another plan."

Benaiah bowed. Zadok stared at the king, certain of his intention. In the priest's mind, it was folly. "My lord, when all is revealed, people of the same fabric band together. Do not forget this."

The king waved a hand. "You may take your leave."

The two men backed away from the throne. Zadok knew Solomon's heart well enough to understand he had to be silent on the matter.

Nicaule stood between the beds of her two daughters, who slumbered peacefully in nests of white linen. What bliss to be so oblivious to the pain harbored in hearts, to the slow bleed of long-open wounds.

Taphath, her youngest, was still suckling; Basemath had turned four just two weeks before, but her birthday was lost in the tumult of preparations for the dedication of Solomon's temple. Such oversights had ceased to matter to Nicaule. After she lost her son, the boy she had planned to one day present to Shoshenq as his seed and heir, she felt as if someone had taken an iron bar to her knees, paralyzing her. It wasn't so much the loss of the child—such things happened—but rather the erasure of the possibility to claim any part of the Egyptian throne. If fate did not allow her to be queen of her homeland, she was determined to wrestle down destiny by giving birth to a future pharaoh.

Even that did not work in her favor.

Her thoughts traveled back to that wretched day. Her labor pains had come in the middle of the night—a sure omen of trouble—more violently than she had experienced with her firstborn. Unable to leave her bed, she called for her nurse. For reasons still unknown to her, the nurse was not nearby.

Because Nicaule lived in her own palace, outside the walled city, no one answered her cries of agony until daybreak, when the servants began work. By then she was shivering and spent and scarcely had the energy to push.

She would never forget the pain during the hours that followed. Drenched in sweat and feeling as if she'd been stabbed in the loins, she labored to deliver the child, whose shoulder was presented instead of his head. She recalled wailing through clenched teeth and gathering the bed linens in her fists as the nurse shouted, "Push hard, my lady. This child is the size of a wild boar."

When at last the head came out, she heard the nurse gasp. Too weak to realize she had not heard the baby cry, Nicaule only asked, "Is it a boy?"

The nurse ignored the question and called to one of the servants: "Get the physician. Hurry!"

Nicaule felt cold and pale. She knew she had lost a lot of blood. Her voice barely audible, she repeated, "Is it a boy?"

Again, no answer. The physician, the Levite Berechiah, threw the door open and did not bother to close it. She realized something was wrong and struggled to prop herself onto her elbows. The effort exhausted her. Berechiah bending over a sickeningly blue boy was the last thing she saw before passing out.

Had the nurse come sooner, the child might have been saved. Having her banished from the kingdom was the least Nicaule could do in the aftermath, but it wasn't going to bring her son back.

Three years later, the thought still haunted her. Though she had valiantly tried after the death to bear another son, she was rewarded with another daughter. She cursed her misfortune, whose cruelty was compounded by the fact that Shoshenq had long since ceased to communicate with her.

She'd read in a palace missive that a son had been born to him and his Meshwesh wife—another blow, and one from which she could not recover. Her dream had all but faded.

She left the children's room and walked the familiar paces to Solomon's chamber. She had counted the steps—six hundred sixty-six—to amuse herself during the twice-weekly march to pleasure her husband. He never went to her, as a matter of protocol. She felt a new pang of longing to be among her own people, where women were revered and walked hundreds of paces by choice, not by obligation. She shook it off. These days, she did not allow such thoughts to linger. She had willed an internal sea change, for it was the only way she could stomach her fate.

Two hundred twenty-one.

Like the leopards of the riverine forest, she watched from a high branch, waiting for the right moment to pounce. Women like her did not forget. It might take years before she could exact her revenge, but the day would no doubt come that the thief of her freedom would pay. And he would never see it coming.

Three hundred twelve.

The memory of her lover grew ever distant. It had been nearly six years since she'd left Egypt. Did Shoshenq think of her? Did he still long for the throne? Did he remember his promise to her on that autumn midnight when the harvest moon cast its shimmer over the Nile?

She had made a promise of her own. "The king of Israel will never know my heart," she'd told him. Though the notion of reuniting with her beloved seemed hopelessly remote, she held true to her promise and always would. She'd given her flesh and the illusion of amity but nothing more: it was all a facade for an empty treasury.

Five hundred.

She felt short of breath. She stopped and clutched her chest. She had to see Shoshenq. Surely the sight of her would stir him, as it had so many times in the past. His Meshwesh wife was an insignificant obstacle. No desert dweller could hold a candle to Nicaule Tashere's beauty or match her seductive powers. She was certain of that. All she had to do was present herself to him, and she could win him back.

She had to escape to Egypt. And she believed she knew how.

She quickened her step. *Five hundred ninety-five . . . Six hundred six.*

The heavy double doors of Solomon's chamber were within eyeshot. She ran the last few paces, arriving breathless at the king's threshold. She barely had knocked when he opened the door. He had been waiting for her.

He swept her into his arms and kissed her greedily. He had abstained from relations during the seven days of the feast, and his hunger had mounted. His beard needled her face as he devoured her mouth.

He pressed her against the wall. His perspiration

seeped into her night tunic. Judging by his rapid, desperate breaths and his unyielding eagerness, tonight's strike would be quick. But she had something else in mind.

She pushed him back gently. A bewildered look crossed his face, but with a sideways smile she made it clear the change of plans would be worth his while. She led him to the bed and untied his tunic until it was loose enough to easily slip off his shoulders.

She kissed his neck and whispered, "Lie down."

He lay naked upon the sheepskins, his chest rising and falling like the waves of a raging sea. His eyes were fixed upon her as she walked to the table on which he kept a pot of thick thyme honey. He took a spoonful every night before retiring; said it helped him sleep. She tipped the pot and let a drop fall on her fingertip. With her gaze locked on his, she slowly licked her finger until all the precious nectar was gone.

Honeypot in hand, she walked to him. She put the vessel down on the sheepskin and stepped out of her tunic, exposing a slim brown body, still taut despite three births and shimmering with a fine veil of perspiration.

"You may be king, but tonight I am in command. Do you trust me?"

He nodded, though there was apprehension in his eyes. He clearly had no idea what was coming. No Israelite nor Ammonite nor Shunammite knew the love secrets of the Egyptians.

She held the honeypot above his torso and tipped it, letting two drops fall onto his navel. She leaned down and swept them onto her tongue. He shuddered.

Satisfied with the reaction, she dripped the honey lower, then lower still. His eyes grew wide as she spread the golden liquid where she wanted it. She blinked slowly and smiled, then lowered her head, moving her hair away so he could watch.

As she took the first taste, his body jolted. She continued steadily until his soft moans melted into rapturous cries.

It was a power she had over a man—any man. She didn't use it frequently; only when she wanted to be sure things went her way.

Nicaule lay beside Solomon and waited until he regained his composure.

He stroked her hair. "My lily, my dove, you have taken my breath away with your exotic ways. You have made me soar to a place whose door was shuttered until you opened it."

"A man as powerful as you deserves to know every hue of love." She sounded like she meant it.

"Tomorrow I shall have the king's goldsmith fashion for you a pendant with new rubies from the traders from the East. They have brought me a very rare stone, as big as a lion's paw. It is the only one in the Levant—nay, in all of Mesopotamia. I want you to have it."

"But, my lord, I do not wish for more jewels." She looked away and sighed.

He propped himself on an elbow. "What is it that would please you, then? Name it; you shall have it."

She stroked his forearm. "It is my father . . . He has

been ill. I fear he may—" She willed a sullen look upon her face. "I want to go to him, my lord."

He started to speak but was interrupted by a rapid knock. He turned to the door.

She sat up and pressed her body against his. "Don't answer it."

He gave her a perplexed glance.

"You said I could have anything that pleased me." She kissed his shoulder. "I want only two things: permission to go see my ailing father"—her lips moved up his neck to his ear, and she whispered—"and your love at this moment."

The knock came again. A man's voice—she could not tell whose—called, "My lord. My lord!"

Solomon ignored it and searched for her lips. He had made his choice.

Nicaule pitied him for his weakness. But it was of no consequence to her. Even as she feigned passion, she plotted her return to her homeland—and to the only man she loved. She would leave at first light.

Zadok lay awake that night, consumed by the imminent danger. Hadad and his band of malcontents were on the move. According to Judahite informants in the desert, they had left Edom and were moving north through the Wilderness of Zin. It was not inconceivable that they would be in Jerusalem by dawn.

He had tried to warn Solomon, but his urgent pleas had gone unanswered. In all the years Zadok had served

Solomon, he had never encountered such brazen disregard. What could be more important than the security of the state?

He knew the answer, though he was loath to accept it. That the king put the love of a woman ahead of matters of defense—the safety of his own people—was unthinkable. Ire churned inside him. He closed his eyes and implored the Lord to grant him equanimity.

The hard knock on the door shattered the peace of his meditation. The breath of his son Ahimaaz rose and fell at the other end of the one-room hovel Zadok called home. Quietly he rose and went to the door.

He spoke through the slats. "State your purpose."

"It is I, Zadok. Let me inside."

The king? Coming in the middle of the night to the priest's house? He flinched at the improbability of it. He opened the door. Solomon stood on the other side of his threshold, dressed in a simple gray tunic and covered with a pauper's mantle. "My lord. This is highly unusual."

Solomon pushed his way inside. Zadok closed the door and felt for the oil lamp in the dark. It was almost empty but he lit it anyway, releasing a fragile light. He scrutinized his visitor. Despite his humble appearance, Solomon was alert, strong, confident—every bit a monarch.

He lowered his threadbare hood onto his shoulders, revealing a tousled mass of black curls. It was unlike him to be so ungroomed. It was as if he was trying to disguise himself. "Do you know why I have come here, Zadok?"

"Perhaps to explain why you ignored my calls earlier this night?" Zadok's rebuke was harsher than he intended. "I had come to warn you. Hadad the Edomite is planning a strike against you."

"And you do not think I know this?"

"How is it you know? We got word only while you were—" He held his tongue.

"You surprise me, Zadok. You should have more faith in your king."

Zadok leaned on his cane and released a long stream of breath. "Forgive me."

"When word came that Hadad had returned from Egypt, I installed a mole in the Edomite palace at Sela. He reports on Hadad's every move. I have known since yesterday Hadad's men are in the desert of Zin making their way to Jerusalem."

"If you know all this, why have you not taken action?"

"I have no intention of mobilizing an army, if that is what you are asking. My tactics are different." Solomon glanced at the sleeping Ahimaaz, then lowered his voice to a near whisper. "I know what Hadad plans. He means to go through the old Jebusite water shaft and ambush the city. Perhaps he thinks it ironic to enter Jerusalem in the same way my father did so long ago. The only difference is, he will not succeed as my father did."

Zadok nodded. The king was a step ahead of him. He should have known. "Then you have fortified the water shaft."

"Benaiah and his mighty men are camped inside the shaft, lying in wait for the Edomites. When Hadad and his men arrive in the city, likely under cover of night, nothing will stir. They will believe we have no defenses and they have the advantage. They will not expect a counterattack. But that is what will await them, for I have instructed Benaiah to fall upon the Edomites and leave no one alive."

"But, my lord, if Benaiah is in the shaft, who will guard *you*?"

"I have thought of this, too. I intend to leave Jerusalem."

Zadok started. "The city will be under attack and you will . . . flee?"

"You have not heard me, old friend. This will be a swift blow. Hadad will not be given the chance to storm Jerusalem. He will come to death at Kidron, well outside of the city."

"Even so, why leave?"

Solomon hesitated. "There is something I must tend to."

"Something more important than this?" He gestured toward the city.

"The pharaoh is gravely ill; a lung ailment, according to the missives. Berechiah has the gift of healing, the power to restore Psusennes to health. I will take him with me to Tanis."

Zadok ran a hand through his coarse, silver-threaded hair. "My lord, this is folly. You would have to travel through Zin. With Hadad mounting an offensive through the wilderness, the route to Egypt is not safe."

"I am not taking the wilderness road. My caravan will travel the Way of the Sea. The men are saddling the camels now. We will leave before dawn."

Zadok stared at the king. It was obvious his decision had been made and no man, not even the one he trusted most, could hold sway over him. A sudden premonition needled his gut. Perhaps this wasn't about Psusennes and his life-threatening lung ailment. "The queen . . . Is she going with you?"

"She is going but not with me. She leaves at first light. Eldad is driving the caravan to Tanis."

His suspicion was correct. Either Solomon could not bear to be away from Nicaule's side, or he did not trust her to go to Tanis alone. But why travel separately? "I don't understand. Why not have a woman arrive with her husband?"

"I needed to create a distraction. Nicaule's caravan will go through Zin and likely encounter Hadad. That will slow him down and allow me to leave the city undetected."

Zadok's eyes widened. "But you are sending your wife and your men to their deaths."

Solomon shook his head. "Hadad will not harm Nicaule. She is Egyptian. He has pledged loyalty to the pharaohs he served—one of whom is her father. He would violate that vow on pain of death."

"You are using her as a decoy."

He didn't answer. He didn't have to.

"Even if you are not worried about what he might do to her, you should worry about what she might say to him. Search your heart: do you have enough faith in her to believe she would not betray you?"

"The hour grows late." Solomon raised the mantle over his head. "I must go. The men wait for me."

Zadok took hold of the king's wrist as he was moving toward the door. Solomon looked at him, puzzled. "Tell me this, Solomon." He dispensed with the honorifics. He wanted to ask this question man to man. "Does she know you are going to Tanis?"

He pulled away from his grip but did not break eye contact. "No. She does not."

Zadok understood. Solomon's trip to Tanis was not a healing mission at all. It was his way of ensuring Nicaule did not stray—or catching her if she did. Such was his obsession with her. He wanted to spew a litany of warnings but decided against it; Solomon would deny it anyway.

As if reading Zadok's thoughts, Solomon said, "It is for her safety that I do this. She cannot be forced to concede what she does not know."

"We can convince ourselves of anything. But the Lord knows what is in our hearts."

"My heart is pure before God, as is my love for her. Do not doubt this." He nodded toward the bed. "Wake Ahimaaz and tell him to meet me at the gates. He will ride with us to Egypt."

Solomon placed a gentle hand on Zadok's shoulder, as if to reassure him, and took his leave.

At the sound of the door slamming shut, Ahimaaz bolted upright, sweeping a *khopesh* from under his pillow. Zadok's youngest son had mastered the art of the blade. Solomon knew this and wanted him by his side.

"That was the king," Zadok said. "He has called for you to accompany him on a journey."

Wasting no words, Ahimaaz rose swiftly and gathered himself for his appointed task.

Zadok glanced beyond the window, watching Solomon as he walked toward the gates. His hooded figure grew smaller and smaller until it was consumed by the darkness.

CHAPTER FOURTEEN

On the fourth night of the journey out of Jerusalem, the caravan carrying Nicaule Tashere to Tanis reached the Wilderness of Zin. The camel jostled its passenger as it tried to gain footing on the rocky ground.

Nicaule removed the long head veil that shielded her identity and gazed at the passing landscape. The caravan had entered a passage between two flat-topped mounds, and the camels were treading on a dried-up riverbed. Every ripple frozen into the crags over centuries of battering winds was magnified by the pewter glow of the waxing moon.

The stones had stories to tell. It was through these lands that the Hebrews passed hundreds of years ago, searching for a new place to scratch out an existence after the exodus from Egypt. They wandered through here for forty years, it was said, walking in circles, unable to find their way. *It served them right*, she thought. How ungrateful they were for the eleemosynary asylum they had been granted by the Egyptians. When they were made to work, they cried slavery when in fact they were earning their keep. That was how it was with inferior peoples: they always wanted something for nothing.

She sat back on the cedar saddle seat, made specially for her use by the carpenters of Solomon's kingdom, and listened to the chorus of crackles as the dry limestone crumbled beneath the weight of laden camels. It was a day's crossing, perhaps two if the beasts couldn't find brush for sustenance, into the Wilderness of Shur: the Egyptian border.

Her heartbeat quickened. She gazed at the indigo sky embroidered with stardust and considered the flawlessness of her plan. She would pose as the concerned daughter, there to nurse her father to health. She would tend to him day and night and wait until his army captain called for audience. When a pharaoh was ill, it was customary for his top officers to assemble by his bedside rather than the throne room. Sooner or later, Shoshenq would come—and she would surprise him.

She imagined the look on his face when he'd encounter her after all those years. Though she'd had scores of perfumes made for her since becoming Solomon's queen, she would wear her old, familiar scent, the one that made Shoshenq delirious with delight. She would wear his favorite dress, a one-shoulder, figure-hugging sheath of white linen woven with golden thread that shimmered like the stars. She had not worn it since she left Egypt but kept it hidden in a trunk, waiting for that moment.

She smiled. This was a seduction she would savor.

One of Solomon's officers, Eldad, rode next to her. "My lady, it is my duty to inform you there are two routes up ahead. One will quicken the crossing into Egypt but may be more treacherous. It is said there are bandits in that part of the desert."

"And the other route?"

"It is longer by a moon."

"Are your men armed?"

"They are, my lady. But we do not number many. It is risky."

Nicaule scanned the retinue. They numbered a score, all able-bodied and alert men with *khopeshes* and double-edged bronze swords tied around their waists. None wore armor; in an attack, that would be a disadvantage.

"My lady," Eldad prodded. "What will you have us do?"

She thought for a moment. She longed to reach Tanis as quickly as possible. But she also knew attacks by desert bandits could be deadly. To have come this far only to be robbed, hurt, or worse by outlaws was a risk she was not willing to take.

The short route Eldad proposed was known as the badlands. Nicaule knew it well. Because of its hostile terrain, it had been used historically by Egyptian soldiers as a hideout when mounting an offensive into Canaan land. Boulders were strewn throughout, making it difficult to know where danger lurked.

If bandits hid among the boulders, an attack was likely—and that would no doubt cripple the caravan. But such a confrontation had not happened in years. The strong relations between Solomon's Jerusalem and her father's Tanis had kept lawlessness at bay.

She clutched the lapis lazuli amulet that hung between her breasts. It was carved in the shape of a heart for her great-grandmother, a member of the Theban elite, and passed down to the women of subsequent generations for magical protection. It was said to symbolize the source of earthly life and to grant the power to choose between good and evil. Nicaule always wore it during long journeys or when she needed the grace of the gods.

The image of Shoshenq's face floated into her mind's eye. If all went well, taking the alternative route would give her one more day with her beloved. She looked to the sky for the *Ba* of her ancestors, whose souls were thought to take the shape of stars. She had hoped for a message, but the clouds, hanging motionlessly over the high heavens, obscured the full celestial panorama that so often held the answers.

Heat radiated from the smooth surface of the talisman into her palm. She took it as an omen. She turned to Eldad. "We will go through the badlands."

The officer's face tightened, but he said nothing. He rode to the assembly of men and uttered a string of clipped instructions before taking the lead. The caravan fell into place and followed the prescribed route.

Nicaule leaned back on her saddle seat and exhaled slowly. She felt a pang of doubt but willed it away. She was convinced she had made the right choice.

The distant howl of a jackal startled her out of deep slumber. Nicaule sat upright, unsure for a moment where she was. She rubbed her eyes, coaxing the world into focus. As the fog that had enveloped her mind lifted, she heard the howl again.

The fine hairs on the back of her neck stood on end. That was not the cry of a jackal.

Eyes wide, she looked about her. Something was happening up ahead, but it was concealed behind a cloud of silver-hued dust.

"Eldad," she called out. When she received no answer, she took up the crop tied to the saddle and whipped her camel's hind quarters. The burdened beast groaned and picked up the pace with Nicaule guiding it toward the dust cloud.

As she rode closer to the skirmish, she heard the urgent cries of men and the clashing of swords. Warm blood rushed to the pit of her stomach. What Eldad had warned of had come to pass.

A frightened camel without a rider raced out of the cloud, hurtling toward her. Before Nicaule had a chance to maneuver her camel out of the way, the two beasts collided and crashed to the ground. The impact forced the wind out of her lungs.

Her field of vision was filled with the tawny hide of the animal whose neck was sprawled across her chest. She struggled to regain her breath. She felt hands reach under her armpits and drag her out of the trap. She rolled to her side, clutching her aching ribs and heaving.

A man walked within view. She saw his legs first, great hairy stumps culminating in sandal-bound feet so dusty and hard-skinned it appeared he had been walking the desert for eons. She lifted her gaze and saw him: a stout, dark-faced stranger whose wiry black beard could not hide the scowl that had overtaken his countenance.

Squinting, he studied her. "I know your face."

She wiped the dust from her mouth with the back of her hand. "I cannot say the same."

He offered a hand. She did not take it, using every vestige of strength to stand on her own. "Who are you?"

"The name is Hadad." He nodded toward the east. "I come from Edom." He folded his arms across his chest. "And you are from the Egyptian court. I have seen you. You were younger then."

Nicaule suddenly remembered his face. Could it be? She looked about her. The Israelites had either fallen or were cowering beneath the Edomites' swords. It appeared Hadad's men were well trained in military tactics, which was consistent with her recollection. She turned to their leader. "When were you in Egypt, Hadad of Edom?"

"I grew up an Egyptian. I was taken in by the pharaoh Siamun and raised in his court. I learned the ways of the sword and, upon Siamun's death, fought for his successor."

Nicaule's memory had not failed her. The man she remembered was a brooding foreigner with a taste for blood and a master's command of spear and sword.

"Siamun's successor," she said, "is my father."

The whites of Hadad's eyes flashed, and his nostrils flared. He looked like an animal in attack mode. He took a step toward her. "You are the one. The one who married David's son." At the utterance of *David's son*, spittle escaped from his mouth and dribbled down his beard.

The glint in his eyes terrified her. He obviously had a grudge for the Israelites—and perhaps those who associated with them. "I married Solomon at the behest of my father. It was a marriage of political convenience."

His face relaxed slightly. She took it as permission to continue. "My heart belongs in Egypt. I journey there this night. I pray you will let me go."

Hadad waved to one of his men. The Edomite approached, leading an Israelite prisoner by the hair. The battered Israelite stumbled and fell to his knees, but the Edomite pulled him upright and held a *khopesh* to his throat.

Hadad spat at the prisoner's feet. "Judahite scum." He turned to Nicaule. "Let's see where your allegiance really lies."

At his leader's nod, the Edomite pulled his knife arm back and, with a primal scream, swung at the Israelite's throat.

Warm blood sprayed on Nicaule's face and stained her dress. She blinked rapidly, her eyes adjusting to the shock of seeing a man executed. Before that moment, brutality was, to her, a foreign concept. She had heard the stories but could never fully grasp how cruel men could be. She stared at the Israelite's severed head, eyes still open and blinking, his blood watering the arid soil of the wilderness. She bent at the waist and retched.

"Kill the others," she heard Hadad say. "You. Princess. Look at me."

She slowly looked up. He was leaning over her, his coarse black curls hanging around his plump face. As much as she loathed him, she knew she'd have to play his game to stay alive. "Why did you do it?"

"Revenge." He looked away, his mouth twisting into a scowl. "Long ago, David's men came to my father's village in the middle of the night. I still remember the stench of the smoke from their fires and their foul cries: 'Kill the king!' A Judahite who called himself Joab dragged my father and mother out of their palace and smashed their heads on the stones over and over. He beat them to death before my eyes." He turned to Nicaule, wild-eyed. "I was a boy!"

She placed a hand on her mouth and looked down. She thought it best to stay quiet.

"Joab found me cowering behind the storage jars. I will never forget his words: 'In the name of David, king of Judah, the seed of the Edomite king must perish.' He pierced my side with his spear and left me for dead."

A man on a blood mission was capable of anything. Nicaule knew he would kill her too, if she did not sympathize with him. "To slaughter a child is unthinkable. It is, perhaps, the gods' justice that you lived."

"The next morning at dawn, a passing caravan found me. I was the only one to survive the carnage. They nursed me to health and sold me as a slave to the Egyptians. The pharaoh took pity on me and raised me as his own. He showed me love, and I was loyal to him. But I always knew I would return to my homeland." He spat on the ground. "I swore on my father's memory I would smite David's breed. Now his son will pay in blood for the massacre of my people."

"I understand your plight. But Solomon is a formidable foe. Your band of outlaws does not stand a chance."

"Our only hope is an ambush." Hadad smirked. "I reckon you can help us. If yours is truly a marriage of convenience and your loyalty lies with Egypt, you should have no trouble betraying the Israelites."

Nicaule swallowed hard. It seemed she would have to bargain for her freedom. "What is it you want of me?"

"There is a water shaft leading from the spring to the city. David used it to defeat the Jebusites and claim Jerusalem. We will enter the city using the same tunnel and attack Solomon as he sleeps." He licked his lips. "I need to know where the entrance is. You tell me that, and you will be free to go. My men will escort you to the edge of Tanis."

She shifted her gaze to the line of *khopesh*-wielding Edomites waiting for their leader's command. The Israelites' bodies littered the wilderness. She regarded her husband's would-be assassin. "What if I do not know?"

He glared at her. "I think you do."

She did know. But to betray Solomon to his death, to open the door wide to his enemy . . . No matter how she despised him, such an act would haunt her forever.

Hadad continued. "If you choose to keep silent, we

will abandon you here. It's a long way to Egypt when you do not know the way."

Her eyes bulged. "But . . . I would be as good as dead. Why not kill me instead?"

"No Egyptian blood will be shed by my hand. When in service to Siamun, I took a vow. I cannot forsake that."

Her decision amounted to this: her life or Solomon's. Nicaule gripped her heart amulet. It felt cold and lifeless. She began to weep.

Hadad turned to his men. "On your mounts. We ride now to Jerusalem." He addressed Nicaule. "We will find the entrance to the shaft another way. Give my regards to your father . . . if you make it to Tanis alive."

She watched him walk toward his camel, his husky silhouette lined in silver beneath the moonlight. The rest of the men had lined up, ready to ride.

It's a long way to Egypt when you do not know the way. A frigid sensation rippled down her spine. "Wait."

Hadad turned to face her.

"There is a cave above the Kidron Valley, east of David's city. That is all I know."

He nodded, letting a moment pass. He called to his men. "Sair. Beor. Lead this woman to the Tanis border."

Nicaule exhaled. She told herself what she did was preservation of self. To purposefully go to one's death was the most heinous of sins, worse still than betraying another. Yes. It was what she had to do. It was what the gods wanted.

She watched absently as Sair and Beor took her

saddlebag off the fallen camel and tacked it onto another, ensuring nothing was lost in the skirmish.

Yet so much was.

Hadad whipped his camel and shouted a string of profanities, goading the animal to a gallop. A thick cloud of dust rose beneath the beasts' hooves as the band of Edomites rode in the direction of Jerusalem.

When the caravan crossed into Lower Egypt and the Nile Delta, Nicaule felt a knot rise to her throat. She did not realize until that moment how much she had missed her homeland.

Everything assaulted her senses, overwhelmed her: the clear, bright sunlight dancing upon the water, the fecundity of the orchards lining the riverbanks, the dulcet lament of the sacred hoopoe, the sweet scent of ripe dates.

She gazed at the slaves working by the river, their black, sweating skin glistening in the sun as they gathered mud to make bricks. When one moved a little too slowly, the Egyptian overseer hit him with a crop and shouted profanities. It was not a pleasant thing to watch, but neither was it unnecessary, for the lazy would always slacken their pace if left to their own devices.

The Egyptians were a productive lot and did not tolerate anything less from the inferior peoples. Justly so. What other nation had crafted pyramid tombs that soared to the sky? Or discovered the secrets of embalming the dead to preserve their bodies unto all eternity? Or was so accomplished in art and literacy and music? Her people had earned the right to command respect. Her chest swelled with pride.

The pharaoh's palace came into view behind the rows of date palms. It was as if she had left a fortnight before; nothing had changed. Rising out of the river with great columns and chapiters, gates and pylons, and a courtyard profuse with orchards and reflecting pools, the compound radiated a pink hue in the midday sun. The flags whipped in a rogue breeze, welcoming her home. Thoughts of her carefree childhood inside those walls rushed to the forefront of her mind, and she came undone.

By the time they had reached the edge of the Nile, she had willed away all trace of sentiment. She did not want anyone from the court to see her tears, for in her country that was considered a sign of weakness.

She was met at the riverbanks by two handmaidens from the court, attendants to her father's new wife. They would be appointed to her service for the next few days.

That was all she had—a few days—to win back Shoshenq and alter the route of destiny.

For some days, the pharaoh had been confined to the bed in his chamber. As a servant announced her, Nicaule stood at the doorway and watched her father's reaction.

Psusennes turned his head slowly toward her and held out a hand. His voice was feeble as he said, "Come forth, my daughter."

She approached and kneeled by his bed, as was the custom. She kissed his hand, surprised at how light it felt, like a boneless mass of desiccated, creased skin. "I bow before the Lord of the Two Lands," she said, using the pharaoh's formal title referring to Upper and Lower Egypt. "May the presence of this humble daughter please the king." She rose and sat at the ivory-inlaid wood folding stool the servants had arranged for her.

Psusennes had aged a disproportionate number of years. His eyes had sunken within dark eye sockets, and the skin on his cheeks had sagged and grown pale. The hard lines of his bones were visible beneath the white linen sheets that covered his body. Lying on the ebony bed with lion's claw feet and gilded likenesses of the gods carved into the headboard, he looked like a corpse in wait for an undertaker.

"My illness has robbed me of my strength," he said. "Forgive me."

"It pains me to see you like this, Father. What illness has taken such hold of you that the physicians cannot cure you?"

He swatted the air weakly. "They do not know anything. They say my lungs are withering to consumption, and there is no medicine for it. I say they are charlatans and we should call for the Greeks." He coughed, and it was apparent his lungs were full of liquid. As he struggled to take a breath, the cough escalated into a whoop.

The nurses rushed to the pharaoh's bedside with compresses soaked in herbs, which they placed over his air passages. After a while, he calmed down but was visibly weakened by the fit.

"Tell me, Daughter," he croaked. "Have you come to bury me?"

She smiled. Even in his compromised state, he was blunt as ever. "I am here to nurse you to health. Nothing more."

He changed the subject. "I hear you and the Israelite king have children . . . a son."

She swallowed hard. "Yes. A son was born unto me . . . and two daughters also." She decided against telling him the whole truth.

"Splendid. Then it has been a happy union."

"I hope it has produced fruit for Egypt likewise. That was the intention, was it not?"

He stared at her with obsidian eyes that looked too big for his gaunt face. "We have prospered from the alliance. But Israel has prospered far more. I fear someday it will overshadow Egypt." He coughed again but got it under control that time. "Alas, I have grown too weak and Solomon too strong. Perhaps the next pharaoh will put the Hebrews in their place."

She sat up straighter. "And have you named a successor?"

"It is not a matter I can discuss with anyone but my closest advisors. He who will be named pharaoh upon my death has been informed. That is all I will say."

"What can I do to make you feel better, Father?"

He thought for a moment. "Rub my feet."

She nodded and went to the other end of the bed, which was elevated slightly higher than the head. A female attendant moved the stool and helped her sit, then brought a pan of warm water scented with aloe vera.

Nicaule lifted the white linen and exposed Psusennes' wrinkled soles. She was repulsed but dutifully did what he asked. She soaked a cloth in the water and washed his feet twice, then dried them with fresh linen and went to work. First she squeezed the feet, reviving circulation. She pressed on points she knew would relieve tension and watched her father's pained expression fade. With long, gentle strokes she relaxed him further until he finally fell asleep.

She covered his feet and stood. She watched his chest rise and fall with strained effort and heard the froth gurgling in his lungs. His death was close at hand.

For three days Nicaule went to her father's bedside and did little else. She suffered through the ennui, waiting for word of Shoshenq's arrival from the Upper Nile Valley, where he and a small regiment had gone to recruit new soldiers among the villages. When she asked about the company's arrival, she was told, "Tomorrow." But tomorrow had come and gone without sign of him.

When the rooster crowed before dawn on the fourth day, Nicaule woke with a sense of clarity. She knew what she had to do.

She sprang from bed and dressed in a hurry. She wanted to be out of the palace before the morning's commotion began.

It had been a long time since she'd seen Anippe. She had sought the seer's advice years ago, when she'd first met Shoshenq. Anippe had confirmed what Nicaule had known in her heart: she and the army captain were destined to be together. Anippe had foreseen a marriage to a king and two children, one of whom would bear a queen. At the time, Nicaule believed it to be a prophecy: before their union, Shoshenq would hold the crook and flail of the pharaoh. She never imagined a different marriage or a different king.

She slipped on a glossy black wig and a simple ribbon headband that would not betray her social standing. She swung a mantle around her shoulders and slipped out the door.

Nothing stirred in the city save for a few old women doling out feed to their animals. A chill in the early morning air carried the promise of *peret*—the emergence. Soon the waters of the Nile would retreat, leaving behind the fertile soil her people would plant for their yearly crops. It was her favorite time of year: a quiet time of sowing and nurturing, of waiting for the harvest.

Anippe's home was at the far end of town among the hovels of the poor. The seer lived alone; she'd never taken a husband, nor did she wish to. Men were too much trouble, she had always said; they clouded the clarity of her oracular powers. The truth was, men stayed away from her. They thought her dangerous, said madness dwelled in her.

The campaign to defame her began years before, when Anippe—without being consulted—publicly predicted the fall of a Theban regiment that had launched an offensive into Meroë. It happened as she said it would, but instead of celebrating the oracle, the stricken military men viewed it as a curse.

For her part, Nicaule dismissed the accusations. It was in the interest of Egypt's most powerful men to contain seeing powers within the priesthood, where they could be manipulated. A gifted woman who spoke her mind had no place in that world.

Nicaule stood outside the one-room mud-brick house, hesitating. A part of her was afraid of receiving bad news. She sighed and rapped lightly on the door.

The lady of the house opened right away. She had aged considerably in the years since their last encounter. Her hair, which she did not bother to cover with a wig, was cut short, disheveled, and streaked with ribbons of gray. Her clothing was that of a pauper, draped so loosely it hid her figure and made her gender ambiguous. She greeted her guest with a subtle smile of recognition.

"Hello, old friend," Nicaule said. The two women grasped each other's arms and touched foreheads.

Anippe closed the door. "Much has happened since we last met. Life has not taken the direction you expected."

Nicaule was surprised at how quickly the familiar choke hold of emotion overtook her. Tears welled in her eyes. She could not utter a word.

Anippe put a hand on Nicaule's head. "You are safe here. Be as a babe in its mother's arms."

With that permission, Nicaule lowered her head into her hands and felt her body quake with sobs.

"Someone so young should not be so troubled," Anippe said. "Such is the cruelty of men."

Nicaule looked up and dabbed her eyes with a linen handkerchief. "I beg you, old friend. Tell me what will become of me. For if my fate continues along this path, I surely will die of grief."

Anippe brought down an alabaster jar from a shelf and sat on a floor cushion, gesturing to her guest to sit opposite her. "I will call upon the creatures of the Earth to divine the future. What do you wish to know?"

Nicaule sighed. "Does the man who owns my heart still love me?"

The seer lifted the lid of the jar and released thirteen black scarabs onto the floor. She waved a hand over them and chanted something in a tongue Nicaule did not understand. Bewildered by the light, the beetles scurried in circles, and then they fell into a curious formation, as if enchanted by Anippe's voice. They held their places for a moment, then scattered.

Anippe turned to Nicaule. "It appears he still values you. There is something you have that no other can offer him."

Nicaule let out a quiet gasp. In the depths of her heart, she knew it. "When will we be together?"

Anippe rubbed her hands for some time, then offered them to her guest. Nicaule was surprised at the heat they radiated; not warmth but a searing sensation that sent needles through her nerves to her spine. Though it was uncomfortable, Nicaule did not let go. Both women closed their eyes and bowed their heads.

There was a long silence. A spasm shook the left side of Anippe's body. At last, she spoke. "He will come for you when the mountain burns and all dignity has passed from the Earth."

Nicaule opened her eyes. "What does that mean?"

Anippe's gaze was blank, unfocused. She appeared to dwell in another realm. "Those answers are not given to me. They are only made clear in time."

"And what of Solomon, my husband?"

"It is up to a woman to tame a man and bend him to her will."

"He is strong and obstinate. He does not bend easily."

Anippe stood and walked to another shelf. She chose another jar and a juglet and placed both on a rough-hewn wood bench. She removed some of the jar's contents and placed them on a linen square, then turned to Nicaule. "This will help you subdue his spirit."

Nicaule walked to her. "What is it?"

"Dried petals of the blue lotus from the Upper Nile. You take three petals—only three—and soak them in his wine for exactly the time it takes to fill this juglet. Not more, not less. When he drinks of this wine, he will enter a state of such euphoria that he will not deny you a thing. But you must follow the directions exactly."

Nicaule accepted the bundle. "I am in your debt."

"Speak nothing of this, or I will be sent into exile . . . or worse. This must be our secret."

She grasped the seer's hands. "You have my word."

Anippe's gaze darkened. "My lady, this you must know: there is a price to making your own destiny."

"What punishment can there be for one who loves

so deeply? Surely the gods can forgive such transgressions when no less than the human heart is at stake."

Anippe fell silent for a moment. She seemed to hold something back. "When you pray, offer tribute to Bastet—the cat goddess, she of dual nature. She will understand and protect you."

Nicaule glanced out the window. The sun had come out in earnest, painting a golden morning. "I have to go." She reached into her mantle and removed a purse full of coins. She placed it in the seer's hands. "Thank you for your precious gift. I will not forget your kindness."

Anippe bowed slightly and unlatched the door. "May the gods watch over you."

Nicaule lifted her mantle over her head and exited into the light.

Psusennes' bedchamber was a hive of activity. Nurses came and went, carrying vessels with compresses, jugs of sweet wine said to warm the body, herb potions for cough, and all manner of food that went mostly untouched. Three physicians tended to the pharaoh, each making his own proclamation about the state of the ailing man's health.

Psusennes looked toward the door and spotted his daughter. "Ah, Nicaule. Come, dear girl."

Nicaule hurried to her father's bedside and kneeled beside him, kissing his hand. She glanced at his face, expecting to see the vacant look of imminent death. Psusennes' eyes were as intense as ever, perhaps even sparkled a little. "You called for me, Father."

"Yesterday, all the physicians declared I would be dying within a fortnight. There is nothing to do."

Nicaule lowered her head.

"I have called in all the viziers, priests, and generals. They all ride to Tanis now to gather before the dying king." He let out a shaky sigh. "But I will have a surprise for them."

She looked up.

"I, Psusennes II, son of Pinedjem II and High Priest of Amun, do not plan to give up my throne without a fight."

"Father, what are you saying?"

"I have no plans of dying, dear girl."

"But fate isn't yours to change. It is up to the gods."

"Bah!" The exclamation brought on a hoarse cough. He caught his breath and with fragile voice added, "It is up to medicine."

"But. . . I thought the physicians had tried everything."

"These physicians have. So I have decided to bring in others from outside the walls of this kingdom."

She wrinkled her brow. "But who? Who knows more than the Egyptians?"

He patted her hand. "You will know soon enough."

The door opened wide and a servant announced, "Her Highness the Queen and the royal daughters." Nicaule stood and waited by the foot of the bed, within eyeshot of the king.

A striking woman with glossy, waist-length raven hair entered accompanied by young children. Psusennes' first wife had died years ago, as had Nicaule's mother, and the king had replaced them with younger consorts.

One of the children, scarcely older than her own Basemath, had a haughty demeanor and eyes too intense for her years. The girl ran to Psusennes' bedside.

"Ah, Maatkare," he said. "My favorite daughter."

Maatkare kissed her father's hand, glanced at Nicaule, and backed away.

The procession continued with Nicaule's half-sisters and their husbands, some of whom were ranking court officials, and two half-brothers who were princes in name only. Then came the priests, most of whom she did not recognize, and the viziers, the two men appointed by the king to govern Upper and Lower Egypt.

It seemed an eternity before Shoshenq entered. For a moment, her breath was trapped inside her lungs, rendering her unable to exhale. Her bottom lip trembled ever so slightly.

Shoshenq I, son of the great chief of the Ma and commander of the Egyptian army, entered with head held high, a man certain of his fate. He was as beautiful as ever: broad shoulders framing a tapered torso, hard and sculpted as the chiseled rocks at Memphis, as smooth and dark as polished amber. His almond-shaped, kohl-ringed eyes were almost too big for his head, which was bare and marked by a new scar. He had seen some action.

Nicaule caught his glance and held it. His face betrayed surprise and, she thought, delight. He didn't take his ebony eyes off her, ripping social convention to shreds. In her peripheral vision she saw some heads turn toward her. It made her uncomfortable enough to shift her gaze.

Shoshenq bowed on one knee before the king.

"Rise, Commander," Psusennes said. "What news from the borderlands?"

Shoshenq stood. "My men have successfully stopped a raid by the Kushites in Karnak. They had come to claim the treasures in the temples of Amun-Re." He rubbed the scar above his ear. "Some blood was shed, but the precinct is safe. All the invaders, down to the last, have been slain."

"Fine work." Psusennes turned to the gathered. "You may think I brought you here to announce my successor. I have not." He folded down his bedcovers and swung his legs around until his feet touched the floor. A servant girl rushed to his side and helped him step into leather sandals.

The pharaoh stood on shaky legs and put a hand on Shoshenq's shoulder, a telling gesture. "When the time comes, I will name a successor. But that time is not now. I have been given new life, brought back from the gates of Anubis by Osiris himself.

"The gods have sent an unexpected messenger to deliver this precious gift for which I will forever be grateful." He turned to the door. "Enter the physician and his master."

A slight man hunched at the shoulders entered with head down. He was dressed in a long striped tunic, waist cinched with a leather sash and shoulders covered with an indigo *kethoneth*. Abundant black curls spilled beneath a white turban.

Nicaule shifted to steady herself. The sight of the physician who had tended to her during her stillbirth scrambled her thoughts and robbed her of breath. How had this happened? How had Berechiah, the Hebrew priest-healer, come here?

No sooner had the questions crossed her mind than they were answered. Solomon stepped into the doorway, scanning the faces in the room before entering. With arms outstretched, Psusennes shuffled over to his Israelite counterpart and ally. Solomon mirrored his movements until they met halfway, locking arms.

Psusennes turned to the members of his court. "It is to this man I owe my restoration to health. King Solomon, my Hebrew brother and husband of my daughter, has brought his healer to my doorstep." He turned to Solomon. "My days had all but ended, and you gave me new life. For so long as I draw breath, you have my favor."

Solomon tilted his head. "I was only repaying the favors Egypt has bestowed upon Israel. I am the one grateful, my lord Psusennes, for you have granted my kingdom many resources and have held back my enemies. And lo, you have given me"—he gestured toward Nicaule—"the immeasureable gift of your daughter's hand."

Nicaule narrowed her eyes. Of course. It was in Solomon's best interest to keep Psusennes, one of the mildest and most permissive pharaohs of the New Kingdom, in life. Psusennes was no threat to Israel, as his successor might have been. He wasn't doing his moral duty but rather securing the interests of his state.

And he was buying Psusennes' loyalty. *Held back my enemies*. That was no doubt a reference to Hadad. Surely Solomon's miracle came with a price.

But that was inconsequential. What mattered now was her plan: with Solomon present, it would be near impossible to execute. Once again, he had clipped her wings before she could take flight. She cursed him silently.

She searched for Shoshenq's eyes, but they were riveted on the pharaoh. Each man was playing his own game. It was time for her to mobilize her plan, whatever the consequences.

In the thick of night, Nicaule rose from her bed and went to the window. She could not sleep. Her mind was racing like a chariot, consumed with thoughts of him.

Seeing Shoshenq's face after all those years rekindled a fire that had been reduced to embers. She wanted him more than ever. She gazed at the garden outside her window and the softly breathing black mass of the Nile beyond. She recalled clandestine walks with Shoshenq in that very garden. With the stars and moon bearing witness, they would profess their love to each other and pledge devotion for all eternity.

They were mere children then, and so much had happened since. She had become a queen, albeit of a foreign land, and—she was certain—he was soon to be named king.

She saw something move between the grasses lining the riverbanks. She blinked to focus in the dark. Again, movement. Who else was restless this night?

His figure emerged in the shadow of the date palms. Her heart hammered within her chest, and her mouth went dry. He gazed toward the palace, searching, she hoped, for her window.

She clutched her chest and glanced around the room, looking for her mantle. She saw it draped on a bench, reached for it, and threw it haphazardly over her shoulders. She did not give herself time to ponder what she was about to do or whether anyone was watching. She quietly exited her chamber and walked barefoot down the long corridor leading to the garden.

Looking over her shoulder at the darkened palace, with nary an oil lamp burning, she assured herself everyone was asleep. She launched into the orchard, skulking between the trees. With quick gait she followed the path down to the river, her mantle billowing behind her and rustling the brush.

She was nearly out of breath when she reached the riverbank. She stood still for a moment, watching and listening. The night was as quiet and dark as a tomb. She pushed through the shoulder-high grasses, walking toward the thick stand of date palms where she last saw him.

Her woolen mantle got caught on the teeth of the grass blades, hindering her progress. Despite the hard chill in the air, she removed the outer layer and let it lie on the brush. She felt cold, exposed. Her bedclothes consisted of a thin cotton nightgown that sat just below her bare breasts and was held up by V-straps.

The grass hissed as she continued forcing her way through the thicket. She could see the tops of the date palms outlined in a halo of moonlight. Her pulse quickened. Just a few more steps.

She heard a crunching sound coming from the ground and stopped in her tracks. A snake? She could not see well enough to gauge the danger. She held perfectly still, her eyes wide and ears alert.

She heard it again, then felt a hand grasp her arm. Before she could scream, another hand covered her mouth.

He stepped out of the shadows. The strong angles of his face were illuminated by pale light. He relaxed his grip. "I knew you would come."

"The years I have waited for this moment have felt like an eternity." She fought back the onslaught of emotion.

Shoshenq wrapped his arms around her and kissed her, exploring her mouth with his tongue like a desert animal searching for water.

Breathless, she devoured him. Her hands traveled down the hard contours of his torso, searching for the tie of the girdle that held up his pleated *shendyt*.

He stepped back, and for a moment she thought he resisted her advance. Then he bent down and kissed her bare breasts, suckling her nipples. She whimpered as thunderbolts shook her body.

Suddenly he stopped and stood up straight. He looked as if he was listening for something.

"What—?"

He put up a hand.

A vague rustling sound came from the distance. It could have been the breeze mussing the grasses.

"Someone's there," he whispered.

"No . . ."

He grasped her arms. "Hear me, Nicaule. We haven't any time. There is something I need you to do."

"Tell me what it is."

"Your father has appointed me to succeed him. Sooner or later, I will be king. But my plans for Egypt are different than Psusennes'. Your father does not see the threats all around us . . . beginning with Solomon's Israel."

She studied his face. There was nothing tentative in his gaze.

He continued. "I want you to ascertain Solomon's movements . . . who he's allied with, what he's building, where he is stashing the treasure he stole from Egypt."

"Stole?"

"He has no right to the gold from Ophir. That belongs to our people. Your father gave it away without regard for the pacts of our ancestors. If we are to expand the empire, as is my plan and duty, we need every last *shematy* of it."

She took a step toward him. "For you, I will travel to Tuat and back."

"Not for me; for Egypt."

The rustling sound was heard again, this time closer.

"Record his movements and report to me." His whisper was barely audible. "When the time comes, my armies will strike. And I will come for you."

There was a crunching sound, like footfall.

Something— or someone—was indeed there. Nicaule instinctively turned her head but saw nothing. By the time she turned back to Shoshenq, he was gone.

As she realized she was alone with a potential intruder, a chill rippled down her spine. She felt abandoned by Shoshenq but in an instant realized he probably was crouching nearby like a hidden tiger, scanning for danger. She trusted him enough to believe he would protect her.

She heard the swishing of grass again, then a low, throaty growl. An animal. Her heart galloped, and she stepped back gingerly, gaze darting to and fro.

The pharaoh's leopard revealed itself, snarling and baring its canines. It was the first time Nicaule had seen the cat away from a human companion. Aware a leopard was first and foremost a wild animal, disloyal and capable of anything, she lowered her head in submission and stood still, buying time until Shoshenq came to her rescue.

The leopard growled, a cry to wake the dead.

Her blood turned cold as mountain water, and her teeth chattered. Where was he? What was he waiting for?

She stepped back slowly. The cat walked toward her, mirroring her movements. "The pharaoh's blood runs in me. Be away!" As she addressed her stalker, her mouth was dry, her voice strangled.

The leopard gazed at her coldly and crouched as if ready to pounce.

"No . . ." Nicaule shook her head. Perspiration trickled down her temples as she realized Shoshenq was not coming. She wanted to scream, to run, but knew it would trigger the beast's attack. Unsure of what else to do, she kept inching away. Jade eyes glinting in the dark, the leopard followed.

In the instant she felt despair grip her, a hand touched her shoulder. "Great beast, your place is in the green grasses by the river. We are intruders in your home. Be still and let us pass, and we shall go in peace."

The male voice was distorted in her adrenaline-riddled consciousness. She glanced at her shoulder where his hand still lay. She saw the ring first. Four stones, alive in the moonlight.

The leopard let out a faint whimper and sat on its hind legs as if charmed by his presence. Nicaule exhaled and turned to Solomon, too stunned to speak.

He cast a long glance at her bare breasts before meeting her eyes. "Surely you are cold, Wife." He held up her mantle.

She took it from him and covered herself. "Why are you here?"

"I might ask you the same."

"My affairs are my own," she hissed.

The leopard stood on all fours and snarled at her.

Solomon raised his ring hand to the cat; she sat back down.

"Pray tell, Husband: what is it you really want from my father?"

"I am merely doing my moral duty: one man helping another."

"And this has nothing to do with enemies at the gates of Jerusalem? With Hadad?"

His eyes scrutinized her. "How is it you know so

much about my enemies?"

She hesitated as she framed her lie. "His men ambushed my caravan in the wilderness. They wanted information . . . I told them nothing."

The leopard walked to Solomon and curled itself at his feet. "Hadad has been planning an attack on Jerusalem," he said. "I have informed the pharaoh of the scheme, and he has withdrawn all support to the Edomites. Psusennes' loyalty is to me." His gaze traveled slowly down her body. "As is yours."

She wrapped the mantle more tightly about her.

"You are trembling." He smiled. "You should go and rest. We leave for Jerusalem in the morning."

She recoiled. "But I must—"

He placed a hand on her lips. When she quieted, he began walking toward the palace. The leopard followed him.

Nicaule stood alone amid the grasses, watching Solomon's darkened figure diminish as the distance between them grew. Surely he thought he'd outsmarted her, extracting her from her own temptations and ensuring her loyalty, if by force. None of it mattered: she felt triumphant.

Though it was only a fleeting moment, it was enough. Her beloved had professed his passion and had entrusted her with a grave task—the gravest, perhaps, of their lifetimes. He still loved her. Even if she could not have him, that knowledge would sustain her every day as she waited to be freed from her gilded prison.

With the taste of Shoshenq still on her lips, she drew a long breath and followed the path to the palace.

CHAPTER FIFTEEN

"*Kohain*! Come quickly."

The voice at the other side of his door roused Zadok from deep sleep. He opened his eyes to darkness. A pale shaft of light entered through the narrow opening near the ceiling of his bedchamber, indicating the full moon was still high in the sky. An urgent knock followed.

"*Kohain*, you must see this."

It was the voice of Zuriel, one of the Levites who lived permanently near the temple compound and ministered within it. Zadok rose slowly, steadied himself on his cane, and shuffled to the door.

He cracked the door open and peered at his acolyte from the shadows. "What is it that cannot wait until morning?"

Zuriel appeared disturbed. "I have come from Mount Zion. I went up to the high place to make an offering and saw the most wicked, horrible thing."

"Say what you mean."

"On the high place of the mountain lies a bronze statue . . . of a cat." Zuriel's face collapsed into a look of disgust. "Flowers are strewn around its base. They are still fragrant. Someone has put them there this very day."

Zadok's jaw tightened. Only one person could be responsible for such an abomination. "Take me to it."

The high priest and his acolyte walked east toward the holy mount that was once home to a Jebusite stronghold conquered by David. Adjacent to Mount Moriah, it had long been viewed as sacred, a haven for Yahweh's faithful sons and daughters. The thought of it being defiled by foreign idols was so detestable Zadok could not speak of it. If all Zuriel said were true, this would be a grievous violation of the laws of Yahweh. Anger seeped into the corners of his being, and he fought hard against it, for it was not his nature to be hot-tempered. He meditated upon the rise and fall of his breath and the evenness of his gait to regain his composure.

The full moon cast its long silver beams as Zadok and Zuriel made their way to the top of the mount. They stopped beneath a tree just before the summit and stood over the foul object, a statue the size of a newborn child, depicting the Egyptian cat goddess Bast. The bronze creature sat on its hind legs with chest protruding and haughty head held high. At its feet were freshly cut narcissus blossoms.

His memory traveled to Solomon's negotiations with Psusennes in Zoan. "She must be free to practice her customs and worship in her own way," the pharaoh had said of his daughter. Zadok knew then it was a mistake to accept such terms. Now, seeing evidence of the Egyptians' detestable idolatrous religion on the top of the Hebrews' sacred mount, the high priest felt deep in his old bones the onslaught of Yahweh's wrath.

He turned to Zuriel. "I will speak to the king. In the meantime, destroy this and restore virtue to the mount."

"Yes, *Kohain*." Regarding the statue, the Levite shook his head. "What Israelite could have done this?"

"None did. The cat goddess is sacred to the Egyptians."

Zuriel's eyes grew wide. "The king's wife?"

Zadok nodded.

"The king will be angry at us for destroying it."

"I do not fear his ire. My lord and master is not of this earth. My first duty is to him. Now make haste."

Zadok turned on his heel and started down the hillside. It was not the first time he'd encountered such indignity. Two winters prior, he'd found a statue of Molech, the beast-god of the Ammonites, near the Valley of Ben-hinnom. It was in that cursed valley, not far from Jerusalem, that apostates long ago had made their children to walk through a raging fire as a hideous form of sacrifice to the Ammonite deity.

The practice predated Solomon's Jerusalem, but the statue was new. Someone among them had placed it in the valley to glorify Molech, defying the Hebrew laws that forbade such a thing. Zadok suspected Naamah, Solomon's Ammonite wife and mother of Rehoboam, his heir apparent. But she never confessed to it, and Solomon ordered Zadok to drop the inquisition.

The priest proceeded to destroy the stone statue with his own hands, beating it against a massive boulder until nothing remained but shards. The act had at once taken everything out of him and fed him strength.

He thought then it was an isolated incident. He did not expect to find more evidence of idol worship so soon after. It whispered of Solomon's permissiveness with his wives, his refusal to hold them to his own religious standard. The king was in direct defiance of Yahweh's warning, which had come as a dream-oracle during the first years of his reign.

When destiny favored them, men became too full of themselves, quickly forgetting that what had been given them could just as easily be yanked away. Zadok had hoped the wise king would not fall into that trap, but the years had proven him wrong.

He clenched his teeth and quickened his pace. This time he would intervene, lest the entire nation suffer from its king's licentiousness.

In the cold gray light of daybreak, Zadok arrived at the palace gates and stopped in his tracks. Two figures were in the courtyard, heads together in conference and whispering words he could not hear. One was cloaked, his—or perhaps her—identity shielded. The other cut a familiar figure. It wasn't until the man turned his head that Zadok realized who he was.

Jeroboam, the Ephraimite to whom Solomon gave

work when the temple was in early construction, stood beneath the canopy of a pomegranate tree. He looked around, then whispered something in haste to his companion. The hooded figure dashed away.

The high priest waited a moment before approaching. "Ah, Jeroboam. What brings you to the palace at this hour?" He acted as if he had seen nothing.

"I seek audience with the king. It is a matter of utmost importance." His face was pinched, his onyx eyes hard beneath a thick brow. "And you, Zadok. I would have expected you to be at the temple."

Zadok did not like the way Jeroboam addressed him—as an equal rather than as a holy man. Since being promoted to overseer of the laborers of the house of Joseph some ten years prior, the Ephraimite's confidence had taken a dangerous turn toward outright arrogance.

"I am here to counsel the king. As always."

"Good. Perhaps you can bring him to his senses."

The priest pointed his cane at him. "This is no way to speak about your king. I caution you to show respect—or face his wrath."

Jeroboam smirked and walked away, pacing among the sycamores until a footman announced King Solomon was ready to grant audience.

Zadok entered the throne room first and noted that the king had positioned himself on the formal seat of judgment. His throne sat at the apex of a six-stepped structure carved of ivory. Each step was flanked by a different set of gilded beasts—each symbolic of the Lord's commandments to the king of Israel. On the left side of the throne sat the unclean beasts that represented evil; on the right were the righteous ones, representing the divine.

Though only the king sat upon the throne, there were seats around it reserved for the high priest and the judges. Zadok stopped at the base of the seat of judgment, kneeled, and bowed deeply before the king. He took up his place on Solomon's right.

To the king's left sat twenty-three judges—the *sanhedrin*—and two of his children, Rehoboam and Basemath. As Solomon's heir, Rehoboam was frequently present in affairs of the state. The reasons for Basemath's presence were a little more obscure, but Zadok understood. Solomon's eldest daughter was his favorite child, and he often treated her as he would a male heir, sometimes to the chagrin of the men in the council.

The footman announced Jeroboam, and the superintendent of the *burnden* entered. He stopped before the throne and gave the requisite genuflection.

"You have sought this assembly, Jeroboam." Solomon's voice boomed in the cavernous chamber. "You say you seek judgment about the Millo. Say what you have come here to say."

"My lord," Jeroboam said, "the people are restless. They do not understand the purpose of the Millo. They believe there should be no walls round about the city."

Solomon tapped his fingers together. "The common people do not always understand a higher purpose. The Millo fortifications are there to protect them, to guard the city against enemies."

"But, my lord, these common people are the pilgrims coming from all parts of Israel, who have traveled on foot for days to come worship at the temple. They can no longer come and go freely. They are having to camp, sometimes for days on end, until they are deemed worthy to enter the city simply so they could worship. It is an outrage."

Zadok watched Solomon's reaction. The king's body stiffened as he listened to the criticism from one of his own mighty men of valor. Jeroboam's harsh proclamation was the first indication of a conflict stirring among Solomon's own people.

"I have placed my trust in you, Jeroboam," Solomon said coldly. "I have appointed you overseer of all the labor of the house of Joseph. Your purpose is to ensure the people carry out their duty for the kingdom, not to sympathize with them."

"My lord, it is not only the laborers for whom I speak. There are rumblings among the people of Joseph—my people." Jeroboam addressed all present. "They feel they are being unfairly taxed for the building of something they deem unnecessary. They are calling the Millo an iron curtain, a vanity project for the king and nothing more."

Solomon raised his own voice in response. Zadok could see his anger was mounting. "The people need not question; they need only follow. You tell them their king knows what is best for them. You are dismissed."

"My lord, have you been so blinded by power that

you disregard the desires of your own people? Is your own glory all that matters to you?"

Zadok started. Jeroboam had gone too far. Surely he knew such displays of disrespect came with catastrophic consequences.

Solomon rose from his throne and descended the steps to the base, where Jeroboam stood. He struck his servant across the face with the back of his hand. The king's heavy iron ring left a streak of raw skin on Jeroboam's cheek. "Do you know to whom you speak, Jeroboam, son of Nebat?"

Jeroboam's eyes blazed, but he said nothing.

"You are hereby stripped of your title and discharged from royal service." Solomon was breathless. "I should have you put to death for your disloyalty. I will forgive your folly this once for the service your father gave to my father. Now be gone."

Jeroboam hurried out of the room. When he was out of sight, Solomon clenched his fists and turned to Zadok. "That fool. Does he not realize what powers are rising around us? Does he not know what simmers in Egypt? Psusennes is dead. His successor is a Libyan warrior with a taste for blood. Shoshenq is not the peace-loving king my father-in-law was. He is a threat to us. It is my duty to guard the people against such dangers."

Zadok studied Solomon's eyes and saw in them something he did not recognize. It was a cross between fear and arrogance. "My lord, I respectfully ask for private audience."

Solomon stroked his beard, now more silver than

black. Though he was nearing the fiftieth year since his birth, his gaze was still as intense as it was when he was anointed king. He dismissed the others with a wave and turned to his high priest. "Say what you have to say."

Zadok waited for the last person to leave the room. He spoke softly. "I am not justifying Jeroboam's actions, but you must take heed of his words. There are indeed enemies at the gate of Jerusalem, but some wear the garments of your people."

Solomon scoffed. "You speak nonsense."

"Perhaps you trust too much." Zadok steadied himself on his cane and rose from his seat. "My lord, our faith is our foundation. When that falters, everything we have built upon it crumbles to dust. It pains me to say I have seen evidence of this.

"Some time back, the widow Tirzah took to the streets, begging for food for her four boys. I bade her come to the temple and take of the animal sacrifices that they may not go hungry. But she did not come. When next I saw her, she was with Nahash the elder. He was groping her openly."

"Nahash? The married, old merchant?"

"The very one. He followed her to her house before sundown on the Sabbath. Neither of them came to the temple that night. I fear she is selling her flesh to him for bread."

"That is shameful. They must be punished. See to it, Zadok." He sat at a table on which lay a pile of scrolls. He opened the one on top and shifted his attention to it.

The dismissive attitude raised Zadok's ire. "My lord,

this is not about mere punishment. It is an omen of the depravity that has settled among the people."

"It is one incident, isolated to a man and a woman." Solomon spoke calmly, never raising his gaze. "You cannot judge a people by the actions of a few."

"Open your eyes, Solomon. Your subjects' spiritual armor has been breached. The winds have changed in Jerusalem. People like Nahash and Tirzah are taking what they want without regard for judgment. They seek immediate pleasure without restraint, and that is a certain sign of moral decline. Surely you see that."

The king pounded his fist on the table. "Enough! The people's faith is intact. They come in great numbers to the temple, offering their livestock for sacrifice, and our coffers are full. That is what I see. Rein in your pessimism, lest it become its own, misguided prophecy. The people need guidance; it has been that way since the time of our fathers. It is your duty to lead them down a spiritual path. If they do not follow, it is you who have failed."

Zadok could not believe his ears. "Solomon, how can you—?"

"I will hear no more of this, Zadok. Go." He bent over the scroll and said not another word.

Zadok could see it clearly: Solomon had become a victim of his own legacy. He had created a machine of such monstrous proportions that it had consumed him, leaving little time for matters of the spirit. He was not blind to the unrest stirring around him but rather had chosen to ignore it, focusing instead on fulfilling his destiny. For a leader, it was the gravest of missteps.

"There is something else you must know," Zadok said. "This morning I stood upon the Mount of Olives and saw the most abhorrent sight. Someone had erected a statue in the likeness of a cat. There were signs of worship . . . spent incense, fresh flowers."

Solomon obviously understood the inference. "When I took Nicaule to wife, I made a promise. It would be dishonorable to go back on my word."

Zadok tapped his cane on the floor. "Idol worship is an abomination before the Lord. You must not allow this. If you look the other way, you do so at the peril of your soul."

"My soul is intact before the Lord. Our people do not worship idols. I have no sway over the beliefs of foreigners."

"But they are foreigners on your land. Nay, in your house. Allowing them to worship their gods on Israel's soil is in direct defiance of the laws of Yahweh." Zadok paused to catch his breath. "God will not tolerate such abominations. He will raise up enemies against your kingdom. It has already begun. For if you don't believe Jeroboam is such an enemy, you are the fool."

Solomon stood abruptly. "Blasphemy!"

The priest's cane slipped out of his hand and fell to the floor.

Solomon must have realized the gravity of his misstep, for he lowered his head and softened his voice. "Forgive me, Zadok."

"It is not too late, my lord Solomon. Lead the people in the way the Lord demands of you."

Solomon picked up Zadok's cane. Handing it to him, he said, "You must trust in me, old friend. All I have done, I have done for the glorification of his name. It is why I have built him a house and a kingdom that is the envy of people of all nations."

"The Lord does not want buildings and armies and stores of gold. He wants your heart to be pure and you to walk upright before him. Do not forsake what he said to you all those years ago. 'Should you or your children falter, should you break my commandments or serve other gods, I will strike down Israel and cast out of my sight the house which I have hallowed.'"

The king placed a hand on Zadok's shoulder. "I have not forgotten. The years may have passed, but the wisdom granted me has not diminished. I know what is best for the people. Do not burden your old bones with worry. Now, go."

The taste of bile permeated Zadok's mouth. The king's condescension was like the sound of the horn at the sight of the approaching enemy. Solomon was so full of his own pride he could not see it. Zadok could say nothing to alter that. For the first time in his eighty-four years, the high priest of Israel had failed. He gathered himself and walked out of the throne room.

In the corridor, a familiar feeling came over him. As he had few times before, he felt like the conduit for a message. He stood still and closed his eyes, letting it come. In his mind's eye, he saw the face of Jeroboam, bleeding and full of rage. The captain of the *burnden* stood on a golden statue in the likeness of a fatted calf. Beneath him were outstretched hands that numbered so many they could not be counted. The image dissolved into blackness, replaced by a desert. The wilderness of Judea. A wind blew the sand across the parched ground, revealing a buried object. As the sand parted, he realized it was his own staff.

The end was near.

He opened his eyes and knew what he had to do.

CHAPTER SIXTEEN

When night fell upon Jerusalem, Zadok threw a dark mantle over his bony shoulders and crossed the cobbled alleys to the officers' quarters. He knew his visit would bring forth answers as surely as the vines yielded grapes at summer's end.

The light of an oil lamp trembled at the window of Jeroboam's house. Zadok stood in the shadows and waited. A light rain touched his face, but he did not seek shelter. He would wait in that spot until morrow if he had to, for he knew with all certainty someone would come.

Two hours later the rain had soaked him to the bone, making him shiver with a deep chill, but his premonition was rewarded. A cloaked visitor rapped at Jeroboam's door and was quickly let inside, obviously expected.

Zadok skulked across the alley and hunched beneath Jeroboam's window. The voices were soft, whispers almost. From beneath his mantle he drew a horn and placed it on his ear to amplify the sound.

"Three hundred horses and chariots are coming out of Egypt tomorrow for delivery to the palace. My men will meet the caravan in the wilderness at dawn and divert the horses to my stronghold in Zeredah."

The betrayal Zadok had suspected was true. Jeroboam was plotting against Solomon, and he had an accomplice. He listened actively, but the mysterious visitor was silent.

"It is imperative you deliver the message to our allies tonight," Jeroboam said. "Everything must go according to the plan."

Allies? Could there be a support army? If Jeroboam was planning a revolt, surely he needed reinforcements. But who among neighboring kings would raise a hand against Solomon?

"How will we know the time has come?" the visitor whispered.

Though there was something familiar in it, Zadok could not identify the voice.

"The prophecy has been made. God's plan is already at work." He paused. "A few days ago, I was walking along the road outside the city. Ahijah the Shilonite appeared from behind a thicket of sycamore trees and bade me stop. He removed his mantle and rent it before my eyes. I thought him mad and begged him to stop, but he would not do so until it was shredded into twelve pieces. Then he counted out ten and put them in my hand. 'Take this cloth which is a symbol of the ten tribes of Israel,' he said. 'The united kingdom is crumbling, for Solomon has done wrong in the eyes of God. You have been chosen, Jeroboam. You must lead the tribes of the north. Only Judah and Benjamin will remain in the hands of the house of David.'"

So it had been done. Zadok looked to the sky. Even the stars were hiding beneath the black, impenetrable veil that had fallen upon Jerusalem that night. There was no surprise in it. He knew in his heart the day of Solomon's judgment would come. The son of David had everything—power, glory, wealth, vigor, and wisdom— yet he let it trickle away like water through gossamer. Instead of letting himself be guided, he placed his faith in his own sovereignty, disregarding the one who had given it to him in the first place.

Zadok had witnessed pride over and over: it was the great conjurer, luring men like moths to light. Solomon wasn't the only one who had fallen prey to it. Jeroboam was guilty in equal measure. A chill rippled down Zadok's spine as he imagined his beloved Israel in the hands of such a man. He felt short of breath and took it as an omen: he would not be there to see it.

"Very well," the visitor said.

Zadok's ear stirred. Could it be?

"It shall be done." The voice was unmistakably female. "The pharaoh will be pleased. He has waited for this news."

Zadok started when he realized the voice was Nicaule's. Though he had never trusted her, he could not have imagined betrayal of this scale.

"You must distract the king," Jeroboam said. "He must not see this coming."

"Leave Solomon to me," she whispered.

The voices stopped. A moment later, she exited the house and was swallowed by the night. With great effort, Zadok stood on weak legs and walked in the opposite direction. He had to get to Solomon before Nicaule did.

Though he was shivering, he felt his skin burn with fever. His lungs felt heavy, causing him to labor for every breath. He clutched his chest and pressed on. He would warn his king if it was his last task on Earth.

By the time he reached the palace, he was exhausted and gasping for breath. He dragged his feet to reach one of the guards. "Wake the king." His voice was weak. "It is an urgent matter."

The guard nodded and disappeared into the corridor. His hurried footfall grew fainter and fainter as he traveled toward Solomon's chamber. For several moments, Zadok heard nothing but the clipped sound of his own shallow breath. Then the footsteps came again, this time unrushed and evenly paced.

The guard walked back to his post and bowed to Zadok. "The queen gave instructions to King Solomon's private guard: the king is not to be disturbed under any circumstances."

"This cannot wait until morning. In the name of the almighty God, I order you to wake him."

"It is not possible, *Kohain*. The orders were very specific: no one breaches the king's chamber . . . not even you."

She had foreseen the possibility of Jeroboam's plan being exposed and had made provisions for it. But she hadn't counted on Zadok's ingenuity.

"Send Benaiah to my house," he told the guard. "Make haste."

He walked out of the palace gates and started toward his own house at the foot of the temple compound. When Zadok pushed the door open, his youngest son was asleep on a hay mattress in the corner of the one-room house. He bent down and shook his shoulder. "Wake, Ahimaaz."

Ahimaaz sprang from his bed. "What is it, Father?"

Zadok lit an oil lamp and held it between them. His son's honey-colored eyes were alert. "The time has come for valor, my son."

A crease formed between Ahimaaz's brows. He took the oil lamp from his father's shaking hands and waited for instructions.

"The king has been betrayed," Zadok whispered. "One of his officers has raised a hand against him. You and I are the only ones who know."

"Should we not tell the king?"

"He is sequestered and cannot be warned. If we wait, all will be lost. We must act now . . . without orders from the palace."

"What will you have me do, Father?"

A hard, rapid knock sounded. "Enter, Benaiah," Zadok said.

The captain of the army approached the priest and his son. "What is the meaning of this?"

"The king has been betrayed, Benaiah. Jeroboam plans to ambush the Egyptian caravan and steal the horses intended for Jerusalem. He will take them to his stronghold in Zeredah, where he is gathering his forces."

Benaiah's jaw slackened. "How do you know this?"

"I followed Jeroboam and heard him speak about his plans." He glanced at Benaiah, then at Ahimaaz. "Now listen carefully. I want you to ride to Zeredah with a small but able unit. Your approach must be stealthy." Zadok felt a crushing weight on his chest. His jaw was so tight that his words were distorted. "When Jeroboam comes, arrest him for treason by order of the king."

Benaiah eyed him. "Do we have such an order?"

"The order comes from a higher place than the palace." Zadok dragged a chest from under the bed and lifted its lid. He pulled out an object and held it up. "Show this to Jeroboam."

Ahimaaz studied it for a moment. "A piece of cloth. Of what consequence is this?"

Zadok thought back to the day he first laid eyes on Jeroboam. The temple was in the early stages of construction when the young Ephraimite approached Solomon and handed him that cloth, claiming it was the corner of King Saul's tunic that David, then a renegade, sliced off in lieu of killing the reigning king. David had spared Saul's life, for it was against the law to touch the Lord's anointed, however many his trespasses.

So it had come to pass again. Jeroboam surely deserved to die for his duplicity. But if what he said was true and Ahijah truly rent his garment as a prophecy from the Lord, no man—not even the high priest of the kingdom—could pass judgment.

"He will know." Zadok struggled for breath. He knew he would not see his son again. He gazed at his face, still youthful after twoscore and three years. He had groomed Ahimaaz to succeed him as high priest, but now he was uncertain the Zadokite priesthood, like the house of David, would persist. He could see the future written in the stars as surely as the east wind broke up the ships of Tarshish.

Ahimaaz squeezed his hands. "You are unwell, Father. I cannot leave you . . ."

"My dutiful son." A feeble smile crossed Zadok's lips. He felt the Lord's presence as his lungs filled with breath. "Life is as fragile as the song of the hoopoe. My voice will soon be silenced, but yours is as clear and bright as a summer morrow. Take a wife and multiply. Live according to God's law. No matter what darkness falls over this land, the land of your fathers, do not forsake it. Even if you are given no sign from the Lord, even if all the prophets have departed, do not deliver your dove to the hands of wild beasts."

Zadok felt Benaiah's hand on his shoulder. He addressed both men. "Go now. Ride to Zeredah. May the Lord keep you."

Ahimaaz kissed his father's cheeks and clutched the fabric to his breast. He dressed hurriedly, and the two men went on their way.

Though it was a cool autumn evening, perspiration soaked Zadok's gown. His bones ached as if he had been stoned by a raging mob. He stood, ignoring the pressure on his chest, and started toward the temple gates.

The effort of walking exhausted him. He had made it halfway to the temple when he collapsed to his knees. He could go no farther. He let his walking stick drop to the ground, and he clawed at the cool soil of his beloved homeland, clutching it between his fingers. That very dirt had been granted to the sons of Israel by the Lord himself. It had been soaked with their blood and sweat, and that of their children, as they toiled for a great nation worthy of the gift it had been given.

Centuries later, it had come to pass. Zadok spread his fingers and let the soil slip through.

He thought of Solomon lying on the bed of iniquity, oblivious to the damage he had done. For mortal men, drunk with their own power and so easily seduced by earthly pleasures, greatness was not an enduring state but a fleeting fancy. It blossomed like the pomegranate trees, but when the *khamsin* blew, its petals scattered in the wind, floating without direction.

Zadok dropped his forehead to the ground and let his tears water the earth. "O Lord, God of our fathers, forgive the sins of your people Israel," he whispered. "Open their eyes, that they may see your light; unbind their hands, that they may do your bidding. Let righteousness rise again from the ashes of depravity, that your inheritance on Earth may not fall to the hands of the wicked."

A gentle breeze blew across the mount, making him aware of how sodden his robes were. He shivered like a naked man in midwinter, expending energy he could no longer spare. Gasping, he continued, "Take now this soul, O Lord, into the kingdom of heaven and deliver your judgment upon it. May it appease your anger like water quenches the thirst of the desert."

The face of the archangel, pale as wheat and framed by flaxen locks, flashed in his mind's eye. It was time. He lay on his side and looked toward the northern horizon, sending a silent blessing to his son and the men who accompanied him on the clandestine mission. He closed his eyes and exhaled his last breath.

CHAPTER SEVENTEEN

When the rooster crowed, Nicaule woke in Solomon's arms. He was sleeping deeply, probably exhausted from their night of love and still intoxicated by the spiked wine with which she had plied him.

To bring about a state of hallucination followed by stupor, she had soaked petals of blue lotus into the wine, releasing their narcotic substance. It was a practice familiar to Egyptian priests seeking a transcendent state but could be deadly if misused. She held close the formula, a gift long ago from the seer Anippe, close to her breast, using it only when necessary.

In all the times she had used it on Solomon, he had been oblivious, attributing the ecstasy he'd felt to her exotic lovemaking techniques. As they both had grown older, that illusion had been vital, for it was how she maintained her power over him.

More than that, the blue lotus flower became a tool for incapacitating him so she could go about her business undetected. As he slept off the effects, she slipped out of his bed and met Jeroboam, spilling the secrets of Solomon's palace and helping the captain of the *burnden* plot his rebellion.

The most useful bit of information, she'd learned earlier that night. As the blue lotus took effect on him, Solomon had revealed the secret that would be his empire's undoing.

When Nicaule first entered his chamber, he seemed blue, preoccupied. He was draped over a chair, head resting on his fist. His brow was furrowed, and his gaze seemed to travel in distant lands. She went to him, placing on a table the jug of wine she'd brought for him.

She kneeled beside him and wrapped her arms around his neck. "What vexes you, my husband?" She whispered into his ear, kissing his lobe.

He gently pushed her away. "It is a man's matter. Women should not be concerned with such things."

She did not question him further, knowing his tongue would eventually be loosened. "Whatever it is, let it not interfere with our night of love." She pulled the stopper from the wine jug and poured into a cup. She lifted the cup to his lips. "Drink. This will ease your burden."

With three loud gulps, he emptied the cup. He wiped a few drops from his beard with the back of a hand. "Dance for me."

He didn't ask her often, reserving the privilege for times when he needed a complete escape. Judging by the dark circles beneath his eyes, he longed for a reprieve from the demons dwelling in his mind that night. What troubled him, she suspected, had to do with the confrontation with Jeroboam—and could be vital intelligence for Tanis.

If she were to extract it from him, and subsequently offer it as a prize to Shoshenq, her performance would have to be infallible. She smiled wickedly and stood. She poured another cup of the wine and left it on the table next to an oil lamp. She peeled off her mantle and let it drop to the floor, exposing her costume—a sheer petticoat skirt with a cape crossed at the chest and draped across the shoulders, held in place by a hammered-gold breastplate decorated with a winged amber scarab.

Solomon walked to his collection of instruments and picked up a flute. He eyed Nicaule hungrily and changed his mind, choosing a goatskin drum instead. He returned to his chair and took another sip of the wine. He began drumming softly and slowly.

She took his cue and turned her back to him, following the beat with subtle movements of her hips. She raised her arms above her head and swayed them like papyrus stalks in the wind. Her fingers performed their own dance, gliding and intertwining in delicate, hypnotic patterns.

He picked up the pace ever so slightly. Tilting her head so her hair could fall to one side, she dropped her hands to the back of her neck and stroked her nape with her fingertips before unfastening the silk string that held together her breastplate. She let it fall onto a sheepskin rug and gazed at him over her shoulder, watching his reaction as she untied the cape that covered her upper body. She let the gauzy garment slip over one shoulder, then the other until it draped loosely around her waist, exposing a slim, tawny back glistening with almond oil.

Without taking his gaze off her, he took another sip of the wine and slowly licked his lips. He kept drumming, louder now.

Shoulders rolling to the drumbeat, she bent at the waist, letting her head drop backward until her hair grazed the floor. Her upper body pulsed in harmony with the sound. Noting his admiration of her undulating, naked torso, she teased him by using the cape to alternately veil and reveal her skin.

The lamplight shuddered. Sensing his desire, she slowly returned to the upright position and assumed a more rapid pace. Holding the white gossamer fabric, she moved her arms up and down, creating the illusion of a swan in flight.

As the drumbeat grew louder, she spun round to face him. Her gaze riveted on his, she untied the petticoat skirt and let the fabric drop to the floor, exposing a loincloth that was damp against her perspiring body. She pirouetted several times, twirling the gauzy cape as if it were a cloud encircling her. She moved faster and faster in a blur of fabric and skin, keeping perfect pace with the escalating beat.

With a swift movement, she draped the diaphanous fabric over her head and let it veil her body as if she were a bride on her wedding night. She removed the loincloth. The drumming expanded to a frenzied crescendo, mirroring, she imagined, his heartbeat. She stepped closer to him. Drumming with one hand, he reached for her with the other, but she moved back, letting his desire swell.

Nicaule glided to a stone column and wrapped her arms around it. Ensuring he had a full view, she dropped her head back and ground her hips against the stone. The veil was plastered against her moist body, revealing all the curves. He moaned softly but kept drumming.

When she sensed his longing was complete, she dropped to the floor and inched toward him. As she moved closer, she let the veil fall away and swayed before him, just beyond arm's reach. The rhythmic throb of vibrating animal skin filled the space between them.

Solomon's chest heaved as the drumming reached a fevered pitch. His mouth dropped open, and his eyelids fluttered rapidly. The drumming stopped. His chest tightened, and a breathless groan left his throat. A few moments later he exhaled loudly and let the drum fall from his hands. Panting, he lay back.

She smiled in triumph. She wanted to believe it was all due to her talent, but she knew the lotus-spiked wine contributed to his impulsive ecstasy. She had moments to extract the information she needed before he fell sound asleep.

She sat on his lap and leaned against him, her head nestled into his drenched neck. His pulse thumped against her brow.

He stroked her back with a feather touch. "O fairest among women, how do you please me so? Wives I have in great number and concubines aplenty, but none moves me as you do. Water from all the springs of Jerusalem cannot quench my love for you."

She spoke in Hebrew. "It is a wife's duty to her husband, my lord, King Solomon. It also is her duty to listen to his woes and guide him as only a woman can." She placed a hand on his jaw and turned his face until their eyes met. "Won't you tell me what troubles you?"

He sighed. "All these years I have not known enemies. Now, one by one they gather against me. I fear for the future of Jerusalem . . . of the kingdom."

"Who dares to conspire against you, my husband?"

"One from within my ranks." He looked away. "It is of no consequence. I cannot reverse what has been done. I can only fortify our defenses and ensure the safety of our people."

"But Jerusalem is already fortified. The Millo—"

"Nothing would please my enemies more than to destroy the capital. It is the obvious place to strike. This is why I have instructed my most trusted men—governors, warriors, priests—to leave the city at the first sign of conflict."

She jerked back. "Leave the city? But where will they go?"

"I have made provisions for everyone to hide at Megiddo."

"My lord, is that wise? Megiddo is the chariot city. It is not the fortress Jerusalem is. There is nowhere to hide."

He smiled like he was keeping a secret.

She bit the inside of her lip. She was so close. "Is there, my lord?"

He cast a long glance at her, as if trying to gauge her sincerity. Pressing her breast against his chest, she kissed his lips softly and explored his body with her hand. "Do you not trust your queen?"

He closed his eyes. His chest rose softly and evenly. He was drifting.

She pressed on. "Should conflict arise, I can help the women and children take cover. Tell me, my lord. Tell me where to lead them."

"There is a tunnel," he said, eyes still closed, voice trailing off. "A hidden passage between the palace gardens and the spring beyond the tell. No one knows . . ."

Sleep took him. Thanks to the drug, he would remember none of this when he woke.

Nicaule extracted herself from his embrace and gathered her clothes. As she dressed, she watched Solomon sleep. How vulnerable a mighty king could be in the web of a cunning woman.

Some part of her, a compassion long stifled, felt remorse for doing that to him. She immediately dismissed the sentiment. Her mission was bigger than that; beyond a man and a woman, it could decide the future of nations.

She gathered the wine jug and tucked it into her mantle. She bent down and cupped her hand behind the trembling flame of the oil lamp. She cast a last glance at Solomon and blew, plunging the room into darkness.

She tiptoed out and closed the door quietly before launching down the corridor. She was eager to exit the king's palace and retreat to her own, where she could wait for word from Shoshenq's emissaries. The plan was flawless: the Egyptians, en route to Jerusalem with a consignment of horses, would look like victims attacked by bandits, when all the while they were arming Jeroboam and forging a new alliance with the soon-to-be-anointed king.

At the courtyard of Solomon's palace, a group of women wailed and rent their clothes. Mourners. She spotted Azariah, son of the prophet Nathan and chief of Solomon's governors, walking briskly toward the king's chamber.

"What has happened?" she asked one of the guards.

"Zadok the priest is dead. He fell sometime in the night."

She exhaled, thankful her fears that the plan had somehow gone awry were unfounded. That Zadok had passed was an unexpected gift. For years he had despised her for no better reason than her heritage. She was glad to be rid of him.

She continued on the path to her palace, stopping first at Irisi's quarters. She knocked once, then twice, the longtime signal between her and her old friend and scribe.

Irisi was still wearing her nightgown when she came to the door.

"Any word?" There was impatience in Nicaule's voice.

Irisi nodded and let her lady in. She closed the door and bolted it with an iron bar. "At dawn, the messenger came to the appointed place. The exchange has been made."

"Good. Jeroboam has his horses and chariots, and Shoshenq has his Israelite rebel army. It won't be long before we are free."

"Are you sure this is the right path, my lady?"

"Twenty-five years I have waited to return to my homeland and to the arms of the only man I have loved." She smiled. "Yes, dear one. This is our appointed path.

Now I must go. Speak to no one of this."

"What will become of the girls?"

"Taphath will stay here and marry. Basemath will accompany us to Tanis."

"Forgive me, my lady, but Basemath is old enough to make her own choices."

"When she knows the truth about her heritage, she will choose Egypt. I am certain of it."

Irisi shook her head. "My lady, Basemath believes she belongs here. She would sooner fight for Israel than seek solace in Egypt."

Nicaule cupped Irisi's face with both hands. "Dear Irisi. Basemath is naïve. Her allegiance is to Solomon because she thinks he is her father. When the time is right, she will know she is the daughter of a pharaoh. And that will change everything. You will see."

Irisi sighed and pulled away.

Nicaule contemplated her friend's posture. Though Irisi had proven her loyalty time after time, her eyes were often veiled with skepticism. Each time Nicaule questioned her, Irisi did not acknowledge it. But she could not hide it.

Nicaule decided to let it go this time, for one woman's emotions were trivial in light of the grand plan. She unbolted the door and left the room.

On her way to her chamber, she stopped at a window opening and gazed at the ascending sun. She whispered a tribute to the sun god Amun-Ra. She had so much to be thankful for.

At sundown the next day, Nicaule was summoned to the throne room. That happened only on rare occasions, when there was a matter of diplomacy or a major event of which she needed to be informed. Otherwise, she was left out of the affairs of state, which suited her just fine.

Solomon was seated on the throne of meeting, a gilded chair whose carvings mirrored those on the seat of judgment. The king's throne was on an elevated platform, flanked by four chairs two cubits beneath it. When Nicaule entered, he was finishing a conversation with Benaiah.

Solomon sent Benaiah away and motioned to Nicaule to sit on his left. She sat at the edge of the seat and looked up at him. How he had aged. Beneath his golden crown, deep creases marked his forehead. His beard and hair, thick despite the advancing years, had grown gray as the mourning doves of Kidron Valley.

"My wife, I have splendid news," he said, though his expression betrayed more concern than joy. "Our daughter is to marry."

Nicaule assumed he meant their younger daughter, Taphath, who was being courted by an army officer. "Nepthador has asked for her hand, then."

Solomon shook his head. "I speak of Basemath."

For a moment, she was unable to breathe. She felt as if someone had driven a spear into her abdomen.

"You don't seem happy, Wife."

"Forgive me, my lord, for this is a surprise." She

struggled to compose herself so as to not rouse his suspicion. "Basemath has seemed uninterested in marriage. I have considered she might be a spinster for all her years."

"How little you know of her." He stood and walked down two steps. He paced the floor in front of the throne. "Basemath is destined for greatness. Of all my children, she has the most intelligence, passion, humility, and closeness to the Lord. She is of fine enough character to lead this nation. But alas, the people need a king."

Nicaule did not see her daughter as a leader of Israel but rather as a future queen of Egypt. Basemath was a splendid creature, raven-haired and honey-skinned, with a slim physique and breasts like lotus blossoms. She was a purebred Egyptian, destined for the love of a pharaoh, whether she knew it or not. But more than that, Basemath was the expression of Nicaule's own passion for her beloved. She was what bound Nicaule to Shoshenq, now and always.

Solomon stopped in front of her. "Are you not curious as to her betrothed?"

Nicaule looked at him without expression. Inside, she was crying. "Do reveal, my lord."

"Ahimaaz, son of Zadok."

She bit her bottom lip and tasted the bitter red ochre stain. "A priest . . . Why?"

"Ahimaaz is Zadok's heir. That alone makes him worthy. But there is something else for which I owe him allegiance."

"What is that?"

He hesitated. "Since it is a matter of interest to Egypt, you should be aware. The horses sent to Jerusalem by the pharaoh have been seized and diverted to the north. The Egyptians were attacked last night before dawn."

She feigned shock. "Who would do such a thing?"

"I cannot reveal it, for it is a matter of national security. But I will say this: the perpetrator was confronted by a band of warriors led by Ahimaaz."

"Ahimaaz is a priest, my lord. He is not capable—"

Solomon laughed. "Ahimaaz has been trained equally in the ways of Yahweh and the ways of the sword. He is a silent but sure force in Jerusalem's arsenal. One of the best stealth warriors we have."

"And how is it he was privy to such intelligence as to uncover a secret plot?"

"Zadok had uncovered the scheme. He gave the capture order to his son and Benaiah before he died."

Her veins felt as if mountain water trickled through them. Had Zadok followed her? Had he overheard? Who else knew? She placed a hand on her throat. "How could he have known?"

Solomon shifted his gaze upward. "That vexes me. Perhaps the Lord appeared to him." He turned to Nicaule. "Alas, it will remain a mystery. However it happened, it was a blessing, for he thwarted an imminent attack by sending an army to confront the traitor."

A trembling breath left Nicaule's lips. "Where is this . . . traitor now?"

"He escaped captivity and has fled from Israel. The men pursued him to the edge of the wilderness before losing his tracks." His gaze traveled down her body. "But let us speak of happier things. The wedding will be in a fortnight."

She stood abruptly. "Why so soon? I have not prepared . . ."

"You need prepare nothing. I have seen to the matter of the *mohar.*"

"Does Basemath—?"

"Yes. She knows everything."

Nicaule clenched her jaw. How could he leave her out of something as important as the negotiation for her daughter's marriage? The blatant disregard for her, and for all womankind, was yet another reminder of why he deserved to be deceived—or worse. He had brought it on himself with his abhorrent actions.

And yet, once again, he had won. But not for long. Her plan would come to pass sooner or later; she would make sure of it.

"Let us rejoice, Wife, for it is a happy day." Solomon offered her a hand.

She did not take it. It was the first time she had defied him. "You decided alone; therefore, you must rejoice alone." She brushed past him on her way to the door.

"I have not dismissed you, woman."

She stopped but did not turn around. She was shaking.

"I expect you in my chamber. Go now and wait for me."

She tried to fight back the tears, but they came anyway. She wiped her cheek, and the kohl around her eyes left a black trail on her palm. Without facing him, she bolted out the door.

CHAPTER EIGHTEEN

Solomon had grown old when Makeda, the queen of the vast and remote empire of Sheba, came to Jerusalem. It was the first state visit in many years, for the leaders of neighboring nations had pulled back their support as conflict marked Solomon's kingdom.

Nicaule watched her husband prepare for the queen's arrival. He had new clothing woven for all the palace staff: tunics of pristine white linen, striped linen robes for the men and brocade ones for the women, head coverings of blue and purple held in place by golden bands. He appointed potters to make special vessels stamped with the king's insignia—the winged lion that symbolized the immortality of Judah—and servants to fill them with honey, oil, seeds, and olives, all gifts to the queen. He ordered fragrant flowers to be planted along the path leading to the walled city and perfumes to be made using the same scents so that Makeda would remember her visit long after she'd departed. His cooks spent weeks butchering milk-fed animals, gathering fruits, and procuring fish for the royal feasts.

It was disgusting, and perhaps a little desperate, this wanton display of wealth. Though Solomon insisted it was standard protocol, Nicaule knew it was merely an attempt to put on a show of opulence and abundance for a monarch famed for her untold treasure. It was as much for his own pleasure as for hers. In his latter years, when he became full of himself, Solomon had grown fearful of losing his once-undisputed status as the greatest king ever to reign in the holy land. In the sunset of his life, his mission was no longer to rule justly but rather to secure his legacy for the generations that followed.

Makeda's caravan appeared in Jerusalem on an afternoon in late spring, but it was evening before all the camels—five hundred of them, the rumor had it—had made their way to the city and been tethered outside the Millo.

Nicaule watched from the window of her palace as the queen was carried to the city on a grand palanquin, said to have been fashioned in the Orient exclusively for her use. Four black men, possibly from savage lands of her realm, wearing white loincloths and turbans, held each of the poles of the royal conveyance. The passenger was hidden behind lavishly draped curtains of gold-fringed red silk.

Solomon's lute players assembled as the men placed the palanquin onto a platform, welcoming Makeda with traditional Hebrew melodies. From behind the curtains emerged a radiant creature. Her skin was black as midnight and glistened in the afternoon sun. Beneath her bejeweled diadem, a waterfall of tight curls tumbled down her back.

The queen's clothes were unlike anything Nicaule had seen. She wore a long dress dyed in exotic shades of blue and embroidered with golden thread. A swath of the same fabric trailed her, and a mantle decorated with peacock feathers was draped over her shoulders. Her waist was cinched with a sash studded with turquoises and tiger's eyes.

Makeda entered the city followed by her retinue of servants and handmaidens holding trays piled high with gifts for her host. Nicaule saw mounds of spices, bales of frankincense, wooden chests big and small, and cages crowded with white doves. Sheba's queen was known both for her wealth—it was said the streets of her kingdom were paved in silver and gold dust—and for her generosity. It appeared she had spared nothing to ensure her visit to Solomon's fabled kingdom was well received.

Nicaule walked to her dressing room, where Irisi was laying out clothes and jewels for her lady. Solomon had ordered new dresses for his favorite wife, beautiful confections made of brightly dyed linen with an overlayer of luminous spider's silk. Nicaule picked one up, studied it for a moment, and put it back down. All the finery in the world could not stand as a substitute for her freedom: a splendid cage remained a cage.

She picked up a round bronze mirror, a gift from her own mother, and regarded her reflection. Without the benefit of makeup, her eyes were marked by deep lines and dark sockets. Her jowls had sagged and the corners of her lips pointed toward the floor, both telling of nights spent crying, dreams smothered, and anger repressed.

It had been seven years since Jeroboam's failed attempt to stage a rebellion. According to dispatches from Tanis at the time, Jeroboam had fled to Egypt and was under the protection of Shoshenq. But the letters had stopped coming. Her own missives asking about plans to take Jerusalem were met with frustrating silence from the pharaoh's palace.

She considered the possibility that a plan had been put into motion but had not been revealed to her for security reasons. If that were true, Shoshenq would not have risked a letter falling into the wrong hands. Though she knew she should have faith in her lover, it killed her to not know. She felt like a ship adrift in a sea cloaked in winter's fog.

At least she had Irisi, her only connection to her roots. And she had Basemath, though their bond had always been tenuous. She was a respectful and dutiful daughter, but Basemath had never revealed the fire in her heart, at least not to her mother. Nicaule would have dismissed her as a haughty swan had she not witnessed her ardent devotion to Solomon.

If Nicaule had ever doubted it, it was plain the day Solomon told Basemath she was to marry Ahimaaz, twenty years her senior, and move to Shechem in the northern provinces, where Ahimaaz was to serve as governor. Her role, however, would be more than that. She would have to be Solomon's spy, moving in political circles and reporting to her father any stirrings of rebellion or treasonous behavior.

It meant putting her life on the line.

Nicaule had protested, but Basemath ignored her. She dropped to her knees and kissed Solomon's ring, pledging her allegiance to him and to the state. She and Ahimaaz left Jerusalem after the seven days of their marriage ceremony and had been in Shechem since. Less than a year later, one of Solomon's servants informed Nicaule she had a granddaughter.

"My lady, would you prefer the scarlet or the white?"

Irisi's question jolted Nicaule back to the present. She was to meet Solomon in the throne room so they could receive the illustrious guest together. She smiled. "Give me the scarlet."

The queen entered the throne room with much fanfare. A harpist came first, heralding her arrival. Her ladies-in-waiting walked in next, singing softly in a language unfamiliar to Nicaule. Then came Makeda, floating within a golden gown whose ample skirt was embroidered in brilliant colors like birds' plumage. Her gossamer mantle was sewn with glass beads that captured light, dazzling Nicaule's eyes. Two men with fans of palm leaf flanked the queen, renewing the air around her as she glided toward Solomon's throne.

At the top of the throne structure, Solomon and Nicaule awaited Makeda's arrival. As she approached the steps, Solomon stood. He stared at his guest as if he were in a trance. It was obvious he was taken by her exotic presence and poised demeanor.

Even the gilded beasts on the edge of the throne's steps seemed to gaze at her in wonder as she ascended. Her perfume, a pleasing scent of jasmine and Oriental spice, preceded her. As she reached the top step, Nicaule noted her flawless skin and eyes as bright as polished onyx and felt her own youth so far behind her. The claws of jealousy dug into her core.

Solomon took her hands. "Your legend is known far and wide, but even the most praising tales do not do justice to your splendor." He bowed slightly. "Welcome to Jerusalem, O fair queen."

"Solomon, son of David and exalted king of Israel, I have waited long years to walk amid the majesty of your fabled city. But more so, I have longed to meet the man whose wisdom is celebrated across the land."

"I pray I will not disappoint you." He waved a hand toward Nicaule. "May I present Nicaule Tashere, daughter of Psusennes II of Egypt, and my first wife."

Makeda placed her hands in Nicaule's. They were soft as the petals of a new rose. The queen smiled kindly and bowed, then took a seat at Solomon's right.

"What news do you bring from the kingdom of Sheba?" he asked.

"I have not come to discuss my humble home but rather to witness the opulence of yours and to learn from your intelligence and insight. But first, I must test you to determine if you are the sage about whom I have heard so much."

"What is it you wish to know?"

"In my kingdom, we enjoy riddles—making them and answering them."

He raised an eyebrow. "We have that in common."

For nearly twoscore years, Solomon had never looked at another woman in the same way he had Nicaule. She remembered still the enchantment that had overtaken him like a sorceress' spell when he first laid eyes on her in Tanis. On the day of Makeda's visit, Nicaule saw the same look in his eyes—only it was no longer directed at her.

She did not care. The king of Israel disgusted her more now than he ever had. But seeing that impossibly serene woman, who was powerful and rich and capable of bewitching any man without sacrificing her independence, filled her with fury. Makeda was everything Nicaule wanted to be.

Makeda leaned back in her chair and crossed her wrists on her lap. "Good. Then you will not mind answering the riddles I have prepared for you."

"It will be a privilege to engage in games of the mind with so lovely a challenger." He smiled. "Perhaps you will have something to teach me."

"What woman can say to her son, 'Your father is my father; your grandfather, my husband. You are my son, and I am your sister.'"

Solomon took no time to think. "The two daughters of Lot, who lay with their father and bore his sons."

Makeda nodded. "You know the history of your people. Now I shall put another question to you."

"May the Lord grant me wisdom to answer it."

"What are the seven that halt and the nine that enter,

the two that put forth drink and the one who drinks?"

Solomon scratched his white beard. "Seven are the days of menstruation that stop when the nine months of gestation enter. Two breasts put forth milk, and one child drinks it."

"That was too simple, perhaps." She clapped her hands. One of her attendants entered with a group of small children, all the same height and dressed in identical robes, with hair shorn close to the head. "Tell me, wise king. Who among these children are boys and who are girls?"

Solomon thought for a moment, then signaled to his servants standing nearby with trays of food and drink. The men spread nuts and dates on the floor in front of the children. The young ones bent down and collected the treats. Some tied a few to their aprons; others stuffed great amounts securely inside the hem of their gowns.

The king called forth all those who tied the nuts and dates to their aprons. He turned to Makeda. "These are the girls. They are too timid to take more than their share and too bashful to lift their skirts so as to tie the treats to their undergarments."

The queen of Sheba smiled, revealing teeth as white and shimmering as the breakers crashing on the shores of Tyre. "Very clever, my king. You seem to have a great grasp on the spirit of females. Not all men are able to understand women."

Solomon placed a hand on his heart and lowered his head. "My queen, it pleases me to please you even in so small a way." He looked up. "My days are spent among men, but I delight most in the company of women. Women are like the river reed—delicate yet strong, able to bend with the wind and spring back, so buoyant as to be unsinkable. Knowing the female soul is a great privilege."

"Only for the strongest and wisest of men." She signaled to her attendants, and they fell in line for the exit procession. She stood. "My journey has been long. If you will forgive me, I must retire."

He rose and extended a hand. She placed her palm on his.

"Tell me, wise king," Makeda said as they descended the throne together. "In which garden should I walk this eve so I can gaze at the stars?"

Nicaule, who walked behind them, understood the intimation. She had seen it coming. For all Solomon's flaws and despite his advancing age, he had an aura women found irresistible. His wives, Nicaule excepted, clamored for his favor. Women and girls trembled as he touched their heads during public ceremonies. They all were influenced by his power and wealth, but they were spellbound by his raw sensuality. This queen was no different.

"The orchards in front of my palace are most fragrant this time of year," he said. "I beg you come enjoy the beauty of my private grounds. My home is as yours."

He kissed her hand and delivered her to her attendants.

Nicaule stood next to him. "So lovely, this Makeda of Sheba."

"Yes," he said without taking his eyes off the departing queen. "So she is."

That night, Nicaule went down to the orchard and hid in the shadows. She had a perverse curiosity about Solomon and Makeda. She didn't care to spy on her husband. She was more interested in observing Makeda's ways of seduction.

The queen's white gossamer gown gleamed in the starlight as she glided along the cobbled paths, stopping every so often to smell a rose or an apricot blossom. Her golden bracelets, stacked in multitude upon her wrists, chimed in concert with her gentle movements.

As sure as the stars embroidered upon the midnight sky, Solomon came. Silently he walked behind Makeda, like a hunter stalking his prey. He watched her for a long while before taking an alternate path and appearing before her.

The queen started. "My king." She crossed her arms in front of her chest, covering her exposed, bejeweled décolleté. "Forgive my immodest dress. I thought I was alone."

"I did not mean to startle you. I wanted to bring you a gift." He handed her a small pot, the type usually reserved for unguents.

She opened it and sniffed the contents. "What intoxicating scent is this? My nose has never encountered such intense sweetness."

"It is spikenard from the Orient—one of the most precious perfumes known to man. Here in Jerusalem, we use its root in worship and the oil to anoint the bodies of high-born mortals."

Makeda dipped her finger in the pot and drew a drop

of the oil. She applied it behind her ear and made a fragrant trail to her throat. She inhaled. "Exquisite. But why give it to me now?"

"I watched you from my window. You looked like a night-blooming flower floating on a dark sea—so ethereal, almost divine. I thought, such beauty can only be a gift from God, bestowed by the angels themselves. The perfume of the spikenard, reserved for the most high, belongs with you."

"Your words are like music. How can one man be so learned and wise and have a psalmist's way with language?"

"For whatever graces have been given me, I am in debt to the Lord Yahweh, God of the Hebrews. He is my rock and my guide."

She took a step toward him. "I do not know your god, but if he made you, he is a master artist."

He leaned down and kissed her.

"The kisses of your mouth are better than wine," she said.

"Your lips are like honeycombs, and your tongue drips of milk and honey." He kissed her again, this time more passionately. "With one look of your eye, one turn of your neck, you have ravished my heart."

She closed her eyes and sighed. "Rise up, O north wind and blow upon my garden. Rouse the blossoms and awaken the spices, that my beloved, a king among men, may partake of them." She untied her gown and let it drop to the ground, exposing taut, shimmering ebony flesh with buttocks as round as the moon and thighs like bread loaves. The vague scents of myrrh and aloe floated upon the air. If butterflies fluttered at night, they would have alighted on her fingertips. "Whatever you ask of me, O fair king, I shall give it."

Solomon lifted Makeda's naked body into his arms and, with his eyes fixed upon hers, carried her into his lair.

Nicaule's face flushed. She felt the blood rise to her head and throb in her temples. She was suddenly aware of the departure of her youth, of the once-supple skin that now sagged upon her bones, of the cloudy veil that had descended upon her eyes. Time, that wretched thief, had vanished with her beauty and her dreams, and all that remained were the bitter leaves of regret and longing.

Her husband had loved many women, but none had ensnared his heart. Nicaule alone had that privilege, and it gave her power. That night, all that changed.

Makeda's love was different. She genuinely was enthralled by him with an enthusiasm Nicaule never could muster. With Nicaule, Solomon wrestled away love that wasn't freely given and sometimes begged on his knees for it; with Makeda, it flowed as easily as the mountain water after the spring thaw. That, coupled with the young queen's exotic beauty, political power, and untold wealth, was a heady brew that surely warmed his soul like spring melts the snows.

Nicaule felt alone and powerless. She suddenly saw herself dying in the hills of Jerusalem, becoming one with the ochre dust of the land of slaves. Who was the slave now? She fell to her knees and heaved, repulsed by the pathetic shadow she had become.

CHAPTER NINETEEN

During the summer of her stay, Solomon had not once left Makeda's side. Every day they spent long hours walking together in the gardens, conversing about things Nicaule could only imagine, and every night they spent in each other's embrace.

Nicaule had stopped stalking them, for it was too painful to watch two lovers revel in the rapture she so dearly longed for. Many nights she wondered if Solomon would tire of his new consort and call for his beloved lily of the valley. He did not. He had clearly found solace in the bosom of another. Nicaule had expected to feel relieved, even liberated, by his absence; instead, she was consumed by thoughts of self-pity that mounted into an anger she had never known in herself.

It wasn't anger at losing her husband's heart. It was an emotion that had been building since the day she left Tanis: the resentment for being yanked from the arms of her lover and the embrace of her country by a man who claimed to adore her, who promised her the stars, but who didn't have the decency to worship her to the end.

She was grateful for the day of the queen's departure. The entire court had assembled at the edge of the city to see off the Sheban caravan as it launched into a desert voyage that could last several weeks or months, depending on conditions. The camels, dressed in elaborate saddles of leather and wool and decorated with necklaces woven of goat hair, were loaded with gifts from the king of Israel: wine, olives, wheat, spices, honey, and so much Ophirian gold it took a score animals to carry it. Makeda's men, numbering five hundred at least, and ladies-in-waiting, all attired in desert blues from their turbaned heads to their ankles, lined up in front of the city gates, waiting for their queen's command.

As protocol demanded, Nicaule accompanied Solomon to the official sending off of the royal guest. As they stood at the open city gates waiting for Makeda, with entourage in tow, to make her way down from the palace, Nicaule watched her husband's reaction. Though his hair had the hue of the moon, Solomon had a spring in his step. He stood on strong legs without a trace of a slouch, and his chest was puffed like a peacock's, as it had been when she first met him.

His gaze was riveted on Makeda as she walked toward him. His expression was not one of longing or angst over the impending separation, as Nicaule had expected, but rather one of peace. And perhaps a bit of sadness. For the first time in Solomon's life, he would experience the unbearable weight of loss. A part of Nicaule rejoiced at the justice of it.

Makeda, shielded from the summer sun by a silken canopy held up by her attendants, was a vision to behold. She was dressed not to take a long desert journey but to attend a royal feast. A gown of scarlet silk embroidered with golden leaves clung to her curvaceous frame, teasing the imagination. A short mantle of leopard's hide, fastened with a tiger's eye as big as a child's fist, hung over her shoulders. Her hair was pinned high on her head and draped with a transparent spiderweb veil that covered her face like the cool mist of a waterfall.

Nicaule felt the familiar gnawing at her core. She averted her eyes, lest they be blinded by that intolerable beauty.

The queen approached Solomon and took his outstretched hands. "It pains me to say good-bye," she said.

He was silent. Nicaule imagined he was overcome with emotion.

"You have taught me much," Makeda continued. "Your kindness and generosity are unprecedented. Your wisdom knows no bounds."

He bowed. "I cannot take credit for gifts bestowed upon me by God."

"I will not forget the teachings you have shared with me. I will take them to my people, that their hearts may be fortified. And I will go forth a follower of Yahweh, for any god that made you, dear Solomon, is a god worthy of worship."

Nicaule's brow furrowed. Had Solomon, whose faith had faltered so obviously of late, regained the favor of his god? Had he converted Makeda?

"It pleases me to know this," he said. "It is you, O splendid queen, who restored my faith. In you, I have known true amity. I am forever bound to you."

"And I to you."

Nicaule felt bile rise to her throat. She begged the sun god to put an end to the unbearable charade.

"There is one more thing I must ask of you," Solomon said.

"I will do anything."

He signaled to one of his officers. The man approached, presenting a small package wrapped in pristine white linen. Solomon took it from him and unwrapped the linen, exposing a small alabaster box stamped with his royal insignia. "This is the message of which I spoke. I beg you carry it back to your kingdom and keep it safe."

She accepted it. "I will do as you command. I will guard it until he comes to claim it."

What did she mean? Who was *he*? And what was this message? Nicaule felt like a disinherited child, suddenly left on the streets without a crust of bread while the rest of the clan feasted.

Solomon and Makeda touched foreheads. Nicaule thought she saw tears glisten through the queen's silken veil.

"May the Lord accompany you on your journey," Solomon said.

"Will I see you again?"

He stepped back. "The years have mounted, dear Makeda, and I grow old. I do not know how much longer before the angel calls to me."

She placed a hand on her abdomen. "Come what may, the grace of Solomon will be with me forever." She bowed and walked toward the gate.

Solomon and Nicaule watched as Makeda entered her palanquin and was carried into the caravan. The blue riders spurred their camels, and the royal procession was on the move.

Nicaule turned to her husband. "Perhaps now you will come back to me."

His eyes were riveted on the departing caravan. "Do not wait for me, Wife. There is a long journey I must take. I will be gone by morrow."

"A journey? To where? And with whom?"

"I will go alone. I cannot say where."

For the first time in their marriage, he was shutting her out. The insult made her furious. "At your age, such things are folly. I beg you reconsider."

He turned to her. His gaze was distant. "Worry not about me. The Lord will be my anchor and my ballast."

She could no longer hold back. "Look around you, Solomon. Jerusalem is crumbling to dust. Anger is seething among the people. Your enemies are circling you like birds of prey, and you don't even know it. Open your eyes! Your Lord has abandoned you. Or should I say, you have abandoned him?"

He swung the back of his hand as if he would strike her. Though he didn't touch her, Nicaule instinctively stumbled backward and fell on her backside.

Solomon's face was stern and unyielding as he walked

away. She knew it was the last time she would see him.

Humiliated and bristling with rage, she got to her feet and hastened toward her palace.

Desperate to talk to someone, Nicaule entered Irisi's chamber as she took a midday nap. She walked to the writing table where the scribe's instruments were spread about. A reed dipped in ink lay on the wood, black drops splattered around it. A stick of beeswax sat atop a stack of papyrus sheets next to an unlit oil lamp.

Two stones—one flat with an indentation, the other the size and shape of a pomegranate—caught Nicaule's eye. Unsure of their function, she picked up the round stone. Surprisingly, it weighed as much as a summer melon. On its underside were minute copper filings. Irisi must have mixed them into the ink to make it fast. She replaced the stone on its flat counterpart without taking care to be quiet.

Irisi woke at the sound. "My lady," she croaked. "What are you doing here?"

"I'm sorry to wake you. I needed to talk." She walked to Irisi's bed and helped her to her feet.

Irisi had become so frail. Her spine no longer held up her body, and she bent at the waist as she walked. Her limbs, spindly since her youth, were reduced to skin and bone. Despite her physical limitations, however, her eyes still sparkled with curiosity, and her hands were steady as ashlars in the wind.

The two women sat on a rough-hewn wood bench

next to the scribe's table. Nicaule took her friend's hands and began with a sigh. "O dear Irisi, how life has changed. I once was the rose among thorns, the lily of the valley, the song of the dove at dawn. And now I am nothing, a grain of sand in the desert. If not for you, my dear old friend, I would be completely alone. Shoshenq, I fear, has forgotten me. My daughter does not speak to me. And now, with the arrival of that woman" —she spat out the words—"even Solomon has abandoned me."

Irisi smiled. There was kindness in her eyes. "You still are as you have always been: Nicaule Tashere of Egypt, daughter of kings. No matter what life brings, this no one will take away."

Nicaule scoffed. "Old age has turned us into paupers, though it is not material wealth we want. We are poor in beauty and vigor and therefore deprived of society's favor. Once we made men's hearts stop by merely gazing out our windows, and now the only glances we receive are of pity. No one wants an old woman, Irisi. No one cares about us."

"My lady, old age is merely a reflection of the way we lived our lives, of the choices we made when we were younger. Those who have lived righteously have nothing to fear. No one dies alone who has peace in her heart."

Nicaule bristled at the words. Whether by design or by circumstance, she had not known peace. For a fleeting moment, she considered she might have been to blame. Had she accepted her fate then, had she not tried so hard to swim against the current, she might have grown old without despair.

No, she told herself. She could not be condemned for holding on to her dream. Any woman of principle and steadfast soul would have done the same. It was the most noble of endeavors, and anyone who stood as an obstacle to it was the personification of evil.

The thought was like wood in the fire of her hatred for Solomon, the architect of her misfortune. She shook off the unwelcome sentiment by changing the subject. "I envy you, dear friend, for not having known a man's love. Love is like the *khamsin* that stirs the sea, casting everything upon it into turmoil. In the face of such fury, even a boat with good ballast and sound sail is upended. You are blessed not knowing the power of such a storm."

"It may be long ago, but I have known love. When it is true, love is not a tempest but a woolen cloak that keeps out life's chill."

Nicaule's face collapsed into a look of pity. "O Irisi . . . an arranged marriage has little to do with love. It is merely a comfort for the weak." The thought that crossed her mind was wicked, but she voiced it anyway. "Love is when someone chooses you, not when one is chosen for you."

She stood and walked to the table. She regarded the array of objects for a long moment. "I suppose your love for the scribal arts fills that void in you." She touched the droplets of black ink and withdrew her hand in surprise. "This ink is fresh." She snapped her head at Irisi. "I don't recall giving you a message to inscribe."

For a moment, the space between them was silent.

"You did not, my lady," Irisi said.

Nicaule crossed her arms. "Then what have you been doing?"

Irisi sighed. "The king called for me. He wanted to write an intricate message, and there was no one in his court with the skill to do it. I had no choice but to obey."

"A message . . . to whom?"

"I cannot say. I have been sworn."

The image of Solomon handing Makeda the small alabaster box flashed in Nicaule's mind. So that was the answer. Solomon had given the queen of Sheba a message, inscribed by Irisi, to guard "until he comes to claim it." Nicaule found herself outside the circle of trust, cast there not only by her husband but also by her confidante.

Rage bubbled like stew in a cauldron. "Was it a letter of love to that wretched queen? Answer me!"

Irisi put her hands on her ears. Her face twisted into a look of pain. "Please, my lady . . . I cannot say. The king . . ."

Nicaule's heart galloped, and hot blood throbbed in her fingertips. It was the final indignity. "You answer to me, not to Solomon," she shouted. "How can you betray me in this way?"

Irisi steadied herself on the bench and stood. "Hear me now, my lady." Her tone was calm, almost cold. "My oath to Solomon is not a betrayal to you. It is a matter of honor."

"You consider keeping a secret from your mistress honorable?" She spoke behind clenched teeth. "How little you know about honor."

Irisi stood taller. "No. It is not I who does know not

honor. It is you. Asking me to betray one's confidence is the highest offense. How can you speak of honor after all the schemes you have concocted to ruin one man in a desperate bid for the heart of another?"

"Everything I've done, I've done for Egypt."

The scribe shook her head. "No. All your spying and conniving have been for personal gain."

Nicaule leaned down and shouted into Irisi's face. "May I remind you you have been an accomplice? By writing my missives to Tanis, you have helped betray the secrets of Solomon's kingdom and have helped stage a rebellion against him."

"It is a shame I will take to my grave." Irisi cast a look of pity upon her mistress. "You once were a noble lady of unspeakable beauty and grace . . . a princess destined for greatness. You have degraded into something I don't even recognize."

"Silence!"

Irisi was relentless. "Neither Solomon nor this foreign land on which we have been cast has stripped you of your dignity. With your own hands you have destroyed your life. You have been so consumed with revenge and self-pity that your heart has rotted like a pomegranate fallen from its tree."

Nicaule clenched her fists to steady her shaking hands. Irisi's words sounded distorted, and her face was that of a stranger.

"For years I have watched from afar, my lady," the scribe continued, "and the time has come for me to speak the truth. It is not only your own life you have tainted but also Solomon's. You have poisoned his mind with your potent brew of deception. With glee have you watched him decline. What wrong could be greater?" She pursed her lips and shook her head.

Nicaule's own breath, shallow and shaky, filled her ears. "How could you take up the cause of Solomon, after all I have given you? Where does your loyalty really lie?"

"I can no longer defend you," she whispered. "I will not."

Nicaule glanced at the objects on the table. She picked up the grinding stone and with a primal cry swung it toward Irisi's head. Nicaule heard a crushing sound as the stone landed on the scribe's temple.

Irisi crumpled onto the floor. Blood gushed from her head like water from a spring, forming a crimson pool that grew wider and wider. Her eyes were bulging as she drew her last, labored breaths.

Nicaule dropped the stone and lifted her hands to her mouth, stifling a scream. She was immobilized as she watched the woman who had been her lifelong friend and confidante expire.

What had she done?

Irisi clawed at Nicaule's gown with bloodied hands, leaving a trail of bright red strokes on the white linen. Then her hands went limp and dropped to the stone floor, and she stopped breathing. Her eyes were still open, frozen in a caustic stare, convicting her executioner.

Nicaule looked about her. The walls seemed to be moving toward her, closing her in. She began to hyperventilate. She had to get out.

She threw the door open, not bothering to close it behind her, and ran. High in the sky, the sun assaulted her eyes so violently that tears streamed down her face. The kohl she used to enhance her beauty now stung her eyes. She could hardly see.

She had no destination. She ran to escape the scene of her crime—and her conscience. She stumbled as she made her way down the hillside a little too fast and tumbled twice before regaining her footing. She stopped and, shielding her sore eyes, surveyed her surroundings. She was in the Kidron Valley. Farmers stopped what they were doing and looked at her, bewildered. She looked down and realized they were staring at her bloodied clothes.

"Back to work!" she barked at them in Hebrew and continued down the hillside until she could run no more.

Out of breath, she collapsed by the Gihon Spring. She splashed the cool water on her face and bosom, attempting to cleanse herself of what had just happened. But there was not enough water in Gihon, nor all of Siloam, to wash away her guilt.

She regarded her reflection on the spring. An old woman with wet clumps of black hair clinging to her face and streaks of kohl running down her cheeks stared back at her. She cried with loud, violent sobs.

What had she become? Nicaule Tashere, the daughter and wife of kings whose destiny was brighter than the evening star, died in that instant. Perhaps she had died long before. The recognition of her abomination made her bend at the waist and expel the contents of her stomach until there was nothing but bitter bile.

Thoughts buzzed by without alighting, taunting her and driving her mad. She turned her eyes to the sun, searching for solace from Amun-Ra, king of all deities and keeper of the universe. The midday sun seared her cheeks with the red heat of a furnace, yet it could not evanesce her tears.

She cried out to him: "Shoshenq!" It was more a screech than a yell. Desperation had crept into her voice and strangled it. She called his name again and again until her throat felt so dry that the words would no longer issue forth.

He was not coming. A score and thirteen years had passed since he carried her to his bed and promised her that one day she would be his queen. She had devoted her life to being worthy of that promise: she'd categorically rejected her husband and denounced her new home, keeping her heart pure for the day he would come for her. But the days became years, and the dream grew ever distant.

She could not point to the exact moment bitterness seeped into her soul, nor when it morphed into venom. But she would forever be haunted by the memory of this day: on the banks of Jerusalem's most precious spring, with her hands stained with blood she had drawn, she let hope slip from her grasp and vanish like a leaf carried by the current into the dark heart of the sea.

She no longer wanted Shoshenq to come. Perhaps it was better that her lover remembered her as a ravishing young woman with a heart of fire. Even if he were to ride into Jerusalem now, what he would find would not reward his journey.

She collapsed onto the ground, feeling the warm soil against her cheek. Her tears watered the earth, becoming one with this strange land she could never claim as her own, the one that brought her to the brink of madness. Her gaze wandered across the expanse of red soil and stopped on a graveyard beyond the riverbank. Fresh sobs came as she considered her own mortality.

"O Osiris, lord of the afterlife, do not let your daughter die here." Her words were warped by emotion as she thought of her corpse being committed to the earth rather than embalmed and mummified. "Do not allow tainted soil to cover these bones."

If not for her fear of being buried without proper provisions, she would have drowned herself that day in the Israelites' spring of life. But she was doomed to live and wait for salvation that might never come.

CHAPTER TWENTY

A breeze hissed across the valley, stirring the folds of Basemath's *halub* as she peered through the flaps of her prison tent. Somewhere near, a bulbul trilled in anticipation of the light that would soon crack open the darkness. She drew her arms to her chest to discourage the lingering chill of that awful night.

She closed the flaps and retreated inside. Her pulse pounded in her gut as she awaited Jeroboam's arrival. She reminded herself that the choice was hers, that she was the maker of her own fate.

What would her father do? She ran her fingers over the chain hanging from her neck, and the memories came racing back. She pulled on the chain until the object dangling from it surfaced from beneath her *halub*.

It was the last thing Solomon had given to her. Just days after he entrusted his daughter with his most precious possession, the ring that held the ultimate secret, the king had died. She touched the four stones embedded in a circle of iron on the ring's crown. They symbolized the elements—ruby for fire, aquamarine for water, tiger's eye for earth, and diamond for wind—and beguiled the observer, obscuring the ring's true purpose.

It was what lay beneath the stones that was worth hiding.

Basemath ran her finger across the edge of the crown, searching for the tiny indentation that allowed the gem-encrusted top to open and, lifting it, revealed the ring's golden heart. A layer of pure gold, brilliant even in the scant light of her prison, was inscribed with a five-pointed star.

If her father had not revealed the significance of the symbol that day in the desert, she never would have known. It seemed innocent enough, yet it held the mystery of the ages. She cupped both hands around the ring and closed her eyes.

Solomon had been sitting beneath the shade of a balsam tree, dressed in rags, when Basemath went to him in the wilderness of Judea. He had called for her. A messenger had arrived on horseback at her home in Shechem to summon her in accordance with the king's wishes, and she'd gladly followed. There was nothing she would deny her father.

When she was told she was to meet Solomon in the Judean desert, she was a little alarmed. It was out of character for him to be away from the city he had so painstakingly built. It had been forty days since his departure from Jerusalem, and without its leader, the city was on the verge of chaos.

Basemath had passed through the holy city on her way to the wilderness, out of duty to her mother, who she'd heard was unwell. Before her eyes, one man toppled another and punched him unconscious so he could rip the purse tied to his waist sash. She was appalled at the heinous act, but more so at the indifference of passersby. As she dismounted her horse and went to the victim's aid, wrapping her head veil around his wounds to stem the bleeding, she called for someone to stop the thief, but no one bothered. People scurried through the alleys, pretending not to hear.

It was a small incident, but it was telling. Years ago, when Israelites cared for each other as they did for themselves, such apathy was unheard of. There was a wind change in Jerusalem, and soon it would extend to all of Israel. She could feel it.

There was a change in her father, too. Though she lived in the north and did not see him every day, she could not ignore the gossip: the discontent of certain tribes over taxation, the double standard of religious tolerance for the king's foreign wives, his prolonged absences from state affairs so he could tend to his romantic garden.

Like dogs smelling fear, when the people sensed a weakening in their leader or his regime, they let themselves slip, then slide brazenly into moral oblivion. It had been that way throughout history.

In the desert, Basemath tethered her horse and approached Solomon, her fears heightened. She had never seen her father, Israel's most glorified king, so forlorn. His eyes were tired and bloodshot, his lips cracked from the late-summer sun. Saffron-colored sand coated the hair on his head and face. His feet, bound in worn sandals and peering beneath his faded gray *halub*, were covered with open, weeping sores. It looked as though he'd been walking for weeks.

She stood before him, her gown billowing in the breeze. "Father?"

He stretched out a hand, an invitation to sit beside him. "My dear daughter, how good of you to come."

"How could I not?" She inhaled the dry air laced with the sharp scent of balsam as she sat on the dusty ground. "Tell me, Father . . . why do you come here, in this hostile land of rocks and wild beasts, alone and dressed like a pauper?"

A puff of wind blew Solomon's snow-white hair, unwashed and unruly, away from his face. He squinted toward the horizon. The corners of his eyes were deeply lined, betraying the old age that had overtaken him. "One generation passes away, another generation comes, but the earth is forever. Everything is a cycle, a manifestation of God's will."

He pointed to a stand of spindly bushes in the distance. "Behold the salt cedar. Even in a barren land it flourishes, blossoming every spring and painting the wilderness in the hues of the rising sun. Then winter's frost comes and robs it of its leaves so that only branches remain, twisted fingers clawing at the sky, begging for mercy from the cold.

"No matter how long and hard the winter, the salt cedar will bloom again. No snow nor fire nor an angry man's axe can drive it from this land, for its roots run deep, and its tender shoots will, in time, break through the earth and reclaim what is rightfully theirs."

He drew a deep breath and shifted his gaze to the sky. Basemath could see his heart was heavy, and she let him talk. "I was king over Israel in Jerusalem. The Lord granted me more wisdom than he did any other man who walked upon the fertile ground of this land that was given to our forefathers. I knew the way of all things as they were, as they are, as they will be."

He shook his head. "But vanity got the better of me. I allowed my heart to know madness and folly, that I might increase my knowledge and train my spirit. I partook freely of wine and gave myself unto scores of women, for that was my portion for my labors. I built great fortresses and houses and a temple to the Lord, planted gardens and vineyards, gathered to me silver and gold. No joy did I withhold from my heart. Yet for all I have known and all I leave behind for those who come after me, I depart the Earth an impoverished man."

Basemath could not hold her tongue. "You are the greatest king who ever reigned in the lower heavens. The Lord has given you every privilege and every good thing under the sun. How can you talk this way now, in the sunset of your life, when you should feel gratitude and joy?"

"I have faltered before the Lord, my daughter. I do not deserve his mercy. Yet it is not I but the descendants of my house who will be punished." He sighed. "I have seen the future. I know what will come to pass. All that I have built and all the riches I have gathered shall wither like the salt cedars in winter. Jerusalem's enemies are at her gates."

Her lower lip trembled. "Do not talk like this, Father."

"It is true. My son Rehoboam will see it in his lifetime. His reign will be shaken like the earth in a violent quake. He will pay for my trespasses, as I paid for my father's. All the history of men is a circle." He took her hand, releasing an object into it. "This must go to one who is pure of heart and spirit. You, and you alone, are worthy of it, my daughter. All others have failed in the eyes of the Lord."

She opened her hand and saw the king's ring. She looked up at him with misty eyes. "What will you have me do with it?"

"Keep it safe. Do not let it fall into the hands of the wicked. Let it be possessed only by the worthy, that its secret may not be lost through the ages."

"I do not understand. What secret?"

He reached for the ring in her hand and lifted the crown by inserting a fingernail into an indentation she had not noticed. The golden circle within shimmered in the afternoon sun.

"This symbol is not as it appears," he said, indicating the five-pointed star etched into the gold. "My father came to my dreams one night and revealed the mystery of the ring forged by divine hands: that which is five really is one. The five edges of the star unfold in a straight line, exposing the measuring unit for building the house of the Lord exactly as he commanded. It is not gold nor jewels but this that makes the temple sacred. Any other temple, however opulent, is but an artifice."

He replaced the crown and closed her hand around

the ring. "This must survive at any pain. Promise me, Basemath."

"I promise, Father." Her words were choked with emotion.

A trembling sigh left his throat. "I fear the day will come when my heirs will see the Lord's house destroyed by Jerusalem's enemies. On that day the Lord will abandon our people and cast darkness upon their lands. All will be lost until the righteous rise up again and glorify his name.

"I cannot prevent the Lord's wrath, for it is upon us; I can only plan for the day the temple may be rebuilt. Listen carefully, my daughter. The secret of the ring must be brought together with the plans given to me by my father and drawn by the angels themselves."

A recollection from early childhood flashed in Basemath's mind: her father, bent over a table where a pile of scrolls lay, studying them by the light of an oil lamp. She had not seen those scrolls since. "Where are these drawings? I shall defend them as I do this ring."

"No. It is too much to ask of you to carry both burdens. The plans will be hidden here"—he waved a hand toward the arid wasteland of caves and rock formations—"in the desert of Judea. I have made provisions with Benaiah and his men to inter this most precious of treasures."

"And who will know of their hiding place?"

"There is a riddle that can be deciphered only by one of pure heart. I have sent it away with Makeda, Queen of Sheba. She will safeguard it in her kingdom until my rightful heir comes along to claim it."

"Rehoboam?"

He shook his head. "When the earth shall reclaim my body, my son will be king—but he will never be the leader I intended him to be. An heir yet unborn to the house of Solomon will give Israel the peace that I could not."

She could no longer contain the sadness that welled behind her eyes.

"Do not weep, my daughter," the king said. "I have spent many years in darkness, but now I see the sun. Truly the light is sweet and pleasant for the eyes to behold. My redeemer's face is there, beyond the clouds, calling me to him. I can hear the lyre of the archangel. The time draws nigh for the final journey.

"But death is not bitter compared to the woman whose heart is snares and nets; her hands are ropes that bind with insolence, trapping moral men and feasting upon them in her lair of iniquity. Her sweet unguents are poison, her tears flesh-eating acid."

Solomon dropped his head into his hands. His shoulders quaked.

Basemath placed a gentle hand upon her father's back. She could feel the hard edges of his bones beneath the linen tunic. The forty days in the desert had taken their toll. "You speak of my mother."

He was silent for a long moment before turning his gaze to her. "The Lord said, 'Honor your father and mother.' When I am gone, stand by your mother in spite of her flaws."

She lowered her head. "Yes, my lord."

He took up both of her hands. "When the silver thread is broken and the golden bowl shattered, when the bitter almond tree flourishes, when the birds cease to sing and there is no more music, when the doors are shuttered and only fear and madness dwell in the streets, when the strong men's knees buckle and the maidens' beauty withers, then remember the words of the wise: remove sorrow from your heart, and cast away evil from your flesh, for the dust shall return to the earth and the spirit to its maker. Fear God and keep his commandments, for that is the whole duty of man." A trace of a smile crossed his lips. "Now go, and let me be."

She did as he asked. It was the last time she saw her father alive.

Basemath was startled by voices outside her tent. She quickly slipped the ring back into her tunic, letting it rest next to her racing heart.

CHAPTER TWENTY-ONE

"My lady!" The banging on her chamber door woke Nicaule with a violent start. "Rise now! You are summoned by order of the king."

She sat up and gazed out the window. It was still dark outside. What did Rehoboam want with her in the middle of the night?

The knocks came again, and the door shook.

"Fetch my handmaiden," she called to the unidentified man on the other side.

"There is no time for it. You must dress quickly. It is an urgent matter."

"I refuse to—"

"I have orders to use force if need be." The door rattled.

"Barbarians," she muttered under her tongue. She swung her legs around to the side of the bed and stood with some effort. Age had settled in her bones, preventing her from doing anything quickly. She called to the guard: "Stay out, cursed soul. I am coming."

She slipped out of her nightgown and felt for her clothes in the dark. She stepped into the tunic she wore the day prior—an ample pleated white linen garment that was more comfortable than striking. She'd long since stopped dressing to please the eye. She cinched her waist with a long fringed sash and put on her wig, smoothing the hair with her fingers. She took up her box of kohl and streaked some of the black paste across her eyelids in a blind attempt at beauty.

The door rattled again, then was flung open. Startled, she let the box crash to the floor. The king's messenger, a gangly youth scarcely older than her grandchildren, stood in the doorway.

"Have you no decency, boy?"

"I am carrying out orders. Now make haste."

She huffed and walked out, brushing him aside as she strode through the door.

In the throne room, King Rehoboam sat on the edge of the seat of judgment, twisting his short black beard in the way he always did when he was nervous. Three of his advisors stood around him; one of them was Ahimaaz, Nicaule's son-in-law. Rehoboam saw her standing by the curtain at the entranceway and waved her in.

She approached and stood before him, not bothering to bow. "The rooster has not yet crowed, yet you call for me. What is the meaning of this?"

"Show some respect, woman. You are addressing your king."

She raised an eyebrow. She did not consider Solomon's son, a man so weak he could scarcely use the privy without consulting his council, her king. Word had it his rule was being challenged by Jeroboam, who'd recently come back to Israel after years hiding in Egypt.

Jeroboam, her old accomplice. Years ago, as Solomon's power was fading, she had helped the dissenter plot his rise to the throne. After their scheme was foiled and Jeroboam was driven to Egypt, she'd heard nothing more of him. Even now that he was returned to his homeland and ready to execute his plan anew, he had not sought her counsel or kept her informed. He no longer needed her, so he'd discarded her—like all the others.

"I do not take my orders from lame rulers," she said, a mite too haughtily.

Rehoboam stood. "Curse your defiance!"

Ahimaaz raised a hand in front of the king. "My lord, remember why we are here."

Rehoboam sat back down, eyeing her sternly. He gestured to Ahimaaz.

"My lady Nicaule, wife of the mighty Solomon and mother of my bride, I have come as a fugitive to warn Jerusalem of its impending ruin," the general said.

"Fugitive? From whom do you run?"

"Have you not heard? Are you oblivious to what has been unfolding around you?"

"No one talks to an old woman, Ahimaaz." She narrowed her eyes. "Not even her family."

He ignored the dig. "Before I enlighten you as to what

is coming, it is important you understand the full scope of our predicament." He turned to Rehoboam. "Permission to continue, my lord?"

Rehoboam looked away and waved to Ahimaaz to carry on. The king wasn't much of an orator and often let others talk for him. Nicaule had watched him grow from a shy youth into an awkward adult and knew his lack of confidence, and the arrogance with which he compensated, would one day be his undoing.

"Old enemies, once departed, have returned to haunt Israel," Ahimaaz said. "Jeroboam the Ephraimite has been brought out of Egypt by the tribal leaders of the North. He lays claim to this throne."

She looked at Rehoboam. The king shifted in his chair, avoiding her eyes.

Ahimaaz continued. "Jeroboam demands of the king to lighten the yoke of the people. Long have they suffered, he says. Long have they been taxed unjustly. He does not share your husband's vision of progress, of a dominant world power in the making."

"And what says the king?" Nicaule folded her arms across her chest.

Rehoboam snapped his head toward her. "This was my reply to Jeroboam and his followers: 'Whereas my father burdened you with a yoke, I shall add to it; where he punished you with whips, I shall punish you with scorpions.'" He stood, waving a fist. "No one challenges my rule or the right of the house of David to command this throne."

She found his display comical. He did not have the

wisdom or the charisma of his father and, therefore, had no right to make such proclamations. Where he should have employed diplomacy, he used brute force: the sure sign of the powerless.

"The North is in rebellion against the crown," said Ahimaaz. "The king has tried to appease the people, but they have grown wild. Just this winter they stoned to death Adoram, the captain of the forced labor. They want to raise Jeroboam to the throne and divide the kingdom."

"It sounds like the makings of war," she said.

Ahimaaz nodded. "Jeroboam is staging a war we cannot fight. He has called to him the Egyptian army. Five thousand chariots and tens of thousands of men have marched into Megiddo and the Jezreel Valley, razing villages and towns along the way. We have no defense against that kind of militia."

The pit of her stomach tingled. She had not felt the stir of anticipation in a long time. "Who leads this army?"

"The pharaoh Shoshenq. He rides with his garrison to Jerusalem as we speak."

Her heart thrashed like a demon. The rush of blood made her lightheaded. Was Israel's darkest hour the moment of her redemption? After so many years, would Shoshenq come for her? Would she be delivered from the burden of her captivity now, at the twilight of life?

"The pharaoh means to destroy the holy city," Ahimaaz continued. "We must protect it at all costs."

"You are up against a formidable foe. What makes you think you can win?"

"We cannot win; we are outnumbered. We require your assistance."

She scoffed. "What do I know about such things? I am merely a woman."

"A woman, yes. But the pharaoh owes a debt to you—or rather, to your father. It was Psusennes who appointed him king."

"You think I can stop a king from taking what he wants? Are you mad?"

"If you are clever with your tongue, he will listen to you. You must convince him to leave Jerusalem standing. It is the spiritual heart of our people." Ahimaaz took a step toward her. "Solomon was good to you. Not one moment did he not adore you. Your actions on this day can repay his kindness"—he dropped his voice to a near whisper—"and deliver you from what haunts you."

"Kindness?" She let out a short burst of laughter. "You want me to act charitably toward the man who imprisoned me, who tore me from my homeland against my will? I owe nothing to Solomon"—with a vile look she turned to Rehoboam—"or his spawn."

"Then do it for Basemath. She and Ana have been taken captive by Jeroboam and the Egyptian army. If your daughter learns you let the heathen king destroy her beloved city and the temple of the God she cherishes, she will not forgive you for all your days . . . if she even survives to meet your gaze again."

A foot soldier flung open the door of the throne room. All heads turned toward him. Flushed and panting, he said, "Forgive my intrusion, my lord. The Egyptians are here. The farmlands at Kidron have been set ablaze."

Rehoboam stood. "Sound the horn. Our men have been armed. They are ready to fight."

"Yes, my lord." The soldier bowed and took his leave.

The king addressed his men. "Let us prepare for battle. We will defend Jerusalem with the courage and resolve of our fathers." He turned to Nicaule. "If there is any good left in you, you will do this thing."

Rehoboam stepped down from his throne platform and, followed by his advisors, hurried out of the room.

A thick puff of gray smoke billowed skyward as the houses on the foot of the eastern hill blazed. The Egyptians' rapacious flames, like streams of molten copper against the dark sky, consumed with a vengeance. To the west, the Kidron Valley was burning, part of it already reduced to cinders. In the infernal glow, the damage was apparent. Where once were fecund orchards now stood smoldering rows of charred tree stumps, their leafless branches like gnarled hands begging the heavens for mercy. The air smelled of scorched earth.

From Nicaule's vantage point in the palace arcade, everything seemed to unfold in slow motion, like images from a dream. The torches hanging from the palace walls cast a trembling golden light on the scene. She watched Rehoboam's troops come and go, ants marching to their doom. With their primitive weapons—slingshots and sickle swords—and soft constitutions resulting from decades of not being called to fight, they did not stand a chance against Shoshenq's finely tuned killing machine.

A column of white-robed men, heads bowed toward the earth and palms together in prayer, made its way up the hill toward the high place. Though she could not hear over the din of horses' hooves and men's cries, she imagined the Levites were chanting psalms of salvation. What fools, she thought: it was too late to beg. The fate of Jerusalem had been decided years ago, when Ahijah the Shilonite rent his garment before Jeroboam, delivering the Hebrew god's will.

Too restless to wait, Nicaule stepped out onto the courtyard and passed through the palace gate, making her way toward the city. She was the only civilian on the streets that night; all the inhabitants of the holy city had crouched in their homes. She kept to the edge of the cobbled path lest she be trampled by the horsemen and foot soldiers heading to battle.

She had no clear destination. She knew only that Shoshenq was somewhere in the midst of the chaos, perhaps looking for her. The thought of facing her lover both bolstered and terrified her. She wasn't the woman she once was—her beauty and her charms had long departed, leaving behind an empty shell of misery and pain. Would he still love her?

She sought his visage in the torchlight, but the smoke stung her eyes. She stopped to gather herself, and her lungs filled with the insidious vapors. The cries of men were carried downwind, harbingers of the slaughter.

A horseman cantered toward her. Through her hazy vision she could not make out his identity but recognized the pointed helmet that marked him as an Israelite. She ran in the opposite direction, into the curtain of smoke that grew ever thicker.

He caught up with her in an instant and blocked her path. She looked up and met her son-in-law's eyes.

"We are out of time," Ahimaaz cried over the uproar. "You must come with me." He bent down and offered her a hand.

She let him lift her to the back of the saddle and held on to his waist as he spurred his chestnut mare to a gallop.

He shouted over his shoulder. "The pharaoh and his men are at the temple gates. He has called for a meeting with the king."

Anxiety gnawed at Nicaule's gut. She did not think of the confrontation that could tear Jerusalem apart; she considered only her own fate. In mere moments, it would all come to pass as the gods willed it.

Squat stone houses, ashen in the moonlight, streaked past as they rode to the top of Mount Moriah. The horse's hooves pounding the ground matched the cadence of her own heartbeat. A deep breath admitted the stench of smoke mixed with dust, and she longed for the scent of blue lotus and wet earth. She closed her eyes and did not reopen them until Ahimaaz halted his horse.

He dismounted and helped her down. At the temple gates, a row of Levites stood still as columns, guards to the spiritual fortress. She could hear the faint sound of their soft, monotone chant. In front of them stood a swarm of Egyptians with spears at the ready. They waited for their pharaoh's command.

"King Rehoboam is inside," Ahimaaz said. "Follow me."

She followed him through the gates, looking over her shoulder at her gathered countrymen. She thought she saw Shoshenq's golden chariot, but her eyes cheated her in the dark.

Rebohoam stood at the temple forecourt, surrounded by his mighty men. Metal scale armor covered his chest, and a *khopesh* hung from his waist sash. His face was pinched, his brow heavy with worry.

"The time has come to lift the veil," he told her. "Where does your allegiance lie?"

She raised her head. "I am loyal to my country. Whatever the pharaoh asks of me, I will do."

"So be it, then." The king motioned, and two soldiers approached Nicaule. One pushed her to her knees, and the other bound her hands with jute rope.

"What are you doing?" she shouted, trying to break free of their grip. "I am a free woman!" She turned to her son-in-law. "You drove me to the den of lions. Shame be on you."

"There is no shame, nor civility, in war," Ahimaaz said. "You have made your choice; now we must do what is best for our people."

"I am not a sack of grain to be bargained with. I demand you release me."

"You will not be harmed so long as you cooperate.

Let us hope for a speedy end to this atrocity."

A trumpet sounded. Egyptian officers holding spears and shields marched through the gate two by two until they numbered twelve. The pharaoh walked in behind them, followed by another dozen soldiers. With Shoshenq in the middle, they arranged themselves in a semicircle in front of the Israelites.

She looked up at him. Her lower lip trembled as he met her gaze. He had changed so little in the forty years since she left Tanis. His physique was still as solid as fired iron, his eyes fierce, and his skin taut but for a few creases on his forehead and around his mouth. Ashamed for the way she had aged, she averted her eyes and sobbed softly.

Rehoboam stepped forward, and Shoshenq did the same until they stood no more than a cubit apart.

The Egyptian king spoke first. "Rehoboam, king of the Hebrews, I come in peace to strike a deal with you."

"It seems to me you have claimed all you want," Rehoboam said. "What remains that I can give you?"

Shoshenq pointed up to the temple. "What is inside that house belongs to Egypt."

"All that is there belongs to the Lord, God of Israel. Every object has been consecrated and dedicated to him. I call upon your moral decency: take our livestock; take our homes. But stay away from our most sacred place."

The pharaoh bared his teeth. "I do not care about your sacred place or your greedy god who must be appeased with vast quantities of gold." He banged on his breastplate. "Our gold. Every bit of it belongs to my people. And I mean to take it back."

Rehoboam twisted the ends his beard. "You said you have come to strike a deal. What exchange would satisfy you?"

Nicaule watched Shoshenq's reaction. The pharaoh was absolutely still, staring into his enemy's eyes as if to weaken him. He did not cast a glance in her direction.

"As we stand here, my ally, Jeroboam, son of Nebat, is being crowned king of the ten tribes of Israel. He will make his palace in Shechem and will rule the Israelites with the guidance of Egypt." His biceps rippled as he crossed his arms. "The tribes of Judah and Benjamin have been less cooperative. They seem to be loyal to you. But my men have weakened them. They have killed their sons and raped their women, burned their homes and taken their horses. It will not be long before they turn from their leader"—he smirked—"the one who is not strong enough to protect them from their adversaries."

Rehoboam spoke through clenched teeth. "What is it you want, Shoshenq of the Ma?"

Shoshenq drew his sword and ran his fingertip across the edge. "Two things. All the gold from the house of your god"—he nodded toward Nicaule—"and the woman you hold prisoner."

Her heart leapt. He had come for her, after all. The elaborate campaign, the atrocities and demands, all were ruses to mask what he really wanted: the woman who had seized his heart and held it captive all those years. She was desperate to run to him but could not for her bonds.

Rehoboam looked over his shoulder at Nicaule, then

back at his rival. "If I do this . . . what will I receive in exchange?"

"What remains of your kingdom. You will continue to reign over Benjamin and Judah in this new, divided Israel."

"And if I do not meet your demands?"

"My honor commands that I fight you to the death. We shall draw swords, and he who remains alive shall keep the spoils."

"I require a moment to speak with my council," Rehoboam said. Shoshenq nodded, and the king retreated to a huddle of men.

Nicaule did not shift her gaze from him. He rewarded her with a glance and a half smile, then looked straight ahead. Whatever Rehoboam's decision, she was certain she would soon be in Shoshenq's arms. Even if the Hebrew king chose to fight, he could not win against a man bred for war. Shoshenq's ability with the sword and his battle instinct were legendary in all of Egypt and across the deserts of Libya. He had skewered opponents far worthier than Solomon's fainthearted son.

Rehoboam stepped out of the circle and walked toward the pharaoh. "Take the gold and the woman, and leave me my crown."

Nicaule was not at all surprised. She expected no more of the weakling who reigned in Jerusalem. A king who chose not to fight for his honor or on the moral ground of his faith: it was a spectacle worse than a massacre.

Rehoboam motioned toward her. "Release her."

Behind her, hands cut her jute bonds. She stood on

shaky legs and regarded the man for whom she had waited so long. There was no tenderness in Shoshenq's eyes, only the hard glare of a warrior. She searched her depths for the emotion she had expected to feel at that moment, but it would not come. Time had robbed her of even this.

She went to him. They stood in silence before each other for a long moment. "You came for me. After so many years, I thought—"

"The men of the Ma do not forget their promises," he said. "Where is my son?"

She lowered her gaze. She felt ashamed for the lie she had told in a moment of weakness and never retracted. Irisi's prophetic words, spoken as she committed the invention to a scroll of papyrus, floated to the forefront of Nicaule's consciousness: *You cannot escape your fate, my lady. Whatever it is, it will hunt you and draw level to you.* Even if it meant ruin, there was nothing to do but tell the truth. "There was never a son. A daughter was born unto me of your seed."

"You have deceived me." His voice thundered like stones tumbling in a quake.

"Do not judge me, my lord. I wanted only to hasten our reunion. If you had known the child born of our love was a girl, I feared you would not come."

"Did you not trust in my integrity? Did you not know I would keep my promise regardless of circumstances?" His face was tight, his kohl-rimmed eyes narrow, his fists clenched. She thought he might strike her.

"Never have I questioned you, my lord; you must

believe that." A knot rose to Nicaule's throat, causing her voice to shake. "Our daughter's name is Basemath. She is in the North, taken prisoner by your men and held in Jeroboam's custody. I fear for her fate. She is a spirited one, like her father."

He called to a soldier from his personal guard and had a conference in private. The soldier nodded and mounted his horse. He galloped down the mountain, leaving behind a cloud of red dust.

Shoshenq turned to Nicaule. "Go into my chariot. We ride for the Jezreel Valley."

She took his hands in hers and bowed. "Thank you, my lord."

"I am a man of my word. I will take you and my child back to Tanis. But your trickery I cannot forgive." He pulled his hands away.

His words stung like a strike across her face. She had been granted her wish to return to her homeland, but without his favor it was a meaningless victory. She searched his raven eyes for any trace of the lover she knew. "What will become of us?"

"There is no returning to the past."

Her body tensed, and her breath was trapped inside her lungs. "Do not speak such things. I have been a wife to you, if not in flesh, in spirit. I have grown old waiting, not once wavering in my devotion." Her words were not getting through. His unyielding expression made her feel like a beggar.

His gaze traveled down her body, and she felt the heat

of his judgment. "You have acted dishonorably. The code of my ancestors requires me to exact retribution."

She swallowed hard. There was nothing left to say in her defense. Whatever he dealt, she would have to accept.

His words came down like an iron hammer. "You will live in the royal court as a servant to my first wife."

She lowered her head and wept. A high-born Egyptian ministering to the whims of a Meshwesh tribeswoman: it was the ultimate indignity. She imagined tending to the woman who shared Shoshenq's bed—drawing her perfumed baths, stuffing her into dresses for feasts and state visits, applying unguents to her russet skin—and wanted to fall upon his sword. What purpose would there be to such a life?

Perhaps it was the punishment she deserved. She had brought this upon herself. All the lies and deception, executed in the name of loyalty to her country but really done for the favor of a man, had trapped her in a fiery circle of betrayal whose flames she had lit and now could not escape.

Images of Solomon, serene-faced and young, flashed in her mind. He had loved her unto his death, yet she rewarded his affection with spite, selling his secrets to his enemies at the cost of her own soul. All the while, she was a pawn in a man's game and could not see it. At that moment, when the curtain at last was lifted, she cursed the hubris that had blinded her to the truth in all its ugliness: Shoshenq desired her when he was young and naïve. As time had passed and power shifted, she'd become more useful to him as a spy than a lover.

Shoshenq's voice boomed as he addressed his men. "Pillage the temple of Solomon. Leave no gold unclaimed."

"What of the city, my lord?" one soldier asked.

Shoshenq gazed at the temple, then at the settlement tumbling down the hillside. "Leave it be." He turned to Rehoboam. "Keep your kingdom." With a sneer, he added, "Such as it is."

With swift steps he walked to the chariot. Nicaule followed without hastening her stride. As the fragile pewter light broke through a gathering of clouds, she gazed at the smoldering ruins of Solomon's city and felt the claws of regret pierce the armor of her heart. She knew it as surely as the breeze stirred from the east: the gods demanded her atonement.

CHAPTER TWENTY-TWO

Jezreel Valley

The rustling of fabric had never sounded so profane than at the moment Jeroboam entered the tent of captivity.

Basemath stood at the far edge with her arms wrapped around her, gritting her teeth. Her gaze was nailed on his as he approached with slow, arrogant steps.

He stopped a few palms' width away from her. "The night is long, yet morrow comes too swiftly for the hunted."

She stared at him with hard eyes.

"Day breaks, and your judgment is upon you. What is your decision?"

She had made up her mind but was not ready to utter the words. "I want to see my daughter."

"She may be otherwise engaged." He smirked. "Passing by the officer's tent last night, I could hear her cries, like a dog howling at the moon."

Searing blood filled Basemath's face. Through clenched teeth she said, "You lie."

He shook his head. "I'm afraid not."

With a primal yell she lunged at him, striking him with her fists.

He grabbed her wrists and bore down on them until she shrieked with pain. He hurled her onto the ground.

She landed hard on her side. At that moment she felt defeated, as if all hope had left her. She wanted to die.

Trembling, she sat up. "Tell me, Jeroboam." She spat out the words. "How does it feel to forsake your people and sell your soul to the enemy?"

He tossed his head back and laughed loudly. "You dare ask me this? The only one who forsook his people, Princess, was your father. He did not heed their cries against oppression but tightened their yoke instead. I am fighting for the tribes of Israel in the name of God, who has appointed me. The alliance with Egypt is nothing but a means to an end. Of all people, you, who were born of such an alliance, should understand this. But I suppose you are too taken with your childish idealism and your blind loyalty to the house of David, even though it is woefully bereft of glory."

"You know nothing of loyalty, traitor."

"Enough!" he barked. "I am here to get your decision, nothing more. What will you have—exile . . . or death?"

The sound of horses' hooves came from the distance. It grew loud and steady, like a drumbeat. Jeroboam parted the tent flap and peered toward the commotion.

"The pharaoh's horsemen." He turned to her. "Wait here."

Basemath exhaled. Thoughts of Ana swirled in her mind, heightening her anxiety. She wanted to believe

Jeroboam lied to weaken her spirit, but she knew better. She put nothing past the Egyptian barbarians. She shivered as terror's cold hand gripped her body. Whatever fate she chose for herself, she could not leave her daughter to the savages.

She missed Ahimaaz. Though she did not regret sending him off to Jerusalem to warn the king, a part of her longed to have him by her side at this critical moment. It grieved her to know she would never see him again. She had grown to love him and, perhaps more importantly, to respect him for his piety and steadfastness. It took an extraordinary man to have the heart of both a warrior and a holy man.

Surely Ahimaaz had reached Jerusalem. Had he gotten to Rehoboam in time? Was the holy city under attack? She recalled her father's words—*I fear the day will come when my heirs will see the Lord's house destroyed by Jerusalem's enemies*—and realized for the first time Solomon was a prophet. By divine guidance, he had foreseen this moment. He knew the future just as he knew the nature of all things. She was grateful he had the foresight to hide the treasures of his kingdom. Even if it would take a thousand years, the moment would come when Solomon's righteous heir would find them. It gave her comfort to believe it.

"The captain calls for you."

The Egyptian guard's booming voice startled her. Basemath drew a deep breath to steady her nerves and exited the tent at his command.

Morning's brilliant white light flooded her eyes, and

she raised a hand to shield them. She squinted to focus on the guard's spear, which pointed to a group of men standing by the spent campfire. She straightened her tunic and felt the hard outline of Ahimaaz's *khopesh* resting against her hip. She was ready.

With the guard's spear in the small of her back, she walked toward the four Egyptians dressed for battle in fish-scale leather chest armor, white linen kilts, and tasseled leather helmets. Jeroboam was standing among them, clutching a papyrus scroll. His forehead was pinched, the corners of his mouth downturned.

The guard delivered her to the circle of men. She stood stone-faced before her captor. The morning breeze blew coarse ungroomed strands of hair across her face, and she did not bother to push them away.

"There have been some interesting developments." Jeroboam held up the scroll. "It seems your lot has been decided for you."

Basemath parted her lips, but no words came out. Obviously the scroll was a decree from the pharaoh. But why would the Egyptian king care enough about her fate to send his messengers to the Jezreel camp?

"The pharaoh and his men reached Jerusalem in the night," he continued. "They have plundered the palace and the temple and taken the treasures back to Tanis. Solomon's imprint on the city of the Lord has been obliterated. The generations to come will know nothing of his glory." He grinned. "As it should be."

She shifted her gaze to the magenta-plumed sky. She

could no longer bear to look at him.

"As we speak, Pharaoh Shoshenq rides toward Jezreel . . . with your mother."

She snapped her head toward him. "What did you say?"

"She will return with him to Egypt. It has been her wish since she married your father."

"Do not profess to know my mother's wishes."

"Perhaps you are the one who doesn't know your mother. In fact, there is much to which you are oblivious. Let me lift the shroud from your eyes, Princess." He revealed Nicaule's long-held secret.

The bitter potion of the past rose to Basemath's mouth. Though she did not justify her mother's behavior, she finally understood it.

Had Solomon known of his wife's love for another? His wisdom and foresight were unmatched among mortals; surely something so grave had not escaped him. But if he had recognized the trap, why had he allowed himself to be ensnared by Nicaule's cruel heart?

She thought of the words her father spoke in the wilderness. *Stand by your mother, in spite of her flaws.* He knew what she was, but he could not help loving her. A wise man was still a man.

Jeroboam crossed his arms. "Have you nothing to say?"

Basemath did not want to reward the traitor with a reply.

"No? What if I tell you that her lover, Shoshenq, had promised all those years ago to release her from her bondage to the Judahite king and reclaim her as his own? This is the day of her liberation."

Basemath's throat convulsed, and she raised a hand to her mouth to contain the reflex. Jeroboam's words marched in her mind like bone diggers, unearthing the skeletons of the past. She recalled her mother recounting a terrifying encounter with Hadad the Edomite in the wilderness of Zin while she was journeying to her dying father in Egypt. A few hours after, Hadad's men had attempted to storm Solomon's palace.

Images flashed in her mind of emissaries constantly riding from Jerusalem to Egypt, supposedly to deliver news of happy occasions in the royal household. None but Nicaule and her scribe, Irisi, knew what words were really written on those papyrus scrolls.

It was all coming together. It wasn't Hadad or Rezon of Assyria or even Jeroboam who was Solomon's worst nemesis; it was the woman who shared his bed.

Jeroboam shook his head and laughed in his usual mocking tone. "Not what you were expecting to hear, is it? Perhaps you'd hoped to blame the brutality of the Egyptians rather than the treachery of your own blood. It is a shame indeed when those we trust are, in truth, the perpetrators. It illuminates the wickedness of human nature. And lo, you will witness it every day for the rest of your life."

Her forehead creased. "What do you mean to say?"

He unfurled the papyrus scroll and read from it. "Let it be known that the pharaoh Shoshenq orders the preparation of Basemath, daughter of Nicaule Tashere, for immediate removal from Israel and relocation to Tanis."

Basemath's eyes grew wide. She shook her head. "No. I will not."

Jeroboam took two steps toward her. He crumpled the papyrus. "It seems to me you have no choice. The pharaoh has spoken." He turned his head toward the Egyptian officers. "Men!"

The four approached. Two grabbed Basemath's arms and pulled her away.

She dug her heels into the dirt and struggled against them. "Let me go, pigs! I will not follow. I would sooner die!"

The men clamped down on her arms. One spat out something in Egyptian she did not understand or care to. She kicked his shin. He drove an elbow into her midsection.

On her knees and doubled over, she let the tears trickle down her cheeks. She did not mind being crippled or killed, but the loss of her freedom was an indignity she was not prepared to suffer.

"It is said life comes full circle," she heard Jeroboam say. "It happened to your mother all those years ago: leaving the land of her fathers and the man she loved for a strange, unfamiliar place where she would be held captive in a prison of gold. Now it is your turn. Your history and your destiny are one and the same."

Hatred flashed in her eyes. "Curse you, Jeroboam. May your altar be scattered to the four winds and your house perish as wheat in the jaws of locusts."

Jeroboam ripped off her veil and hoisted her by the hair. His mouth was twisted in a snarl. "Evil whore, I ought to kill you here and now. But it would give me greater satisfaction to watch you die slowly of the worst kind of affliction . . . subjugation and bondage."

"Let her go."

Jeroboam looked over Basemath's shoulder toward the voice. "My lord." He released his clutch, and Basemath's long raven locks spilled around her face. He dropped to one knee and lowered his gaze.

"Face me." The voice behind her was deep and resonant.

She turned slowly and met the pharaoh's austere gaze. Shoshenq stood on a golden chariot pulled by two black horses wearing blankets of fish-scale leather and feathers upon their manes. The middle-aged pharaoh was dressed in royal blue leather armor with a gilded and enameled breastplate covering his chest and shoulders. The *khepresh*, the blue crown worn by Egyptian kings in battle, rested upon his bald head. A quiver full of arrows was slung across his back.

Nicaule was at his side, holding his bow. She was dressed in rumpled white linen with a golden sash tied at the waist. Her glossy black wig, the same one she'd worn during ceremonies over the years, was windblown and slightly crooked. Basemath shot her a somber glance, but there was no comprehension in her mother's vacant eyes. Nicaule looked dazed, almost pitiful.

"Why do you give my men trouble?" Shoshenq asked.

Basemath answered without regard for her life. "I do not take my orders from heathen kings."

The pharaoh narrowed his kohl-ringed eyes. "Is that

so? Then take an order from your father."

"My father is dead."

Shoshenq dismounted and walked toward her. Nicaule followed. He stood so close that Basemath could smell the heavy musk of his perspiration and the garlic in his breath. "Solomon is dead, but your father stands before you."

A chill traveled through Basemath's body like an electrical current. Did she really hear the words? She turned to Nicaule. "Mother . . ."

Nicaule lifted her head, exposing the flacid skin connecting her jaw to her throat. "It is true."

Basemath shook her head. "No. You do not know of what you speak."

Nicaule stepped closer. "Years ago, before I came to Israel, Shoshenq and I lay together. I was already pregnant when I married Solomon. I bore you with Shoshenq's seed."

"Mother, no." Basemath held up her right palm and pointed to the brown stain. "See this. It is the same birthmark Solomon had. It is the mark of the house of David."

Shoshenq turned to Nicaule, his eyes probing her for answers.

"She lies," Nicaule told him. "Solomon never had such a mark."

Basemath did not know whether to be repulsed by her mother or to pity her. Had Nicaule convinced herself of this illusion to the point of believing it, or was she merely manipulating her once-lover to dramatize their reunion? She knew her words were for naught, but she could not keep silent. "Please, Mother. For the sake of Solomon's honor . . . for the sake of your soul, speak the truth."

Nicaule looked away, as she always did when she no longer wished to discuss something.

Shoshenq signaled to one of his officers, who stepped forward leading a horse by the reins. The pharaoh glared at Basemath. His face was tight, unyielding. "You will ride with Nakhti to Tanis. Go now."

As Nakhti came toward her, Basemath reached inside her *halub* and with a swift movement removed Ahimaaz's sickle-sword. She held it to her own throat and felt its tip puncture her skin. Warm blood trickled down and pooled in her jugular notch. "I will not do your bidding. I choose death."

"Bring forth the prisoner!" Shoshenq's urgent words boomed across the valley.

With shaking hands, Basemath kept the blade trained on her throat. An invisible hand held her back, delaying her self-execution. She felt her father's presence.

A moment later, she knew why. A second officer emerged from the cluster of tents, pulling Ana by the elbow.

Basemath gasped. Her daughter's gray tunic was ripped and stained with blood. Her eyes were as a feral animal's, afraid and untrusting. The child's innocence had been sacrificed at the altar of pleasure by the godless brutes who dared call themselves civilized. It sickened her to know Egyptian blood ran through her own veins.

Basemath tightened her grip on the sickle-sword and turned to Nicaule. Even the Lord's commandment could not stop the wave of hatred that came crashing on the shores of her soul. "Was it worth it, Mother? Did your self-indulgent fantasy merit this wanton slaughter of lambs? Will you sleep soundly in your lover's bed by the river reeds, knowing what destruction you have brought upon this land?"

You disgust me, she thought but held her tongue out of deference to her father. It would not have penetrated anyway; Nicaule had fallen too deep into a pit of iniquity and incomprehension.

Shoshenq turned to Basemath. "You are called upon to make a choice. If you stay here, alive or dead, your daughter will be executed." He signaled for Ana to be brought to him. He placed his hands on the child's shoulders. "But if you go, her life will be spared."

Basemath's eyes misted. "What will become of her?"

"She will be taken to Jerusalem this day, where she will live in the court of the lame Judean king . . . your brother." He stroked Ana's hair. "You have my word."

Basemath met Ana's gaze. Trembling in the hands of the barbarian, the child seemed spent but not defeated. Basemath recognized her own ferocity in Ana's eyes. Like her, her daughter would weather the trials and be better for them—if only she was given the chance to live.

A vision flashed in Basemath's mind: Ana had grown and taken Rehoboam's son, Abijah, to husband. Together they led a mighty resistance movement against Jeroboam's rule. She wasn't sure whether it was a message from her father, a revelation from the Lord, or a fool's hope, but she swore it was real.

Basemath's fate was etched in stone. All that remained now was to eviscerate the self and burn its remains on the altar of the greater good. Given the choice between her own peace and peace for Israel, she issued the only judgment she could.

She dropped Ahimaaz's *khopesh*. "I will go."

Shoshenq gave a crooked smile. He turned on his heel and walked toward his chariot.

Basemath called to him. "Wait."

He stopped and looked over his shoulder.

"I need a moment with my daughter."

"You shall have it," he said and kept walking.

Basemath approached Ana. The two looked at each other for a long moment. Basemath choked back tears as she took her daughter's hands. "The time has come to be strong, girl. We no longer live for ourselves. We live for the land of our fathers."

Ana nodded. Tears pooled in her eyes. She blinked, and they rained down.

"The Lord has chosen life for us. There is reason to all things." She pulled the ring out of her bosom and slipped the chain off her neck. She handed it to Ana. "This is your destiny. You must guard it to the end. Even if all testimony of the house of David is erased from the earth, let this be the one thing that survives."

Basemath leaned down and whispered the secret of the ring into the girl's ear. She stepped back and took one last look at her beautiful Ana. "It is the inheritance of our people. Keep it safe."

With a piercing bray, the pharaoh's horses reared. It was time.

Nakhti walked to her. She squeezed Ana's hand and watched her child collapse into sobs. The Egyptian took Basemath's elbow, but she snapped free of his grip. She went willingly.

He straddled his horse, and she mounted behind him. A breeze blew her raven locks across her face as she looked over her shoulder at Ana. "If your father lives, tell him I will not forget him."

Nakhti urged his horse to a trot, and they fell into Shoshenq's caravan.

Basemath lowered her head and closed her eyes. Memory was a tyrant, haunting her steps, tormenting her. All she had known—the glory of Jerusalem, the spiritual fortress of Yahweh's chosen king, the impenetrable solidarity of her people—had fallen to ruin. What remained now? Only faith for the wise and despair for fools.

She offered a silent prayer, vowing to keep the lamp of the Hebrews lit, even against the wind.

She looked up, shielding her eyes from the shimmering light of the midday sun. They were riding west toward a hazy horizon. All was silent but for the rhythmic footfall of horses. The air smelled of almond blossoms both sweet and bitter, and she thought of her father.

When the silver thread is broken and the golden bowl shattered, when the bitter almond tree flourishes, when the birds cease to sing and there is no more music, when the doors are shuttered and only fear and madness dwell in the streets, when the strong men's knees buckle and the maidens' beauty withers, then remember the words of the wise: remove sorrow from your heart, and cast away evil from your flesh, for the dust shall return to the earth and the spirit to its maker.

Solomon knew this day would come.

She inhaled deeply, branding the fragrance onto her olfactory memory. This would be what she would remember, the scent of duality: unification and division, joy and sorrow, virtue and depravity. A soft, warm breeze touched her back, urging her toward her destiny.

Author's Note

It seems obvious to state that historical fiction is based largely on facts, people, and events from the past, laced with just enough literary license to make the story more provocative and to explore possibilities by asking "What if?"

Because history, particularly the ancient kind into which I delve, often leaves us with many blanks, the novelist's insertions—born first of thoughtful research and second of imagination—can illuminate events that were marginally recorded or bring to life characters that were deemed minor by the historians. This is what I hope I have done in *The Judgment*.

Let me explain. A few years ago, when I was researching for my historical thriller *The Riddle of Solomon*, I became fascinated with the stories about King Solomon, son of King David and ruler of the united monarchy of Israel and Judah. Everyone, regardless of nationality or faith, has heard something of the legend of Solomon: the king's untold riches, his wisdom, his building of the first temple in Jerusalem, his affair with the Queen of Sheba, his hundreds of wives, his outsize passion, his ultimate fall from grace. King Solomon has become a cross-cultural symbol for wealth, power, leadership, piety, and insight—all universally desirable qualities.

The interesting thing about Solomon, however, is that most of what we know about his life is written in the Old Testament, in the books of 2 Chronicles and 1 Kings. Aside from a few references in the Kebra Nagast (the Ethiopian book of kings) and in the Qur'an, mainstream theological literature does not reward us with a lot of detail. Worse, archaeology has produced theories but no hard data confirming his existence and the breadth of his empire.

It took a lot of digging in rabbinical literature—the Midrashim—and discussions with rabbis to find answers to my questions: Who was this king? How did he build an empire of epic proportions in a time when such wealth was notably absent in the Holy Land? What was his relationship to Egypt and other neighboring nations? Why did he marry an Egyptian woman (and, subsequently, other foreigners)? Why did he falter in his faith? Was it that lapse that led to the spectacular collapse of the united monarchy after Solomon died in 930 BCE?

In the course of that research, I learned that Solomon likely wrote (his authorship is disputed) the biblical books Proverbs, Ecclesiastes, and Song of Solomon. I had not read these texts before, but absorbing them in the context of my research for *The Judgment* proved to be particularly rewarding. Reading one's writing often opens a window to that individual's soul, and that is certainly the case here. The sage aphorisms in Proverbs, the philosophical questions pondered in Ecclesiastes, and the explicitly erotic passages of Song of Solomon paint a picture of a multifaceted, perhaps even troubled, man.

It was a privilege to tell his story. I chose not to use Solomon's point of view, opting instead to use the voices of three people who knew very different dimensions of him: Zadok, the high priest of Israel in the tenth century BCE and Solomon's spiritual adviser; Nicaule Tashere, the pharaoh's daughter and Solomon's first wife; and Basemath, one of the king's daughters with Nicaule. All of these individuals are historical figures, though information on their lives is scant.

From the Bible, we know Solomon married "a pharaoh's daughter"; no name for her, or for the pharaoh, is given. Through other research, I learned her name was Nicaule and found contradictory theories about who her father was. The assumption that she was the daughter of Psusennes II was my own, based strictly on the timelines of the two kings' reigns.

The Bible also tells us foreign women, and in particular the Egyptian wife he loved with such gusto, caused Solomon to be permissive toward the worship of other gods. This was the main reason (there were others, such as the taxation of his people) for the legendary king's downfall in his old age and the eventual division of the monarchy by his disgruntled lieutenant, Jeroboam, who eventually became king of Israel.

Jeroboam's betrayal is well recorded, as is the massive invasion of Canaan land by Psusennes' successor, Shoshenq I. The fictional part is Shoshenq's love affair with Nicaule and the conspiracy among the two of them and Jeroboam to bring down Solomon's empire.

A word here about Basemath: since history grants no insight to her life, I took some liberties with her character. With her unwavering piety and personal strength, Basemath became a symbol for faith, sacrifice, and the future of Israel.

Toward the end of the story, Basemath recalls the final meeting with her father. To meditate and repent, Solomon had journeyed alone to the Judean Wilderness. After forty days, he called for his beloved daughter. In what probably is the saddest, and yet most hopeful, scene of the book, Solomon tells Basemath that enemies are at Jerusalem's gates and he fears the temple of the Lord will be destroyed. In planning for such an eventuality, he gives Basemath his royal ring and divulges a secret.

Though this ring is documented in the mystical texts, the secret is a fiction inspired by messianic prophecy, which states the Jewish messiah will trace his lineage to the house of David via the Solomonic bloodline. In the book, Solomon's secret is his provision for the temple to be rebuilt by one of his successors in the way God had intended. It symbolizes his atonement for faltering in the eyes of God and of his people. (A modern treatment of this mystery is found in my 2013 thriller, *The Riddle of*

Solomon. The Judgment is a sort of prequel to that book.)

As a final note, I'd like to point out that the descriptions of ancient Jerusalem, Megiddo, and Tanis are authentic. To educate myself on those long-ago worlds, I read countless texts and studied the work of biblical archaeologists and Egyptologists. I believe details such as architecture, diet, wardrobe, hygiene, and, of course, language make all the difference in reader experience.

I hope you've enjoyed this journey as much as I've enjoyed bringing it to you. If you have, please consider reviewing *The Judgment* or recommending it to a friend.